BE CAREFUL WHAT YOU WISH FOR

By

R. K. Avery

Published by
Brighton Publishing LLC
501 W. Ray Road
Suite 4
Chandler, AZ 85225

Be Careful What You Wish For

By

R. K. Avery

Published by
Brighton Publishing LLC
501 W. Ray Road
Suite 4
Chandler, AZ 85225

Copyright©2011

ISBN 13: 978-1-936587-41-4
ISBN 10: 1-936-58741-6

First Edition

Printed in the United States of America

Cover Design by Patricia McNaught-Foster

⟪ *Dedication* ⟫

This book is dedicated to my family: Alan, Kayla, Jared, Ola, Pam and Rita. They allowed me countless hours in front of the computer, which was a sacrifice for all of us.

Also to my many, many friends and co-workers who helped me proofread, edit and re-edit. Not wanting to leave anyone out, I'd rather not mention names, but you know who you are. I am thankful for your friendship and your support.

And last but not least, to my cousins, Benita and Greg. Benita asked me to use her name in a book—and I did! Greg, thank you for allowing me to benefit from your brilliant mind. I love you both!

ᴄ✍ *Chapter One* ✍ᴅ

Bea Miller had been waiting over six, long years for this day to arrive; and once she'd made up her mind, there was no stopping her. Ever since that last fiasco at the Stop-N-Save, she thought she would never get the chance to add to her family again.

Unable to sleep, she had risen early and fidgeted around the trailer, waiting for her four boys to wake up. It was a beautiful day and Bea was anxious to get started. The weather outside was perfect: powder blue skies, not a cloud in sight, and the temperature was expected to get into the high 80s. She was feeling a little jittery; but even so, she made herself a cup of coffee and a bowl of cereal and tried, unsuccessfully, to calm her frazzled nerves. As she sat at the mismatched dinette set, she looked at her wrist as she twirled the old, out-of-style charm bracelet that Henry had been so kind to purchase for her as a surprise. She wondered what her life would have been like if Henry were still a part of it. *Oh, Henry, I continue to miss you every day.*

Bea looked up, thinking she heard someone outside. As she listened closer, she heard a screen door slam shut. *Mrs. Brown is probably going out to get the paper.* She leaned over to peek out the kitchen window. Yes, her neighbor was walking down her driveway to the street where the paperboy had left the *Bunting Valley Gazette*, the only local paper which—in Bea's opinion—*never* covered anything important. Bea didn't care who won the swim meet, or who had grown the largest pumpkin. This was one of the reasons why Bea was never one to pay attention to the news; be it broadcast across the airwaves or in print form. Mrs. Brown, her meddling, next-door neighbor, was quite the opposite. She *lived* to hear what the neighbors and local politicians were up to. Mrs. Brown was wearing a God-awful, flowery house dress, with her hair up in curlers, and big, furry, pink slippers that looked as if she had stuck each of her feet into a wad of cotton candy. On cue, Mrs. Brown tripped over her cotton candy slippers, and then quickly regained her balance, looking around to see if anyone had seen her trip she straightened herself. Bea couldn't help but chuckle. When it appeared Mrs. Brown realized no one had seen, she bent over to pull a few dried up buds from her petunias, as if that was what she had been doing all along.

1

Be Careful What You Wish For

Bea busied herself by straightening up the kitchen and small living room. When she brought her daughter home, she wanted the trailer to be presentable. She stood back and surveyed the room, wishing she could afford new furniture. *Maybe next year.* She took the braided throw rugs outside and tried to shake the dirt and dust from them, but a few were beyond help. As she placed them back on the worn out carpet, she made certain to cover the blood stain that remained. After all this time, the stain still bothered her. She didn't know why. *He'd certainly had it coming.*

She was growing impatient waiting for the boys to get up, so she plugged in the old Hoover vacuum cleaner, banging a little louder and making a little more noise than necessary, hoping to roust them. In the summer, they had a tendency to stay up late and then sleep until noon. However, Bea would not allow it today. Still trying to pass the time, she pulled out her tattered old journal and started a new entry.

July 17, 2010

Today is the day I get to meet my daughter. I wish the boys would get up already. The sooner we get to the lake, the sooner I will find her, and the sooner we will get back home.

I know I will find the perfect little girl there. There will be no mistake this time. I already filled the boys in and told them if they so much as uttered a word to anyone as to what goes on at the lake; I will personally cut their tongues out. And I meant it. I've waited for this day far too long; no one is going to mess it up. I feel like I could literally kill anyone who gets in my way.

I hope she's little, but not too little. I know I don't have the patience to go through the terrible two's all over again. I wonder what her name is. I hope it's pretty, so I don't have to change it.

Not having the patience to wait any longer, Bea closed the journal and placed it delicately on the kitchen counter, to be put away later. She usually kept it under lock and key in her bedroom. She had been making entries in it—on and off—for over thirty-five years now, and it meant the world to her. She still couldn't bring herself to reread the earlier entries. They brought back too many unpleasant memories.

She stood up and walked down the long, skinny hallway, pounding on bedroom doors. "Get up, get up, get up," she screamed.

2

Be Careful What You Wish For

"Oh Mom, just a few more minutes, please?" John implored.

"What time is it, anyway?" Josh asked.

"I don't understand why we all have to go," David said. He was almost nineteen years old, so he tried to talk to her out of it, reminding her of the last fiasco and the way Mikey had joined their family. But Bea assured him she wouldn't make the same mistake again. That's why she wanted to go to Lake Gerber.

"You can't mistake a boy for a girl when all they have on is a bathing suit, *idiot!*" she told him the night before.

"I think this whole idea is absolutely ridiculous! I just have an unpleasant feeling it is going to blow up in your face."

"Don't you fret over it . . . I know *exactly* what I'm doing."

"Yeah, like I haven't heard that before."

"Stop giving me a hard time. We're in this together."

"Just remember, I was against this from the start!" David always tried to be the voice of reason, but Bea lived by her own agenda and didn't care what others thought.

A short while later, just after eleven o'clock, Bea spread an old, tattered, wool blanket out on the sand and sat waiting to find her daughter. She was certain she'd know her immediately. Dressed in a swimsuit and shorts, she thought about wading in the water but decided against it. Instead, she remained on the blanket sitting next to David. The sun's glare on the water was almost blinding, and Bea was grateful she'd remembered to bring a pair of sunglasses. As she took them out of her pocket, she saw one of the lenses had fallen out and was nowhere to be found. *Damnit!* Bea folded the glasses and shoved them back into her pocket, anxious to get situated as families were already starting to arrive. There were several girls at the beach today; all ages, shapes, and sizes. David sat next to Bea on the blanket and kept pointing them out.

"What about that one?" David asked.

Bea shook her head. "No, she's too fat."

"What's wrong with that one?"

"Honestly, David, she looks like she's about twelve years old! I want a *little* girl, remember?"

3

"What about that one?"

"She's probably as old as you are!"

"I know, and she's really cute." David grinned.

Bea raised one eyebrow, "*Seriously?*"

"I was just kidding. Geez, lighten up a bit, won't you? What about that one?"

"Wrong coloring . . ."

"Wrong coloring . . . *what* does that mean?"

"We have to pick one who has the same features we do—one that looks like she belongs in our family. For starters, she should have blonde hair like me."

David looked at Bea sitting beside him. "You're a complete idiot. You don't have blonde hair."

"Sure I do. I just dye the roots brown." Bea smiled as she sat hugging her knees.

David, wearing swim trunks and a black t-shirt, shook his head. "I don't know, Mom. I just can't shake this bad feeling I have."

"How did you turn into such a worrywart? It'll be fine . . . *trust me.*"

The other three boys kept coming down to see if they had a sister yet. Bea finally got exasperated and told them to go wait in the van. She was fearful someone would overhear their conversation, but with the sound of the water splashing on shore, and kids giggling and laughing, it was highly unlikely.

Then Bea saw an angelic little girl in a light blue, one-piece bathing suit. She had the most beautiful, sapphire-blue eyes Bea had ever seen, with long, fluttery eyelashes. She was playing in the sand with another fat girl, whom Bea assumed was her sister. She had baby-fine, wispy blonde hair that fell softly, framing her chubby, pink cheeks. Bea guessed she was either three or four years old. The little girl giggled and kept running to a couple sitting a few blankets over from her. "That's her," Bea said when the little girl ran past.

"Why her . . . ?" David asked, curious.

4

"She's the perfect age, and she's definitely a girl. She has blonde hair, and it looks as if she has a sister. It's not fair they get to have two girls, and I don't have any," Bea said, tipping her head in the parents' direction.

"That's the stupidest thing I ever heard. Why do you get to have four boys when they have none?"

"Exactly my point . . ."

David shook his head. "I wasn't trying to prove a point. I was trying to make you realize how idiotic you sound."

"I don't care what you think. She's the one. As soon as I see an opportunity, I'm going to get this show on the road." Bea giddily clapped her hands together like a child.

It was obvious no matter what David had to say, Bea wasn't listening. "I know you'll do what you want, anyway, so why should I even bother giving my opinion?" He stood and brushed the dirt from the back of his swim trunks. "I'll be waiting in the van."

"Make sure your brothers are in the van, and behaving like I asked. When I'm ready to leave, we have to leave. There won't be time for me to go hunting for them."

Bea sat a while longer, watching and waiting. The lady, whom Bea assumed was their mom, came down and joined them in the sand for a moment; then she and the little blonde girl went out into the water. They were playing a game, but Bea couldn't hear what they were saying from where she sat. They looked as if they were having so much fun, laughing and giggling. Bea looked forward to having that kind of fun with her daughter. She remembered the relationship she had with her Aunt Benita fondly; that was until Papa butted his nose in and ruined everything.

The lady and little blonde girl climbed out of the water, and she left the girls in the sand again. As she joined the man back on their blanket, Bea tried not to stare, but she couldn't help it. The woman and man could pass for Barbie and Ken—flawless in every way. The lady, unusually tall and slender, had such deep red hair it almost looked burgundy. Of course, it was cut and styled in the most flattering way. She had freckles across the bridge of her nose, spaced so perfectly that it looked as if someone had painted them on with a brush. And the man, handsome as a movie star with chiseled features and big, broad shoulders, hung on her every word. *Life is so unfair.* Shortly after the lady sat down, she took out a bottle of suntan lotion and squirted some in her hand. Bea stood up and brushed a little sand from her butt; and then she picked up her blanket, draped it over her arm, and walked down to where the girls were sitting. The man and lady were soon emerged in conversation, so Bea saw her opportunity. *What kind of parent would leave their little girl down by the water and not even watch her? It's a good thing I'm here.*

Bea approached the little blonde girl sitting in the sand. As soon as she looked in her sparkling blue eyes, Bea knew she had finally found her daughter. *Oh my gosh—I knew I would know her when I saw her, but I didn't expect it to feel like this!*

"Hi, little one . . . don't you look adorable in your beautiful, blue swimsuit?" Bea knelt in the sand and looked at the child. She had come to Lake Gerber in search of this little girl. "Is it new?"

"No. Been wearing it all day," she answered, full of innocence.

"Do you like ice cream?" Bea glanced at the fat sister, who was still nearby, but facing the opposite direction.

"Yes, with sprinkles."

"Oh my, goodness . . . ! That's *my favorite*, too!"

The little girl glanced up at Bea, as she appeared to squint from the sun.

"Would you like to come with me?"

She blinked, looked at Bea with her enormous blue eyes, and reluctantly shook her head, "no."

Time was of the essence, so Bea tried again. "My boys and I are going to get an ice cream cone. Are you sure you don't want to come along? It will be lots of fun." The little girl just continued to stare at her. "After that, we might go for a pony ride."

"You have a pony?"

"Yes, I have two of them." *So what if I'm lying . . . ?*

"What kind of pony?"

Be Careful What You Wish For

"A little one with four legs," Bea said, not quite sure what it would take to get the little girl to come with her.

"Is it pink?"

"Pink?" Bea snorted.

"Pink is my fav-oh-right color."

Bea smiled. It seemed the little girl had just learned how to say *favorite*. "Well then, yes, it's pink—both of them are pink—bright pink to be exact. Just give me your hand and we'll go get a chocolate ice cream cone; and after that, you can go for a pink pony ride."

The little girl glanced over at the man and woman she had come with. "Okay. Need to tell Mommy first."

"I already told your mommy, and she said it is perfectly okay. Just give me your hand."

The little girl gave Bea her small chubby hand. As they crossed over from the sand to the grass, Bea kept a close eye on the man and woman as she continued to rub suntan lotion on his back, her flashy, diamond ring sparkling in the sun. The little girl seemed to be having second thoughts, as she quickly pulled her hand away, almost as if Bea's touch had burned it.

"It's okay, sweetie. Don't be afraid. I'll bring you back, right after we get ice cream and ride the pony." She spoke calmly, trying not to upset her. *Just give me your damn hand!*

"With *sprinkles* . . . ?"

"Yes, with *lots* of *sprinkles*, just the way you like it."

"Okay." Bea could tell she was trying to be brave, as she held up her tiny hand again.

Bea's shoulders were turning pink, so she was grateful to get out of the sun. Never much of a sun-goddess, she tended to burn easily. "You can call me Bea, okay?" As they walked hand-in-hand, Bea glanced down at her flip-flops and noticed the band between her toes was coming loose. *My God, what else is going to break today?* Looking over her shoulder, to make sure the man and woman weren't paying attention, Bea said to the little girl, "What's your name?"

"Maggie."

Be Careful What You Wish For

"Maggie's a beautiful name." Bea smiled at Maggie. Bea was average looking, with bleach blonde hair pulled back with an elastic Scrunchie. Today she was wearing bright red lipstick. She wanted to make a good first impression when she met her daughter. She was neither too fat, nor too thin, but she did have a roll around her midsection, which looked like a pile of frosting from a cupcake, falling over the waistband of her shorts. The only thing Bea honestly disliked about her appearance was her teeth. They were tiny – too tiny for her face. When she smiled, all you could see were her pink gums, with extremely small teeth.

Bea held Maggie by the hand and led her up to an older model, dark blue, Chevy conversion van. The van had seen better days, as there were several rust spots on the back bumper and side panels. It had a raised roof, and faded curtains hung in each window. When the side door rolled back, the smell of stale cigarette smoke billowed out. Bea hated smoking more than anything, but as hard as she tried, she couldn't get rid of the stench. Her father smoked Camel unfiltered cigarettes, and to this day, Bea could recognize the scent a mile away.

"Okay, Maggie, climb in." Maggie didn't move.

"C'mon Maggie . . . don't you want an ice cream cone?" Maggie shook her head, "no" as her blonde hair floated around like airborne seeds from a dandelion.

"What about a pony ride? I know you want to ride a bright pink pony. How about we think of this as an adventure, and you can sit in the back between David and Joshua."

Maggie stood on the outside of the van looking in. Bea tapped her foot on the pavement, waiting patiently for Maggie to place her bare foot on the tarnished silver running board, looking around behind them to make sure no one was following. Maggie just kept peering around the inside of the van. When Bea decided she couldn't wait any longer, she finally picked Maggie up and placed her inside the door. Maggie hesitantly walked to the back where the two boys sat on a worn-out bench seat along the rear of the van. Bea knew the van was disgusting, however, with her being a single mom, and with four mouths to feed, it was the best she could do.

"Everyone, meet Maggie, we're taking her to get a chocolate ice cream cone." Bea smiled.

"And a pony ride," Maggie piped up.

"Whatever." David scooted as far away from the empty spot as he could. Bea had to admit, David looked a little scary. He had straight charcoal black hair, parted in the center, which came down to the middle of his ears. He wore dark sunglasses, and a black skull and crossbones t-shirt. *I should have insisted he wear something else. But then, he would have argued, and it would have turned ugly; and I'm not in the mood for ugly today.*

"David, make Maggie feel at home. We are going on a grand adventure!" Bea gave David the evil eye.

"Car seat . . . ?" Maggie tilted her little blonde head to the side.

"No, Maggie. Today is a special day, and you get to ride like a big girl. No car seat, just a seat belt. Won't that be fun?" Bea smiled as she thought of how smart her little girl was.

"Okay." Maggie hesitated. "Don't tell Mommy."

"Oh, I would never tell, don't you worry. Your secret is safe with me. Joshua, please help buckle Maggie in." Joshua buckled Maggie in, and the door of the van rolled shut with a bang.

Maggie's face turned red, and it looked as if she were about to cry. "I want to go back now!" Maggie shouted, as Bea climbed in the driver's seat, glancing at Mikey, who sat next to her in the passenger seat.

"Not yet . . . remember, we're going on a grand adventure."

"But I want my mommy." Maggie tugged at her seat belt release.

"We'll bring your mommy an ice cream, too. Won't that be nice? She'll be so happy." *Just shut up so we can get out of here.*

"Can Mommy come, too?" Maggie looked at Bea.

"No, not this time . . . your mommy's busy, but I promise we'll be back very soon."

Bea looked at her wrist. *Damn it, I lost my bracelet.* Unable to see through the grime on the window, she rolled the window down to see if she dropped it in the parking lot. She didn't see it at first glance, and she was determined not to leave without it.

"Everyone stay in the van. I dropped my charm bracelet somewhere, and I'm going to back track to see if I can find it. Don't open the doors and don't let anyone see Maggie."

Bea went slowly back down to the beach, crawling on her hands and knees through the grass, hoping to find the bracelet. After several minutes of searching, she realized it was nowhere to be found. Bea remembered she had gone to the restroom when they first arrived, so she went back, hoping to locate the bracelet . . . no such luck! Before leaving, she glanced back down at the water and the fat girl was gone, and so were Barbie and Ken. Desolate, she drug her feet as she walked back up to the van.

"It's about time. I thought we were going to melt in here!" David said as soon as the door opened.

"Oh, I wasn't gone *that* long. Don't make a mountain out of a mole hill. Besides, with the windows open, there is a nice cross breeze."

"Maybe up there, but not back here." David huffed.

Bea started the engine, and the older van hesitated, backfired, and then lurched forward.

Bea and David had been sitting by the beach for almost two hours, looking for the perfect girl. When the woman with Maggie turned to put suntan lotion on the man's back, it was her chance. Her plan had worked perfectly, and she was well on her way to making her family complete with the little girl she had always wished for.

ᴄ✍ᴏ *Chapter Two* ᴄ✍ᴏ

Abby and Tim Taylor had made their mind up the day before that they were going to take their girls, Madeline and Margaret, to Lake Gerber for some family fun. It didn't matter how many times they went to Lake Gerber, Maddie and Maggie never grew tired of playing in the sand.

The Taylors were among the first to arrive at the lake, which allowed them to find the perfect spot on the beach, far enough away from the water so they wouldn't get splashed, yet close enough to keep a watchful eye on the girls. The smell of coconut suntan lotion and burning charcoal would soon fill the air, as guests would arrive and start grilling hot dogs and hamburgers for lunch. The sand, separated from the picnic area by a long narrow patch of grass, was the ideal spot for sunbathing. After they picked the perfect location to spread their blanket, the buckets and shovels were dispensed and the girls got busy working on a sand castle.

Lake Gerber, a 732 acre, privately owned resort, was post card perfect. The lake was well known for its giant water slide, the Twirling Tsunami. People came from miles around for a chance to shoot down the slide, as it was ranked in the top-five, *best tourist attractions* in North Dakota. Before long the lake would become crowded, with everything from water skiers, paddleboat riders, swimmers, and guests waiting in line to ride the Twirling Tsunami.

The Taylors had been to Lake Gerber many times over the years, and the memories of those visits still lingered in Abby's mind as if they had happened yesterday. In late August, everyone looked forward to the big family reunion where grandparents, aunts, uncles, and cousins gathered for a cookout and water activities. Laughter abounded as Grandma and Grandpa shared stories of past reunions. Abby would never forget the year Aunt Gracie went down the water slide, face first, and lost her false teeth. It still brought a smile to Abby's face after all these years. Abby wasn't sure which was funnier—the fact Aunt Gracie lost her teeth or the fact they never did find the upper plate. She could just imagine the look on some unsuspecting guest's face when he or she stepped on it.

Be Careful What You Wish For

The lake water glistened from the early morning sun as the girls sat on the white sand, trying their best to make a sand castle. Maddie, born with a lazy eye, squinted to see without her glasses.

"You don't even know what a sand castle looks like," Maddie, the older of the two girls said. Abby noticed she played the role of protector to the hilt, often bossing Maggie around, which wasn't always welcome.

"Do too!" Maggie protested. Even though they were sisters, they resembled each other about as much as a banana bears resemblance to an orange. Maggie, a towhead with fine blonde hair falling over her chubby pink baby cheeks, looked adorable in her muted blue, one-piece swimsuit. "You'll see. I'll build my own castle and I won't let you in!"

"I don't want in your dumb castle anyway." Maddie took after her father and his side of the family, with dark hair and eyes, and she looked like a little sausage stuffed into her one-piece, fire-engine-red swimsuit.

"Girls, stop arguing and be nice. Work together and build a *really* beautiful sand castle." Abby shook her head when she saw Maddie stick her tongue out at her sister.

An hour or so later, Abby decided to leave her spot next to Tim on the worn out down comforter which had lost the majority of its stuffing some time ago. She proceeded to coax the girls into the water one last time before they began to pack up their things and head home. Maggie, her beautiful eyes sparkling like blue diamonds in the sun, took Abby's hands as they played Ring-Around-the-Rosy in the shallow water at the edge of the lake. Each time at "they all fall down," the giggles and laughter from all of them skittered out of control. Maddie stayed on shore, trying desperately to finish the perfect sand castle before Maggie returned and messed it up.

"Okay, girls," Abby said. "About fifteen more minutes and it's time to pack up." Maddie barely looked up. It was obvious to her mother that she was deep in concentration, since she had a tendency to stick her small pink tongue out at the side of her mouth when she really focused on something; a trait she'd inherited from Tim.

"The sand packs better if you wet it, Maddie," Abby said in her direction.

12

Be Careful What You Wish For

"Thanks, Mommy."

Abby went back to join her husband on the blanket while Maggie joined her big sister back in the sand.

"I think I'm getting burned. Can you rub some more suntan lotion on my back?" Tim smiled at his wife.

"Sure I can, but I thought we were heading home soon," Abby grabbed their beach bag to search for the lotion.

"A little while longer . . . besides, Maddie just figured out the trick to building a sand castle."

Tim sat up and turned his bare back toward Abby. Abby took the half full bottle of suntan lotion, squirted some into the palm of her hand, and rubbed her hands together. She then put both hands on Tim's back and covered it generously, rubbing slowly, as they continued to carry on a conversation. Abby knew if she missed a spot and Tim ended up burned, he'd tease her unmercifully.

When Abby had met Tim, ten years earlier, in line at the Department of Motor Vehicles, it was love at first sight. Tim, a consummate bachelor, thought he'd never settle down, but once he met Abby, everything changed. They had decided to marry after only a few dates. The chemistry between them was evident to everyone who knew them; and it was still as strong today as it had been on the day they'd met. When they decided to have children, Tim often voiced his desire to have a son. Now that Maggie and Maddie were here, however, he told Abby he wouldn't trade his situation for the world. He would often joke that he was cursed to live his life surrounded by beautiful women.

"Thanks. It's feeling better already." Tim smiled.

"You are such a liar! You just wanted a back rub," Abby teased.

"You know me so well."

With their legs outstretched in front of them, they both turned to face the girls and the water again. Except . . . something . . . was *terribly* . . . wrong. Maddie was there working on her sand castle, but three year old Maggie had vanished.

Their smiles and laughter, quickly turned to, horror and panic as both Abby and Tim rose to their feet. Abby shot down to the water so quickly, that she couldn't remember if her feet ever touched the ground. Tim was right on her heels.

"Maddie, where's your sister?" Abby tried not to scare her.

Maddie, still deep in concentration, didn't respond.

"Madeline, look at me! Where did Maggie go?" she repeated.

"I don't know, Mommy."

"What do you mean you don't know? She's your baby sister. You always help Mommy by keeping an eye on her!" Abby's voice got a little louder and angrier than she intended.

"I'm sorry, Mommy, but I was busy. See my sand castle?" Maddie stretched out both hands just like a model on *The Price is Right*.

"It's beautiful." Abby didn't even look.

"I'm going to see if I can find her up by the picnic area," Tim said as he turned and ran away.

Abby began to pace back and forth at the shoreline, looking for the little blonde head out in the water.

"Maggie! Maggie! Where are you?" She hoped for an answer. "If you can hear me, you need to come out right now. Maggie, please come to Mommy." Her voice became softer as tears began to sting her eyes. "Please be okay."

Abby took Maddie by the hand and rushed over to talk to some of the people seated near where Maggie had been in the sand. Maybe they'd seen her . . . knew where she might have gone . . . or at the very least, they may have seen the direction she'd been headed in. It sure wouldn't hurt to ask.

"Excuse me. Have you seen a cute little blonde girl? She was sitting here playing in the sand with her sister."

A young man and woman, with an outstretched blanket, were just a few feet from where she and Tim had been sitting. "No, ma'am . . . we just got here," the man replied.

"Maybe you passed her on your way down to the beach?" Abby was hopeful for something—anything.

"I'm afraid not. We had so much to carry, we weren't really paying attention," the lady added.

Abby and Maddie moved on to a group of older people sitting in lawn chairs under a big colorful umbrella. "I hope you can help me. My two girls were sitting down there playing in the sand, and the youngest one decided to wander off. Did any of you happen to see what direction she went?"

"No, I didn't," an older lady wearing a straw hat with a wide brim spoke up. "I do remember seeing her earlier down in the sand. I commented to Harold on how adorable she looked in her blue bathing suit. We didn't see her wander off, did we, Harold?"

"Nope, but I sure do hope you find her. Such a cute little thing," Harold replied.

"Thank you." Disheartened, Abby and Maddie turned and walked away.

Four teenagers were nearby laughing and talking. One of the boys had a water gun and was squirting the girls, who shrieked as loud as a car's worn out brakes when pressure was applied. Abby hated to interrupt. "Excuse me. Did any of you happen to see my little girl earlier? She was down by the water and wandered off. She has blonde hair . . . *very cute*. Her hair was probably wet."

"No, ma'am . . . I'm afraid not, right guys?" one of the girls said to the group. They all shook their heads in unison.

Dejected again, Abby and Maddie turned and headed back down to the shoreline. Abby put her hand up to her eyebrows to shield her eyes from the sun as it reflected off the water. There were so many heads out there. It was difficult to tell if any of them belonged to Maggie. Abby looked at the sand where Maggie and Maddie had been earlier, and she saw a pair of small footprints. *These must be Maggie's.* Abby knelt down for a closer look and touched them with her finger. Next to Maggie's were a set of larger footprints, which looked like a pair of flip-flops. What Abby hoped might be a clue was quickly ruined when the two teenage boys got up and started tossing a football, running, and falling all over the place.

Abby got to her feet when she saw Tim running towards her. Just seeing him without Maggie, tears started flowing down her cheeks.

When Tim saw the tears, it was obvious he feared the worse. "What happened? Did you find her?"

Unable to speak, Abby, still holding Maddie's hand shook her head "no."

"Do you think she went in the water?" Tim asked.

Still unable to speak, Abby shrugged her shoulders.

"I asked several people up by the picnic area and no one saw anything."

Finding her voice, Abby spoke hoarsely, "It's as if she vanished into thin air. I don't understand it. We were right there. We didn't see anything. We didn't hear anything. It seems like no one else did either. Where could she have gone? What could have happened to her that fast?"

"I have no idea but I think we should call the police. The sooner they get here, the sooner we find her."

Tim ran back to where they'd been sitting on the blanket and searched in the beach bag for his cell phone. With shaky hands, he dialed 911, and handed the phone to Abby.

A female operator answered. "911, what's your emergency?"

"We can't find our three year old daughter," Abby replied.

"Who am I speaking to?"

"My name is Abby Taylor."

The operator continued, "How long has she been missing, Mrs. Taylor?"

Abby glanced at her arm, where her watch usually was, but she had taken it off to go in the water. "I don't know, but I guess about half an hour."

"My screen says you're calling from Lake Gerber, is that correct?"

"Yes. We've looked everywhere and can't find her. No one has seen her."

"Who is 'we'?"

16

"Me and my husband, Tim."

"Do you think she wandered out into the water?"

"I don't know."

"Can she swim?"

"No, she can't swim!" Abby was getting frustrated. She just wanted someone to get there and find her baby.

"Calm down, Mrs. Taylor. What was she doing the last time you saw her?"

"She was sitting on the sand with her sister. They were building a sand castle. She was there one minute, and the next minute, she was gone."

"Gone?"

"Yes, gone . . . *vanished!*"

"Okay, I'll radio for a patrol car. Where are you located at the lake?"

"We'll be standing in the main parking lot next to our red car."

Abby and Tim took Maddie by the hand and walked up to the parking lot. It felt as if it took the patrol car forever to arrive. When it finally did, it was a K9 unit.

"Are you the folks that placed the 911 call?" the officer asked through an open window.

"Yes! We can't find our three year old daughter!" Abby almost screamed.

He climbed out of the car and extended his hand. "Good afternoon. I'm Officer Rich Butler, and this is my partner, Max," he said, gesturing to his K9 companion. "Two more patrol cars should be here shortly."

The stereotypical comment about police officers eating a lot of donuts was a misnomer in the case of Officer Butler. He stood tall in a dark blue uniform pressed into clean and crisp creases, and Abby guessed he probably weighed no more than two hundred pounds, if that. He removed his mirrored sunglasses and revealed a pair of beautiful, caring, blue-green eyes.

Be Careful What You Wish For

"I'm Abby Taylor, and this is my husband Tim, and our oldest daughter, Madeline." It was apparent Abby had been crying as her beautiful face was now blotchy and the wet trail of tears still lingered on her cheeks. Tim looked devastated, as if someone had punched him in the stomach and knocked the wind out of him. Madeline, obviously very scared was clinging to Abby's leg.

Officer Butler knelt down to get at Madeline's eye level. "Hi there, Madeline. It's nice to meet you." He extended his hand but Madeline wanted no part of it. Then Maddie spotted the dog, and everything changed.

"I like your dog," Madeline said, as she eased up a bit on Abby's leg.

"Thank you." Officer Butler smiled. Max was always a hit with the kids.

"Where did you get him?" Maddie asked.

Max was a beautiful German shepherd. His black ears were pointed and stood straight up. His slightly wavy fur was black along the top of his back but brown on his sides and underbelly. His long tail was dark and bushy. Max was energetic and playful, but very strong and muscular and knew when to get down to business. "Max came from Holland. He came to the United States to help me do my job better. He's very smart. He was the smartest one in his class."

"Max went to school?" Madeline sounded surprised, furrowing her little eyebrows, probably trying to picture Max sitting at a desk.

Officer Butler chuckled at her reaction. "Yes, Max went to school. He went to K9 School with a bunch of other dogs. Did you know police dogs help out in many different ways, but mostly they help find missing people or things by using their nose? We're going to see if Max can help us find your sister."

"I lost a shoe once. I bet Max could have found it." Maddie reached over and poked Max on top of the head.

"I'm sure he could have." Officer Butler said. "It's okay. You can pet him, if it's alright with your mom."

Abby didn't hear one word of the conversation between Officer Butler and Maddie. She felt like her head was in a bubble and the noise

18

around her was morphed and distorted. All she could think about was Maggie. "Help us find Maggie, please," she said, almost begging. Her beautiful eyes were full of terror.

"Can you give me the details of exactly what happened, Mrs. Taylor?" Officer Butler said, standing back up and brushing the dirt off his knee.

Abby and Tim took Officer Butler and Max down to the water. "Maggie and I were out in the water playing Ring-Around-the Rosy. We came out of the water, and Maggie sat down next to her sister on the sand. They've been working on a sand castle since we got here." Abby, with trembling hands, pointed at what remained of it.

Officer Butler scribbled some notes in a small notepad he took from his breast pocket.

"Then I went up and sat down next to Tim on the blanket. He asked me to rub suntan lotion on his back because he thought he was getting burned. I did, and we talked a moment, and when we turned around, Maggie had vanished." Abby put her hands up to cover the lower half of her face, finally realizing the severity of what was going on. For some reason, saying it out loud to a police officer made it seem so much more real.

"Vanished, you say?" Officer Butler seemed surprised at Abby's choice of words.

"Yes, *vanished*. We took our eyes off her for *five minutes*, if that long, and she was gone. I asked several people down by the water if they had seen her, and Tim did the same thing with the people up near the picnic tables. No one saw her. It's like she vanished into thin air." Abby tried not to cry but couldn't help it.

"Do you have anything that may have the missing child's scent? Some clothes or shoes, or perhaps a favorite stuffed animal?"

"Yes, we have the clothes she wore on top of her swimsuit. They are in the car."

"Good, go get them. I'll also need a recent photo. I'll have Max see if he can pick up her scent. Since she was walking all around here today," Officer Butler motioned with his open hand at the entire area, "it may be difficult, but hopefully Max can tell us which direction she

19

headed last. If he seems to think she went into the water, it will make things more difficult."

Abby placed her hand over her mouth. "What if she went out in the water? She can't swim. My little baby doesn't know how to swim!" Abby put her head down and silent sobs caused her shoulders to shake.

"I'll have to call the department and ask for a dive team. Since we don't have our own diving crew, we'll have to call a certified diver in to assist. Hopefully, that won't be necessary, and we'll find her. I'll also need to call the department to see if the detective is available. He usually likes to be involved in cases such as this, in case there is a news conference or something."

"I think if she went in the water we would have heard splashing or screaming or something. We didn't hear anything. Maddie was right beside her and didn't see or hear anything. How can this be? How can this be happening?" Abby said as Tim turned and headed to the car to get Maggie's clothes.

Abby and Maddie went back to the blanket and Abby searched through the bag for a recent photo. "Being only three years old, the least little thing, such as a butterfly or a loud noise, could capture her attention and cause her to wander off." Abby handed the photograph to Officer Butler.

"I know, I completely understand."

Tim returned a few minutes later and handed Officer Butler Maggie's shorts. He held them up and looked at them, then bent over and showed them to Max. As soon as Max got a scent, he began tracking the area. Max lifted his head and cocked his pointy black ears as he looked up to the picnic area. Then he put his head back down and began tracking again. He headed up, past the grass, past the picnic area and he stopped in the parking lot next to a newer, four door, red Buick Park Avenue.

"This is your car, isn't it?" Officer Butler asked, turning to look and see if the other patrol cars were within sight.

"Yes," Abby said.

"Good boy, Max." Officer Butler bent over and scratched Max behind the ears. "Even though it isn't exactly what we wanted, he needs to be praised for tracking the scent."

Be Careful What You Wish For

Officer Butler placed the shorts back under Max's nose. Max turned and tracked down to the water, but immediately stopped and came back up to where Abby and Tim had been sitting on the blanket. Apparently not satisfied, Max turned and went back down to the water but abruptly circled around and came back up to where Maddie and Maggie had been sitting building the sand castle. Max lifted his leg and relieved himself, right on top of what was left of the sand castle. "I often forget he's still a dog," Officer Butler said. Abby could tell he was somewhat embarrassed.

Officer Butler stuck the shorts under Max's nose again, allowing him to refocus on the scent. He began tracking again, back down to the beach, the sand, the water's edge and again back to the parking lot, all the while everyone traipsing along behind him. This time, however, he stopped at a different spot in the parking lot. Max trotted around a little bit more while he continued tracking, but then returned and sat down. Then Max barked.

Officer Butler looked at Abby and Tim. "Have you parked in or around this area anytime today?"

"No," Abby said.

"Have you taken a walk with the missing child at all today in or around this area?"

"No, not that I recall," Abby glanced at Tim for confirmation.

Tim shook his head, "No."

"I'm going out on a limb here, but I think Maggie was abducted." Officer Butler immediately got on his police radio and told the other two patrol cars to block the entrance and exit to the park. "I need to run up to the entrance and fill my colleagues in on what we know so far. I'll share the photo with them that you gave me so they'll know what she looks like."

"I have another photo in my bag if that would help," Abby said.

"Yes, that would be helpful." The four of them walked toward the beach. "After I get back, I'm going to ask some of the guests a few questions."

"As I said, we already tried that, but no one remembered seeing or hearing anything," Abby said.

Be Careful What You Wish For

"It doesn't hurt to ask again. You are positive you saw nothing out of the ordinary? You didn't notice if there were any strange people around . . . no one was watching your family?" Office Butler asked, sitting his sunglasses back on the bridge of his nose.

"Not that I can remember."

"What time did you arrive at the lake today?"

"We left our house about ten thirty, and it's a fifteen to twenty minute drive, depending on how well you hit the lights."

"About how many people were here when you arrived?"

"Not many. We were probably the third or fourth group to spread a blanket out in the sand." Abby glanced around the beach, which was now buzzing with activity.

"Where were the other groups?"

"Not close. I didn't really pay that much attention. I just know I wanted to get a spot where we could keep an eye on the girls."

"Do you remember what any of them looked like?"

"No, not really—they were just people—here to go swimming and play in the water."

"Do you remember any funny swimsuits? Were they all Caucasian? Did any of them have a camera? Did you notice any tattoos or scars?"

Abby felt like her head was about to explode from all the questions. "Not really. Just normal people like us, I guess." Abby glanced over at Tim. "Oh wait. I do remember something. It just seemed odd to me at the time, and I even mentioned it to Tim. There was a boy wearing a black t-shirt with a skull and crossbones on it. I remember thinking to myself how nuts he was . . . who would wear such a thing to the beach on a hot summer day?"

"That *is* unusual. Did he take it off and go out into the water?"

"Not that I recall, but then again, I wasn't paying that much attention," Abby replied as she shrugged.

"Did he get here before or after you?"

Be Careful What You Wish For

"He was already here . . . he and some lady. She looked as if she could have been his mother."

"Where were they sitting?"

"Right there, where those people are putting their stuff down," Abby pointed at a family who had, apparently, just arrived as they were spreading out a blanket and dropping beach toys on the sand.

"What about the water? Do you need to call the diving team?" Tim asked as Abby squatted on the blanket to search for another photo.

Tim usually let his wife do most of the talking when it came to the girls and their well-being. It was part of their understood role as parents. The one time Tim had to take Maddie to the doctor for her six-month well baby visit, Abby questioned him like a prosecuting attorney when he returned. "What did the doctor say? How much does she weigh? What percentile is that? What is the circumference of her head? Did the doctor say that was normal? Did she get any shots? Did you tell her about the diaper rash?" On and on she went—so after that, they decided Abby would do most of the talking and Tim would stand back and listen.

"I don't think that's necessary, Mr. Taylor, considering Max didn't indicate Maggie was out in the water. Believe it or not, he's been trained to differentiate between new footprints and old footprints. The scent is stronger on the prints that are more current and Max seems to think her feet last touched the ground up in the parking lot." He looked at Abby. "Did you find that photo?"

Abby stood up, looking at the picture as tears spilled down her face. "This was taken on her last birthday. This is all of us singing as she blew out her birthday candles, three of them, all by herself."

"Don't worry, ma'am. She'll have many more birthdays, and you'll have many more photos." Officer Butler finally took the photograph delicately from Abby's hand. She noticed Office Butler couldn't help but smile at the little girl smiling back at him.

"Do you want me to ride with you up to the front gate?" Tim asked.

"No. Just stay here and keep your wife and daughter company. Max and I shouldn't be too long. Keep an eye out and see if you notice anything out of the ordinary."

23

✒ *Chapter Three* ✑

Officer Butler phoned police headquarters as he and Max rode on the shoulder. Dust and dirt swirled in the air behind them as they passed several agitated guests while they sat in line in their vehicles, waiting to exit the park. For what he had in mind, he knew they would need a search warrant. As soon as they arrived at the front gate, he saw the other two officers, Wolfe and Rife. He climbed out of his car and met them near the entrance.

Officer Butler quickly filled them in on what he knew so far, referring to his notes. "She was playing in the sand with her sister, and then when her parents took their eyes off her for a few minutes, they turned to check on her, and she was gone. Max tracked around, and seemed to indicate that her feet last touched the ground in the parking lot, nowhere near the family vehicle. The parents describe the incident as if the child had vanished into thin air."

"Vanished?" Officer Wolfe, a seasoned police officer, asked. Officer Wolfe, a man in his mid-60s with silver hair and blue gray eyes, had already planned to retire at the end of the year. He was a widower and wanted to spend his retirement years on a houseboat out in the middle of a lake. It didn't really matter which lake, as long as there was fresh water and he could fish. During his career, Officer Wolfe had seen his share of missing children. Nine times out of ten, the outcome was not good.

"Yes, vanished. It's the oddest thing. No one saw anything. No one heard anything. She was there one second, and the next, she was gone. I asked the parents if they recall seeing anything out of the ordinary. You know . . . like someone watching them, or something, which may have struck them as odd; however, neither parent was able to think of anything. That is, until Mrs. Taylor, remembered that she'd seen a boy wearing a black t-shirt."

"A boy with a black t-shirt . . . what does that have to do with anything?"

"Probably nothing; however, I did ask if she remembered anyone who was wearing an odd or unique swimsuit, and that was when she remembered the boy in the black t-shirt."

"So what's our game plan?" Officer Wolfe asked, feet spread apart and arms crossed in front of him.

"Both of you stay up here at the gate and work with the attendants. As soon as I get a call from the station, indicating that the search warrant came through, we'll need to search vehicles to see if we can find the missing girl before whoever took her, leaves the area. In the meantime, I'm going to go back down by the lake and talk to a few people." Officer Butler glanced over to make sure Max was still okay in the car.

"Do you have a photo of the missing child?" Officer Wolfe asked.

"Yes I do. I left it in the patrol car, I'll be right back." Officer Butler turned and hurried over to the patrol car. When he opened the car door, the stifling heat hit him like a ton of bricks. He grabbed Max's leash—the signal for him to hop out—since he didn't want to leave him in the hot car any longer than he absolutely had to. Even with the windows open, the temperature was dangerously high. When he returned, he handed the photo to Officer Wolfe.

Officer Wolfe glanced at the little girl and shook his head. "Have you contacted Detective Stephens?"

"I tried. He's not available today. I think I remember him mentioning that he needed to have some tests run over at Crystal Clinic. I'll fill him in, though, first thing tomorrow morning."

"How are the parents holding up?"

"So far, they seem to be doing okay. I don't think the whole thing has sunk in just yet. They seem like nice folks. It's such a shame." Officer Butler shrugged.

"What about the sister?"

"I don't think she understands what's going on. She knows her sister is missing, but I don't think she realizes exactly what that means." Officer Butler started toward the admission station at the entrance to Lake Gerber as the two other officers followed. "Thought I'd help you explain to the attendants what's going on."

Officers Butler and Wolfe entered the small admission station that sat at the entrance to Lake Gerber, about fifty yards from the main road. Max remained outside with Officer Rife. One side had a window for the attendant to collect the entrance fee, and the other side had a window to answer questions and talk with the guests as they finished their visit, and exited the park. Both sides had mechanical arms, which were raised and lowered once the guest had either paid, or was ready to exit the grounds. After brief introductions, Officer Butler explained to the two attendants, Keith and Sue, what had transpired and what the goal was—to find the missing girl *before* she left the park. Both Keith and Sue appeared hesitant. The attendants crossed their arms and then proceeded to shift their weight back and forth. They acknowledged they were newer employees at Lake Gerber and had been hired just a few months prior for their summer season.

Before Officer Butler left, he turned to Keith with one last question. "Oh, by the way, is Lake Gerber outfitted with a security system?"

"Yes," Keith answered.

That was the first *good* news he heard since this whole thing started. "Excellent! Is there a security tape of today's activities that might be available?"

"From what I understand," Keith said, "there are three cameras in the park, but no recorder. This park has been around for over sixty years. It's family owned and not very up-to-date on the latest, high-tech equipment."

"Do you know where the cameras are located?" Officer Butler sighed.

"Yes, only at the stations where money changes hands. There is one here at the entrance." Keith pointed at the camera mounted in the corner. "Also, there's one at the concession stand, and in the paddleboat rental station."

"If there's no recorder, what are they used for?"

"As it was explained to me when I was first hired, management watches the staff from time to time. Since you never know when you're being watched, it tends to keep you honest." Keith shrugged his shoulders.

It wasn't long before Mr. Green, the owner of Lake Gerber, was at the front of the park, wondering what was going on. He had heard about the commotion but had been in the middle of a crisis and had to run out and get more ice. Officer Butler quickly filled him in on the details they had gathered so far in the investigation.

"How many people work here at Lake Gerber?" Officer Butler asked.

"We have grown substantially over the years. We currently employ about fifteen, full time employees in the summer months." Mr. Green ran his hand through his hair—what was left of it, anyway. He was short, round, and reminded Officer Butler of Mr. Magoo—but, with a little more hair.

"Keith told us there are security cameras but no recorder. Is that correct?"

"Yes. That is correct." He nodded.

"If you don't mind my asking, why would you invest money in security cameras, but no recorder?"

"Lake Gerber is family owned and has been for several generations. We pride ourselves in treating our staff like family. If we trust them, they trust us. We find just having the cameras is good enough. We don't need a record of their every movement. Besides, if we did have a recorder, we would record the employees, not the guests, so it wouldn't help with your investigation."

"Okay, then; I guess we're done in here. I'm going to go back over to the lake. The other two officers will start searching the vehicles before they let them leave the grounds. Not a blanket, cooler, bag, container, or box should be left untouched or unopened. Hopefully, we will find the missing girl quickly and this will all be over."

"Please be assured our staff here at Lake Gerber will do whatever they can to cooperate. The last thing I need is bad publicity. I'm a father myself, so I'm determined that this story is going to have a happy ending. Oh, and by the way, I'm not sure if you are interested, but we have a public address system that you are free to use if you need it."

"I appreciate the offer, and I may just take you up on that . . . thanks for taking care of this so quickly." Officer Butler turned to Sue and Keith just as his phone started ringing. "Excuse me, just one minute." Officer Butler answered the phone, spoke quickly with the person on the other end, and hung up. "Our search warrant has been signed so we're good to go. You understand what you need to do, correct?" He asked the employees and the other two officers.

"I think so," Keith answered.

Sue just nodded her head, "yes."

"Make sure you tell the drivers and *all* the passengers to exit their vehicles while you perform your search. Look under the seats, in trunks, wherever you think a little girl might be hidden. If the missing girl is here, we'll find her."

Officer Butler spoke to several guests, both near the water and also in the picnic area. Almost everyone that had been picnicking had finished eating long before and had cleaned off their picnic tables and packed up their leftovers, ready to head home. He talked to an older gentleman and what appeared to be his grandson, just as they were putting the last of their things in their car.

"Hello, there. I'm Officer Rich Butler. Do you have a moment to speak with me?"

"I guess so," the older man answered. "My name is Cecil, and this is my grandson, Tommy. We were just packing up and getting ready to leave. We got here around noon and it's already past two." He looked at his watch. "We've been fishing a couple of hours and I need to get home to take my afternoon nap. Sometimes it's not so great getting old. You feel like you revert back to being a baby. As soon as I get my tummy full," Cecil said, patting his protruding belly, "it's time for a nap. But, I digress. What is it that you wanted, Officer?"

"This won't take long. Have you seen this little girl here today?" Officer Butler asked as he handed the picture over to Cecil.

"Seems like we did see her earlier; didn't we, Tommy?" Cecil remained holding the photo, but lowered it so Tommy could see.

Tommy looked at the picture. "It's hard to tell, but I don't think so, Grandpa."

"Did you catch any fish?" Officer Butler asked.

"Just a few little ones . . . we threw them back. The thrill is in the catch anyway," Cecil said, with his hand on Tommy's shoulder. "My grandson and I enjoy fishing and it gives us something to do together. I don't know how much longer I'll be around; and years from now, when he thinks of his old grandpa, I want him to have fond memories."

"Thank you for your time. Her family is worried sick over what may have happened to her. So, once you leave, if you or your grandson happen to remember anything—anything at all, please call the police department immediately."

"Will do, Officer," Cecil said, bending over to pick up his tackle box.

"Enjoy the rest of your day—and enjoy that nap." Officer Butler smiled as he walked away.

Next, Officer Butler spoke to a young mother and her son. "Both of us were out in the water swimming. I do remember seeing her and a woman playing Ring-Around-the-Rosy. I assumed it was her mother. Tyler went to get in line for the water slide, and then I went up to the concession stand to get a soda. Sorry, I don't remember any more."

"As you can imagine, her parents are worried sick."

"I can't imagine. If anything ever happened to Tyler, I don't know what I'd do," she said, shaking her head.

"After you go home this evening, if you happen to think of anything else, please contact the police department."

Officer Butler questioned an older couple who introduced themselves as Harold and Mildred Billows. They told how they had seen the two little girls down by the water, playing in the sand. They both commented on how cute the littlest one was. Mildred stated that she thought she looked a lot like Shirley Temple had in her heyday, but without the curly hair. The Billows didn't remember anything else, so he moved on.

Officer Butler noticed another family who were just unpacking their towels and sand toys. Even though he was pretty sure they hadn't seen anything down by the water, he thought perhaps they might have seen something in the parking lot when they arrived. When he asked, they explained that they had been the last car admitted into the park before they'd closed the entrance; and, no, they didn't recall seeing anything worth mentioning.

Be Careful What You Wish For

"Thank you for your time." Officer Butler retrieved the photo, and then moved on to a group of four teenagers; two boys and two girls. The boys were busy tossing a football back and forth in the sand, and the girls were sprawled out on a beach blanket, sunbathing.

"Excuse me, I'm Officer Butler, and this is my partner, Max. How long have you been sitting in this spot today?" Officer Butler asked as the two girls flipped over, and sat up.

"We've been here a couple of hours," one of the girls answered as she offered her outstretched hand. "My name is Sandy, and this is Courtney." Courtney followed suit and offered her hand, as well.

"I'm hoping you might have some information that may help me. We've been called out to help locate a missing child. She was last seen, right there on the beach," Officer Butler pointed directly in front of them to the water, "about an hour ago maybe longer." Then he handed the girls the photo that Abby had given him. "This is her."

Both girls looked at the photo, and then exchanged glances.

"We spoke to her mom earlier. She doesn't look familiar, but as we told her mom, we haven't been sitting here the whole time. Earlier we went to the concession stand for some chips and a soda. A minute or two ago we were in the water cooling off before we started sunbathing," Courtney said. Officer Butler believed their story, as both girls were still wet.

"So, you don't remember anything?"

Sandy looked at Courtney and spoke up. "Something we thought was odd *did* happen earlier, but I'm not sure it involves the missing girl. At least not that I know of," Sandy said, hesitantly.

"Go on . . . if you saw or heard anything that might be helpful," Officer Butler urged, "please tell me. It doesn't matter how stupid or unimportant you might think it is."

"Well, there is this really creepy kid in our class at school. His name is David Miller. He's rather quiet and keeps to himself. Earlier we were sitting here, and we saw David with his mom. At least, we assumed it was his mom. She looked a lot older than him, somewhere between forty-five and fifty years old. She had fake blonde hair and bright red lips."

Be Careful What You Wish For

"How do you know her hair color was fake?"

"The roots were showing. They looked like coffee grounds." Courtney grimaced.

Officer Butler smiled as he scribbled a few words on his notepad.

"They were already here when we arrived, but they just sat on a blanket in the sand. Both of them were dressed for swimming, but neither one of them went into the water. At one point, there were three more boys who joined them who were younger. They kept coming and going the whole time they were here, but *none* of them ever went in the water. David and his mom just sat and watched the kids playing. They never really spoke out loud, at least, not that we could hear. Eventually, David got up and left. The woman continued sitting by herself for a while."

"Anything else?"

"No . . . after David left, we stopped watching. When we finally looked back over, the lady was gone, too. It was just really creepy. David was sitting there wearing that black t-shirt, and he had on sunglasses. It just seemed strange to us. I mean, who goes to the beach on a hot summer day, dressed for swimming, but *never* goes in the water and *wears black?*"

"Hmmm, interesting . . . do you remember what the lady looked like?"

"Not really," Courtney said. "We were watching David. I guess she was normal looking. I don't recall anything *odd* about her. She *did* have on bright red lipstick."

"Yes, I believe you already mentioned that. You said . . . they didn't talk?"

"They did talk, to each other—very softly, almost a whisper. We couldn't hear any of their conversation," Sandy said. "But they kept pointing at different kids on the beach the whole time they talked."

"Kids? What kids?"

"Just the kids that were playing in the sand and the ones down there by the water," she pointed to where the two younger girls had been playing in the sand earlier. "I think they were enjoying watching them."

Be Careful What You Wish For

Officer Butler, once again, jotted a few notes down on the pad he carried. "You said David Miller was in your class at school?"

"Yes, we all just graduated from Bunting Valley High at the beginning of June—class of 2010."

"Thank you. You've been a great help. If you remember anything else, please contact the police department."

Max, still busy sniffing wherever they went kept pulling Officer Butler over to the sand where Bea had been kneeling, talking to Maggie. Despite the heat, he was all business when involved in a case.

"Okay, boy . . . *okay* . . . we'll go back down to the water."

Officer Butler let Max lead him down to the water. Max lifted his nose and was sniffing the air. "What is it, boy? Huh . . . what do you think you smell, hmm?" Just then Officer Butler saw something sparkle. He looked down and saw something poking out of the sand. It was a charm bracelet with five charms. Four of the charms were shaped like sports paraphernalia; a football, baseball, bowling ball, and soccer ball. Each of those charms was inscribed with a name: MICHAEL, JOSHUA, DAVID, and JOHN. All, that is, except one. The fifth charm, in the shape of a princess crown, was *blank*. Officer Butler studied it a moment longer, brushed the sand particles from it, and then placed it in his pocket.

⌒ *Chapter Four* ⌒

Bea leaned forward in her seat, trying to get a better view. *What in the hell? It looks like they have the road closed. What in tarnation is going on?*

Bea's van was the eleventh vehicle in line to exit Lake Gerber. She noticed some of the other cars were turning around as they seemed to decide it would be more convenient to go back to the lake and continue swimming, instead of sitting and waiting in a hot, parked car. Bea, too, decided she would turn around until whatever was going on at the front gate played out so she could leave the park. Arriving back at the parking lot, she saw Barbie and Ken and the little fat girl, as well as a police officer, and a dog.

"Oh *shit*, I can't believe it! They've blocked the exit to search for Maggie! I can't believe they got here so fast. I thought for sure we would be long gone before any of this happened." Bea motioned out the open window at all the activity. "This wasn't part of the plan. What are we going to do now?" She opened her hand and cupped her forehead, massaging just above her eyebrows.

Bea drove around the parking lot, trying not to look suspicious. She even managed to wave at the police officer. The officer tipped his head and nodded in return. Bea then drove away, and parked as far from the activity as possible under a huge, American Sycamore. The shade tree stood next to a few other parked cars facing the paddleboat rental station and the lake.

"I need to sit just a minute and come up with a new plan. Think, think, *think* . . ." Bea poked her forehead with her three center fingers. The other passengers in the van were quiet. "I got it, *I got it!*" Bea said, as a new plan popped into her head.

"What kind of *genius* idea do you have now?" David asked.

"We're going on a paddleboat ride!" Bea announced proudly.

"We're going on a *what . . . ?*" David asked.

"They're too busy at the main entrance, so they won't be looking out in the middle of the lake. We'll go out there and paddle around while I think of a way to get us out of here."

33

Be Careful What You Wish For

"Have you *completely* lost your mind?" Sometimes David had to question his mom's sanity.

"David, take this money and rent us a four person boat." Bea completely ignored him as she pulled a five dollar bill from the padded bra of her swimsuit. "Get a life jacket for Maggie and bring it here. If they ask, tell them the life jacket is for your sister. I'll put it on her in the van."

David slid the door to the van open and jumped out onto the steaming, hot pavement. "What if they ask for an ID or something?" He asked, walking up to where Bea was still sitting in the driver's seat, just inside the open window.

"You're a smart boy. You'll figure it out."

David walked away shaking his head. The paddleboat rental stand, only about fifty yards from the parked van, was a diminutive lean-to with a tin roof. It stood on a flat piece of land slightly elevated from the lake. Two teenage girls stood behind the stainless steel counter, which was scratched and worn from years of use, and another staff member—a teenage boy—passed David on the sidewalk as it forked and went down towards the water and the loading dock. David noticed he was going to help some guests; presumably to help disembark the boat.

Each of the girls had long, straight, blonde hair held up with a hair clip. They were tan from working outside and each of them wore a red one-piece suit. They could have been twins, they looked so much alike. LAKE GERBER was printed on the front of the swimsuits in small, white, block letters. Directly behind the counter was a rack with pegs, which held several life jackets and vests. Bea couldn't hear what was going on, but she was ecstatic when David headed back in her direction with a life jacket for Maggie.

"What did they say?" Bea asked as soon as the door opened with a jerk. The fluid motion it once had was lost with years of dirt and grime on the tracks.

David threw the life vest on the floor. "They didn't say much. They asked for an ID and I told them I didn't bring my driver's license, so they made me sign a waiver."

"Did you use your real name?"

"No, I put *your* name."

34

Be Careful What You Wish For

"What? Why in the world would you do that? You are such an *idiot!"*

"Relax. I scribbled it. I seriously doubt they will be able to read it. It looked more like Beau Miller."

"Seriously, David, you have a lot to learn about being deceptive. Oh well, enough about that. Maggie honey, we're going for a ride on a paddleboat." Bea flashed her tiny teeth as she turned her head around to look over her shoulder at Maggie. "Have you ever ridden in a boat before?"

"No. Can't swim."

"You don't need to swim. David got you a really nice life jacket. Bea slid between the passenger and driver seats, and picked up the life jacket.

"Don't just sit there like an idiot . . . help her with the seat belt, Joshua!" Joshua was younger than David, and resembled him slightly. He wore a *Yankees* baseball cap, turned backwards, and his hair, dark and wiry, stuck out from under it at the sides. At the mention of his name, Joshua snapped out of a trance. He unbuckled the seat belt, and Maggie just sat there, the silence in the van, was deafening now.

Finally, Bea spoke up. "Come here, sweetie. This is going to be so much fun." Bea was kneeling in the open door and Maggie hesitantly hopped down and walked toward her. "I haven't gone out on a paddleboat in a really long time, and I'm so excited that you are going with me!" Bea began to pull the life jacket over Maggie's beautiful swimsuit. The color of her suit reminded Bea of the way the Seattle sky looked just after a rainstorm; it wasn't a true blue, and it wasn't grey either. It had small straps, with a ruffle around the middle of her waist. Luckily, the life jacket was more than just a jacket, as it covered most of her upper body. "David, you and Joshua come with us. The paddleboat seats four. John and Mikey—you need to crack the window a little, and stay in the van. Don't go *anywhere.* Don't talk to *anyone.* Moreover, don't do anything *stupid."* Bea grabbed Joshua's baseball cap from his head, exposing a full head of dark, curly hair. "Here, Maggie, you can wear Joshua's cap to keep the sun out of your eyes." The cap was so big it seemed to swallow Maggie's head but at least it covered up most of her blonde hair.

Be Careful What You Wish For

Bea climbed out of the van and picked Maggie up. It was obvious Maggie's mom had carried her many times, as her tiny legs instinctively circled around Bea's hips. Joshua and David followed as the four of them made their way down to the water. Bea instructed them to get the boat and paddle it over to where she and Maggie would be waiting, about twenty-five feet from the spot which was designated for loading and unloading the paddleboats. Bea didn't want to climb on the boat from the wooden dock, which was in plain sight, for fear one of the attendants might recognize Maggie.

Doing as they were told, the male attendant helped them board and get started as Maggie and Bea stood several feet away, obstructed from view by a tall patch of grass. David and Joshua sat in the front two seats and brought the boat around to where Maggie and Bea waited. The two female attendants were too busy laughing, chatting, and text messaging on their cell phones to notice they had not even boarded in the proper area, and the male attendant had already diverted his attention to another boat returning to the dock. Minutes later, Bea, Maggie, David, and Joshua were in the paddleboat, headed toward the far corner of the lake. The area intended for paddleboats was roped off with a line of white buoys attached to a yellow rope. It was a beautiful day. Even though it was hot, there was a slight breeze out on the water. Lake Gerber was absolutely breathtaking. It was surrounded by white, sandy beaches on one side, and tall cattails on the other, with overgrown evergreens in every direction as far as the eye could see. A couple of long-legged cranes were standing near the water's edge, seemingly in search of their next meal. It was quite peaceful. Bea decided she could sit out in the paddleboat for as long as it took the commotion to clear or, at least until she came up with a plan. There was one thing, however, she hadn't counted on; David had only rented the paddleboat for thirty minutes. In a little over thirty minutes, one of the female attendants yelled through the megaphone that it was time to return their watercraft to the dock.

"You, *idiot . . . !*" Bea slapped David on the back of the head. "Can't you do *anything* right?"

David, sat straight up, startled, "*What?* What did I do?"

"Did you rent this thing for *just half an hour?*" Bea was annoyed.

Be Careful What You Wish For

David rubbed the back of his head and turned to face her. "That's all the money you gave me."

"Well, at some point, don't you think you could have mentioned that to me?"

"Sorry, but I thought you knew."

"How was I supposed to know? I'm not a mind reader!"

"You seem to think you have this whole situation under control. I thought you knew *everything*." David turned and sat up straight.

"Don't start with me, David," she warned. "I'm not in the mood. The good news is, however, I did come up with a plan, which I believe will work perfectly!"

"Oh *goodie* . . ." David raised his hands, palms up, making a gesture as if he were raising the roof. Bea reached over and smacked him on the back of the head again.

"The hard part is going to be getting out of this boat without calling attention to ourselves, but I think we can manage."

David and Joshua paddled the boat up to the dock. An older man was at the paddleboat rental station talking to all the attendants, which gave them the perfect opportunity to exit the boat and get out of sight. The man was waving his arms and pointing everywhere. David, Joshua, and Bea climbed up, onto the wooden dock. Several planks had been replaced over the years making the dock different shades of black and brown. Bea stuck her hands out, and Maggie lifted her arms up so Bea could grab her. Quickly, the four of them headed to the van. Once there, Bea opened the van door, stood Maggie inside, and jerked the life jacket off her so violently it left red marks on Maggie's arms. Maggie began to whimper. "Here," Bea snapped as she handed the life jacket to David. "Turn this back in and don't say a word to anyone." Maggie toddled back to where she'd been seated before.

"Do I look stupid?" David turned and went back to the rental station. Just as David was making his way back to the van, the public address system came on with a loud sharp beep and then slight static.

"MAY I HAVE YOUR ATTENTION, PLEASE?" A man's voice rang out clearly over the loudspeaker. **"EARLIER TODAY, WE BELIEVE A CHILD WAS ABDUCTED ON THE PREMISES OF**

LAKE GERBER. THE CHILD IS A FEMALE CAUCASION, SHE IS THREE YEARS OLD, APPROXIMATELY THREE FEET TALL AND WEARING A LIGHT, OR PASTEL, BLUISH-GREY, ONE-PIECE SWIMSUIT. SHE WAS LAST SEEN SHORTLY AFTER ONE P.M. PLAYING IN THE SAND WITH HER SISTER BY THE SWIMMING AREA. SHE ANSWERS TO THE NAME OF MAGGIE. SHE HAS SHOULDER LENGTH BLONDE HAIR WITH BLUE EYES. WE BELIEVE SHE WAS BAREFOOT. THE ENTRANCE AND EXIT GATES TO LAKE GERBER HAVE BEEN BLOCKED. NO VEHICLES WILL BE PERMITTED TO EXIT UNTIL THEY HAVE BEEN THOROUGHLY SEARCHED BY THE ATTENDANTS AND POLICE OFFICERS ON DUTY. IF YOU REMEMBER SEEING, OR HEARING ANYTHING YOU THINK MAY HELP, PLEASE SPEAK TO ONE OF THE POLICE OFFICERS CURRENTLY ON THE GROUNDS, OR CONTACT THE BUNTING VALLEY POLICE DEPARTMENT DIRECTLY. THANK YOU."** More static, and then the PA system went dead.

"Did you hear that?" David asked as soon as he climbed in the van and shut the door.

"Yes, I heard it," Bea said.

"I *told you* this was a *stupid idea*. We're *never* getting out of here." David was actually starting to panic.

"Oh yes, we will. I have a great plan." Bea was so proud of herself.

"I can only imagine," David mumbled under his breath, finding his seat. When he sat down, something bulged in his pocket. He reached in and pulled out the keys for paddleboat number four. *I can't believe I forgot to turn back in the keys.* He thought of mentioning it to Bea but decided against it. He placed the keys back in his pocket and resumed looking out the window.

"Did they ask you any questions when you returned the life vest?"

"No. They were all talking to some man. They didn't even look at me."

Be Careful What You Wish For

"Good!" Bea said as she started the van to move to a spot further away from the paddleboat station. "Maggie," she said, "We're going to play a game. Do you like games?"

"Uh-huh." Maggie nodded her head, "yes."

"It's called Hide and Seek. Have you ever played Hide and Seek before?"

"Uh-huh."

"Do you like Hide and Seek?" Bea stopped and parked at the far end of the lot.

"Uh-huh."

"Good, good . . . okay, John . . . ?" John was twelve years old, and seated in the middle of the van in the captain's chair. The chair originally had a button to make it swivel, but the button had broken long ago, so it swiveled at will, never facing the right direction when it was supposed to. John was chewing bubble gum and had just blown a great big, pink bubble. At the mention of his name, he put his foot on the ground and swiveled around to face Bea.

"*What* do you want?" John sounded irritated.

"I'm going to need your help. I'm going to climb out and slide open the door. I want you to open up that beach chair there in the red nylon carrying bag." Bea pointed at a bag lying on the floor next to John. "Take the chair out and hand it to me. I'm going to put the chair up front on the floor by Mikey. Then Maggie, you climb in and hide in the bag. No one will ever find you. It will be the best hiding spot ever!"

John looked at Bea as though she had lost her mind. "You can't be serious."

"*Dead serious* . . . now *hurry up!* We don't have much time." Bea was already up and standing in the open door.

"What if she suffocates? Did you think of that?" John asked.

"We'll just find another little girl, that's all. Now get up and do what I said. You know what happens when you don't listen to me!"

Maggie began to cry—big, crocodile tears trailed down her chubby cheeks.

"*Shhh* . . . you can't cry, little one. If you cry, they'll find you, and you'll lose the game." This made Maggie cry even louder.

"Oh shut up, Maggie! Stop crying and get in the bag." Bea was losing what was left of her patience. John shook his head.

A scared little Maggie did as she was told. Still barefoot and never buckled in, she hopped off the seat and sat down inside the bag. She lay down on her back and stretched out. Then she curled her slight legs up to her chest and lay perfectly still, while John zipped the bag up over her face like a body bag. Maggie whimpered softly.

Bea started the van, crossed her fingers, and headed toward the exit.

Officer Butler received word that the attendants at the paddleboat rental station remembered a teenage boy asking for a life jacket for his sister. As soon as he arrived, after brief introductions, Brooke began, "A teenage boy, wearing sunglasses, with poker straight charcoal black hair parted down the middle, came in and rented a four-passenger paddleboat. He seemed a little shifty when he asked for a life jacket for his little sister."

"Shifty? What exactly does that mean?"

"Even though he was wearing sunglasses, he never looked directly at us; and when he spoke, his voice was so quiet that I had to ask him to repeat himself a few times. He just struck me as dishonest. Short, precise answers almost as if they had been rehearsed." Brooke stood leaning on the counter, twirling her ponytail around her index finger.

Officer Butler nodded, getting a better idea of what David Miller might look like. "So what happened next?"

"We asked him for an ID and he didn't have one. So, we made him sign a waiver; it's just a legal document indicating that he is a licensed driver and Lake Gerber is held harmless for anything that may result from him taking a boat out."

"Where is the form?"

"It's one of these, here." Tiffany handed him over a stack of about seven forms.

40

Officer Butler looked through them and didn't see any that said David Miller. He did see one where the last name looked like it could be Miller but the handwriting was so atrocious, he couldn't be sure. One thing he knew for sure, the first name on the form definitely was NOT David. "So what happened after that?"

"I asked what size his sister was and he said, 'small'. I asked 'How small?' He said, 'Thirty pounds.' The only time he really elaborated and said more than a word or two was when we asked where she was. That's when he said she was sleeping in their vehicle, and his mom would put it on her, since she was often crabby when she first woke up. He gave us a five dollar bill, which paid for half an hour. I think we told him boat number four, but I could be wrong. Regardless, we gave him a life vest, and a set of keys—and he left with them."

"Don't you keep track of the boat numbers and which ones you rent to which guests?"

"Generally not." Tiffany turned to point to a small peg board attached to the back wall just behind the counter. "This peg board here has all the keys and if the keys are there, the boat is fair game. Besides, Marcus is down on the boat dock. He helps with loading and unloading. It's a simple system. We've never had any issues. If a boat goes out of commission, the keys aren't on the board."

"Did anything else seem unusual about the boy?" Officer Butler was growing agitated at the lack of procedure anyone at Lake Gerber seemed to follow. Security cameras, which did not film anything, and now they just rented out boats to whoever came in with a five dollar bill with no ID required.

"Now that you mention it," Brooke said. "It struck me as odd that the boy was wearing a black t-shirt. It's almost *ninety degrees* out here. Most of the paddleboat renters are in their swimming trunks or swimsuits, not a black t-shirt."

"That's the third time today that someone has mentioned a boy in a black t-shirt. Officer Butler found this incredulous. He looked at his notes and continued, "So, you're sure he said, *vehicle?* Not car, truck, or van, but . . . *vehicle?*"

"Yes, I'm positive. He said *vehicle.*" Tiffany looked at Brooke to make sure they were in agreement.

Be Careful What You Wish For

"Was he acting nervous or jittery?" Officer Butler asked.

"No, he wasn't acting nervous or jittery, just shifty, like I said before." Tiffany continued. "I guess now that I look back on it, it was peculiar we never got a good look at his sister—the little girl who was wearing the life jacket."

"Is that normal procedure?" Officer Butler asked.

"Is what normal procedure?" Tiffany responded.

"That you hand over a life jacket without giving instructions about how to put it on, or even seeing the person it's intended for?"

"No, I guess not. We've never had any problems, and most people know how to put on a life jacket. Besides, Marcus is down by the water and he checks those things. To be perfectly honest, Officer, I was waiting for a text message and I just wanted to get him out of here."

Officer Butler could only shake his head at her frankness. "I need to speak with Marcus. Is he here?"

"I think he went on break. Mr. Green was here filling us in on the details and he sent Marcus on break. He thought Marcus looked a little dehydrated and he was complaining of feeling a little dizzy."

"Okay. While I wait for him to return, I'll have Max see if he can pick up a scent." When Officer Butler turned to leave, he almost bumped right into Marcus, as he rounded the corner carrying a big bottle of water.

"I should know better than to work out in the sun that long without hydration," Marcus said as he took a big sip from his bottle.

Tiffany rolled her eyes. She never really cared for Marcus. He had a know-it-all attitude that she found infuriating. "Marcus, this is Officer Butler. He'd like to ask you a few questions about one of our paddleboat renters."

"Shoot," Marcus, a tall skinny boy, about seventeen or eighteen years old, said. He had longer hair that fell in soft curls, almost as if he had a perm that was growing out. The sun had bleached his hair, and it was currently several different shades of brown, auburn, and blonde. He had on no shirt, but red swim trunks, and a loose braided bracelet around his wrist.

Be Careful What You Wish For

Referring to his notes, Officer Butler began, "Tiffany and Brooke seem to think they rented a paddleboat to a boy in a black t-shirt. Do you remember him?"

"Yes, absolutely yes. He was one of the last boats I helped load before I got light headed."

Finally, an employee with some common sense who remembers something worthwhile. "Who was with him?" Officer Butler asked, as he was beginning to feel encouraged.

"Just some other kid. A boy. About the same size as him, maybe a little smaller."

"So there was no little girl."

"Positive. There were just two boys. One with sunglasses and a black t-shirt, and the other one had curly dark hair. There was no little girl."

Tiffany jumped in, "Marcus, how can that be? When we called for them to bring their boat back in, I saw four people out in that boat."

"You must be mistaken, *Tiffany*. Perhaps you were looking at a different boat out in the water. That far out, it's hard to read the numbers. The boat with the kid in the black t-shirt—there were just *two* riders."

Tiffany stomped her feet and stormed off.

"Sorry about that," Marcus said to Officer Butler. "Tiffany doesn't like it when she's wrong."

Officer Butler turned to Brooke, who was still standing there. "What about you? Did you see them?"

"Yes," she turned to look at Marcus. "I'm sorry Marcus but I'm going to have to agree with Tiffany on this one. There were definitely four people in the boat when we asked them to bring it back in. Perhaps the sun did more than make you light headed. Maybe you weren't seeing or thinking clearly."

"I guess that's possible." Marcus stopped and scratched his head. "But honestly, I don't remember seeing a little girl."

"What about the life jacket? Did you get it back?"

Tiffany looked at Marcus and Marcus looked at Tiffany. She finally spoke up, "I assume so. They all look alike so it's hard to tell."

"Can Max see them? Perhaps he can figure out which one she may have worn."

"Sure," Brooke answered—and then hesitated—"but once a life jacket or vest is returned, we spray them with an antibacterial substance." Brooke pointed at a can of disinfectant sitting on the end of the counter. "The spray is supposed to remove all the germs, but if it works as good as it's supposed to, it may have removed more than just the germs."

Officer Butler picked it up and inspected the can. There was still a bead of disinfectant foam on the nozzle. He turned it to read the label. *Kills 99.9% of germs.* He put the can back on counter and sighed. "It's worth a try. Since this just happened, it should be one of the vests hanging near the front, don't you think? Or maybe you haven't sprayed it and put it back yet?" Officer Butler tried to sound hopeful.

Brooke and Marcus looked at each other and both shrugged their shoulders. Officer Butler led Max behind the counter to the rack where the life preservers were hanging. The rack was huge, about ten feet tall with three rows and seven columns of pegs. Each peg contained at least one—but most often two or three—life preservers of either some sort of jacket or vest. Officer Butler let Max sniff the ones on the lower pegs, but when Max wasn't having any luck, the officer asked if the attendants could pull all of them off and lay them on the concrete floor so Max could have better access. Marcus and Brooke began removing the life preservers from their pegs, and piled them on the floor. There were twenty-nine in all; fourteen life jackets, and fifteen life vests.

"There's twenty-nine here. Is that how many you had this morning?"

"I don't really know. I've never counted them." Brooke was beginning to look nervous as she stood with her arm outstretched, drumming her fingers across the stainless steel counter top.

Officer Butler sighed and let Max smell Maggie's shorts once more, and Max began sniffing. He went around and around, pawing at the pile, causing them fall loosely to the ground. When Max was done, each life jacket or vest laid on its own on the concrete floor. There was only one vest he kept returning to. Even then, however, it wasn't enough to be positive Maggie had worn it, since Max gave no signal to Officer Butler, other than returning to the same jacket.

"Well, it doesn't look as if he's picking up a definite scent. He keeps returning to this one, but even then, he doesn't appear to be certain." Officer Butler held it up to gauge the size. "It appears to be the correct size . . . but, I just don't know." He pulled it close to his nose and sniffed. It smelled of disinfectant. "Do you, by chance, know where they parked?"

"No, not really, but I imagine it was pretty close. For all I know, they may have parked right there." Brooke pointed at the parking spots visible from where she stood.

"So, you didn't see the vehicle?"

Brooke shook her head, "no." "I feel absolutely awful. We should have been paying closer attention."

"I've worked here for the past three summers, and *nothing* like this has *ever* happened before," Marcus said.

"I think Max and I will go out on the dock and see if he can pick up her scent there. What boat did you say they went out in?"

"I'm not really sure. I think it was number four, but I could be wrong," Brooke answered. She turned to look at the pegboard that held the keys. The keys to boat number four were gone. "Looks like we already rented out number four to someone else. The keys are missing."

Officer Butler let Max pull him down the dock, as Brooke and Marcus stood back and watched. A few paddleboats were still out in the water, and the remaining ones were all sitting in a neat little row tied to the end of the dock. There was no sign of Maggie's footprints, or scent anywhere, and Max did not seem very interested in tracking. Officer Butler couldn't even get him to go the end of the dock and was having doubts that Maggie had been out in one of these boats, ever.

"Max can't seem to find anything. I think we'll go look around the parking lot to see if he can detect anything there. Thanks for your help."

"I hope you find her," Brooke said as Officer Butler was walking away.

Be Careful What You Wish For

Officer Butler led Max to the only three vehicles parked near the paddleboat rental station. Ten minutes later, disappointed, and no sign of Maggie ever having been in or around the paddleboat rental area, Officer Butler decided to take Max up to the entrance to help search the vehicles. With Max's keen nose, he'd be able to find Maggie's scent if there were a trace of it anywhere. "I just hope we aren't too late, boy," Officer Butler scratched Max's hindquarters, just above his tail. It was true what Abby Taylor had said earlier; it was as if Maggie had vanished.

ᥱ᥊ᤍ *Chapter Five* ᥊᥈

The row of vehicles at the exit from Lake Gerber had dwindled down to four; a convertible, an older hatchback, a four door family sedan, and a pickup truck with a crew cab. With two police officers and two gate attendants, they could work several vehicles at a time. Keith and Sue worked as a team and searched first, and then officer's Wolfe and Rife followed behind them to make a final check before they cleared the vehicle to leave the grounds.

Bea, John, Mikey, David, and Joshua had already climbed out of their van and stood patiently on the grass as the attendants finished their search of the car in front of them. As the male attendant and his co-worker started towards them, Bea glanced at the boys, reminding them with a single stern look to keep their mouths shut. "How's it going so far?" she asked trying to make light of the situation. The police officers were busy double checking the four cars at the front of the line. One was a bright red Mustang convertible with the top down. There wasn't much room for hiding a three-year-old girl, and the officer finished with his search in less than five minutes. The other three took a little longer, but all of the searches turned up nothing.

"So far so good . . . we haven't found anything, yet. It's been a long, hot day; and just between you and me, I think that little girl is long gone." The male attendant opened a hunter green, Coleman cooler which Bea kept in the back of the van. The cooler was empty except for an inch of water at the very bottom.

"Such a shame," she shook her head. Bea hoped if she kept him involved in conversation, he wouldn't notice the red bag sitting in the middle of the floor. Sometimes, if the answer were the most obvious one, it could get overlooked. Bea hoped by leaving the bag in plain sight, it would be missed. Bea was so proud of Maggie. She hadn't moved a muscle, or made a sound, the entire time while the bag sat, completely lifeless on the floor of the van.

"You don't realize how much stuff people pack up and bring to the beach, until you have to go through it. Some of these people brought enough food to live here for a week," he chuckled.

"I can only imagine. We usually travel pretty light, just a blanket and maybe a drink or two. If we plan on staying longer than a couple of hours, sometimes we bring some snacks—like chips or cookies. Sure beats paying those outrageous prices at the concession stand. With four growing boys, they always seem to be hungry," Bea said.

The female attendant pulled out a rumpled blanket stuffed in the back of the van and sand sprinkled across her feet. Again, their search turned up nothing. One of the officers came back and Bea's heart started to pound loudly. *Oh my God . . . I feel as if my heart is going to jump right of my chest!* "Hello, Officer. I was just talking to this nice young man, and he told me you haven't had any luck today."

"No, ma'am, but it's not for our lack of trying. We've searched one hundred seven vehicles so far, and all of them have turned up empty." The officer shined his flashlight into the van, checking under the seats for something the two attendants might have missed. "How long have you been at the lake today?"

"Oh, quite a while," she answered quickly. "We stopped for a late breakfast on the way and got here about eleven o'clock. My boys love to swim. They've been out in the water most of the day, but now it's time to get back home. I promised them I'd take them swimming this morning if they promised to do a little yard work this evening."

He glanced over at Bea and her boys. "Sounds like a good idea. You help them, and they help you." The officer opened the Coleman cooler for the second time. "This is a great lake for swimming. My wife and I used to bring our kids here when they were younger. They're all grown now. Kevin just turned thirty. He lives in DC and works at the White House as a speech writer. I don't think that boy will *ever* settle down and marry. Every time I talk to him, he seems to be dating a new girl. When they start to get attached, Kevin moves on. A serial heartbreaker is what *I* call him. Kara got married two summers ago, and she and James have a Bed and Breakfast up in the Hamptons. I try to visit a couple of times a year, but, well . . . time has a way of slipping away. One minute they are babies, then you blink, and they are grown adults. My wife died a few years ago; brain aneurism, so it's just me. Family is a wonderful thing. Appreciate them while you can."

"Sounds like you have a wonderful family. Sorry to hear about your wife." Bea smiled. She couldn't believe the officer was telling her so much information about his personal life. *Just shut up and finish with your inspection so we can get the hell out of here!*

"At least she didn't suffer. I hope I go like that when my time comes. My Beverly was a real gem. Put up with *me*, didn't she?" he chuckled. "Okay, this one looks clean."

Bea noticed that the other officer with the dog was slowly edging toward them in his patrol car, driving on the grass. *We have to get out of here before he gets out of the car with that dog!*

"Sorry for any inconvenience. If you happen to think of anything that may help, please contact the Bunting Valley Police Department as soon as possible."

"Will do . . . thank you, officer . . . and enjoy the rest of your day, or what's left of it." Bea shoved the boys toward the van. Just as the officer and his dog climbed out of the patrol car, the van doors slammed shut. *Whew!* Bea waved goodbye and started the engine. As the arm at the exit gate rose and the van pulled out onto the main road, the fake smile she'd had plastered across her face finally evaporated.

"Unzip the bag and make sure she's still alive!" Bea shouted at David. David reached over and unzipped the bag, careful not to pinch Maggie, or catch her hair, with the zipper.

"She's doused in sweat, but otherwise, she looks okay. She's sound asleep."

A real smile crept across Bea's face then. She had wished for a girl for as long as she could remember, and her wish had finally come true. Bea turned on the blinker and moved over to the left lane.

"Where are you going now?" David asked.

"I don't have anything for a little girl at home. I thought we could stop by the secondhand store and pick up a few things. We need to get a car seat and some clothes. She also needs a pair of shoes. I could even see if they have any toys. It's been so long since I was a little girl; I'm not positive what they like to play with these days."

The traffic light turned green and Bea continued to head toward the secondhand store.

Be Careful What You Wish For

"Can't you take me home first?" David pleaded. "Gus is supposed to come and get me, and we're going to see that new horror flick, *The Witch in the Attic.*"

"Did you ask me if you could go see a movie? I don't think so. Tonight is your first night with a sister. I think you should stay home. Besides, we don't have money to be spending on a movie anyway."

"Last time I checked, I'm almost nineteen years old and don't need your permission. *Besides*, Gus said if I drive us, he'll pay for the movie."

"Well now, that's where you're wrong. This is *my* van and I don't recall you asking to borrow it. And before you open your mouth and stick your foot in *again*, the answer is *no!*"

Bea came to a busy intersection and stopped for a red light. She pivoted her body around, so she was facing David. "As long as you live under my roof, you will have to get my permission for *everything* you do, and don't you forget it!"

"Do I have to ask your permission to breathe? You know that movie, *The Witch in the Attic?* It might just be about *you!*"

"Don't be such a smart ass, David. I'm getting fed up with your attitude. In addition, I don't really like Gus and don't want him around my house, especially now that we have a little girl. I just don't trust him. I swear the last time he was over, twenty dollars was missing from my wallet." Bea turned back around when the car behind her honked its horn. The light had changed to green and Bea had missed it. *Geez . . . give me a minute, won't you?*

"He's not going to do anything to your precious little girl, and why would he steal twenty dollars from you? His parents are both doctors, for God's sake. Besides, no matter who they are, it seems as if you *never* like *any* of my friends."

"That's not true. I like that nice boy who used to come around. What was his name? Andrew wasn't it?"

"Are you talking about Drew?"

"Yes, that's it. I like Drew. He seemed to have a nice family, and was very polite. Why doesn't he come around anymore?"

"Well, let's see . . . maybe because he's in jail."

Be Careful What You Wish For

"You're kidding me?"

"No, I'm not kidding you. He stole a car. He's been in jail for about six months. Just goes to show how well *you* pay attention."

"He was such a pleasant boy. It just goes to show *you*, nice people sometimes *steal things*, too."

"Just because someone seems nice and polite, doesn't mean they are. Take you for instance—you *steal kids*."

"Shut up, David. That's a *horrible* thing to say."

"What's so horrible about it? It's the truth."

"Sometimes the truth is better left unsaid. Besides, I don't actually steal them; I simply *remove* them from an unpleasant situation. Someday you'll understand."

Bea flipped on her right turn signal to let the people behind her know she was turning into the parking lot of Second Hand Sam's, a used clothing and household items store. It was located in a strip plaza with a two dollar movie theatre and drugstore. There weren't many cars in the parking lot, which was a good thing. Bea just wanted to blend in and go about her business like all the other shoppers. She parked in a handicapped spot near the front.

"John, can you look at the tag in the back of Maggie's swimsuit and tell me what size she wears? I'm just going to run in and get a few things. No need for all of us to pile into the store."

John moved toward Maggie, who was still curled up in the bag, sound asleep. "I hate to move her. What if she wakes up?"

"Don't be ridiculous. Just look at the damn tag."

Still chewing his gum, John gently moved her blonde hair and folded down the back collar of her swimsuit. "It says three T."

"Great! I'll be right back." Bea entered the store and moved quickly to the children's section. Even though it was clean and well organized, Second Hand Sam's always smelled old and musty. She had been there many times before, and she often brought the younger boys to do their back to school shopping here. After all, they were just *stupid* boys. Why did *they* need brand new things? She quickly strolled through the toys; all of them were old and used. *Maggie deserves much nicer*

51

things. The shoes were about the same; besides, she wasn't positive what size Maggie might wear. She did luck out and find a few outfits on the rack; *size 3T . . . perfect.* One of them still had the original tag attached. She grabbed them and headed to the area where the car seats, strollers, and cribs were. Bea still had an old car seat from when Mikey was a baby, but she hated to use the same one for Maggie. After four boys, it had seen better days. There was only one on the shelf, so Bea took it. The cashier made it a point to tell her that the car seat may not pass all safety inspections, and she seemed shocked when Bea admitted she didn't care. Bea paid for her selections and proceeded to return to the van. When she opened the side door she saw Maggie sitting on the seat, yawning. "I see you're finally awake, princess. Did you have a good nap?"

"Of course she's awake. The way you slammed the door, I'm surprised it didn't fall off the hinges." John popped his gum.

"Yeah, and the way Maggie was screaming, I thought you would have heard her from inside the store." David sat, looking out the window.

"I didn't hear anything. What's wrong, princess?"

"I want Mommy!" Maggie shrieked.

"I know you do, and I know this must seem scary, but it's really not that bad. You'll see." Bea looked at Maggie.

"Where is Mommy?" Maggie had big droplets clinging to her eyelashes, just waiting to stream down her pink, baby cheeks.

"I'm not sure where your mommy is right now. So just for fun, let's play a game and pretend I'm your mommy, okay?"

"No. Don't like that game." Maggie furrowed her eyebrows and crossed her chubby little arms.

Bea smiled when she saw what a stubborn little girl she had. "I'm real sorry, sweetie, but that's how it's going to be from now on. Look, I bought you three outfits and your very own car seat. Tomorrow morning, we'll go shopping, and I'll get you some toys and a new pair of shoes. Doesn't that sound like fun?"

Maggie shrugged her shoulders. "Still getting ice cream?" she asked.

She smiled at her new daughter, *"Absolutely!"*

Be Careful What You Wish For

"And riding a pony?"

"We'll see about that one. The ponies might be resting when we get home." After stopping for ice cream, where Bea only purchased two cones, one for Maggie and one for herself, they finally arrived home.

It had been a long, emotional day and Bea was exhausted. She thought back on how the day had gone and knew she was lucky it turned out the way it did. She'd found the perfect little girl, but as quickly as she'd found her, she could have lost her. Maggie, still in her swimsuit, was sitting on the floor playing with a couple of Match Box cars. *Tomorrow I'll take you shopping, and you can get whatever your heart desires.*

The boys were starving, so Bea made macaroni and cheese. They ate like fugitives—and as if they hadn't had a decent meal in days. Bea looked at them with such disgust. Boys were pigs. She saw her journal still lying on the kitchen counter and picked it up to put it back in the safe where it belonged. As she walked down the hallway, she was so grateful there was finally another female in the house. Things were going to be different from now on. Having a girl would be a breath of fresh air—fresh air that Bea so desperately needed.

Bea was sleeping soundly as the phone next to her bed started ringing. She pounded her feet on the floor and stubbed her toe as she walked over to answer the outdated style of phone connected to the wall. The cord was tangled, so it wouldn't reach the bed. "What?"

"Mom . . . ? It's David."

"David . . . ? Where are you, and why are you calling me at *this hour*?" Bea glanced at the digital clock on the nightstand. It read 2:11.

"I'm at the police station. I've been arrested, and I need you to come get me."

"The police station . . . what in the *hell* are you doing at the *police station?*"

"I . . ." David started.

"You know what . . . *never mind.* I don't care *what* you're doing there." Once she'd hung up the phone and lay back down, she was fuming and realized she wouldn't be able to fall back asleep. She thought about her youth and the one time she managed to get thrown in jail. Her

53

father was so enraged he left her to sit and rot in jail for *five days*. She just couldn't do that to David. Besides, if she made him stay there, he might get vindictive and start blabbing about Maggie. Leaving him to sit in jail would do more harm than good.

"John, wake up." Bea stood over him, trying to shake him awake.

"Hmm . . . *what?*" John sat straight up, blinking his eyes.

"I have to go out. Please keep an eye on things while I'm gone. Maggie is sleeping in my bed. I shouldn't be long."

John fell back onto his pillow. "Fine . . . *whatever*," he said sleepily.

Bea was certain he didn't even hear her. It didn't really matter. She'd be back before any of them woke up. Bea grabbed her purse, went to the kitchen, and took her life savings from the cookie jar and counted it. Then, she hastily walked outside. *Son of a—he took the van! How am I supposed to go get him without the van?* Bea stormed back into the trailer and called a taxi. She barely had enough money to buy groceries, and there was a *lot* of the month left before the arrival of her next disability check. Now, she was going to have to spend it on a taxi and bail to get David out of jail. It had been years since she heard it, but as plain as day, she could hear the words of her father play in her head: *The apple doesn't fall far from the tree, does it Beatrice?*

The taxi took her to the police station where she was told how David was caught driving under the influence. She grudgingly counted out the money and bailed him out of jail. By this time, David appeared completely sober, and Bea was pretty sure he was well aware of how angry she was. To add insult to injury, and after dishing out more cash she couldn't afford because her van was in the impound lot; she and David were finally on their way home.

"What's that horrible smell?" Bea pinched her nose, once the doors of the van closed.

"Oh, God . . . I think Gus puked in here!" David moved his feet around to make sure he wasn't stepping in it.

"Gus? I told you I didn't like that boy. After you clean the van out first thing tomorrow morning, you won't like him either."

54

Be Careful What You Wish For

"I'm really sorry, Mom."

"How *could you*, David? How could you sneak out in the middle of the night, steal my van, and get yourself drunk? *What* were you *thinking*? You could have been in an accident and killed yourself, or, someone else."

"Like I said . . . I'm really sorry, Mom."

"Save it for someone who cares."

They rode in silence the rest of the way home.

⌒ *Chapter Six* ⌒

Across town, Officer Butler had been tossing and turning all night as the events of the day played over repeatedly in his mind. He tried to piece together clues, hoping he wasn't missing something. He knew Detective Stephens would want every minute, sordid detail. Since it was his first time spearheading an alleged kidnapping, he hoped he had asked all the right questions and did everything he should have. Thinking back on it, he wondered why it hadn't occurred to him that he and Max should have checked the vehicles. With Max's keen sense of smell, they would have found her for sure; *if* she were still there to be found.

Knowing he wasn't going to sleep anymore, he finally got up and began jotting down what he wanted to accomplish. He decided he was going to suggest they place an officer at the Taylor house. If the kidnappers called for ransom money, they should have someone there to trace the call. He knew it was a long shot, but he wanted to make sure all their bases were covered. He also wondered if they should have issued an Amber Alert. It would have been difficult to piece enough information together that would have actually helped the case, without knowing the make and model of the alleged kidnapper's vehicle, but he would have liked to try. He also intended to do some checking on the boy with the black t-shirt. Somehow, he was certain that David Miller was involved. It was just too coincidental that three people reported seeing a boy in a black t-shirt on a day when the temperature had hit almost ninety degrees. He wondered what the deal was with the charm bracelet. One of the charms had been engraved with the name DAVID. Was the DAVID on the bracelet the same David as David Miller? He decided to turn in the bracelet as evidence to see if there was a DNA match in their database. Being a small town, Bunting Valley didn't have a forensic staff, so they had to send any evidence off to a larger, nearby city. It usually took several days, even weeks, to provide DNA results, but he would stress how crucial it was to get the results as soon as possible.

Officer Butler showered and dressed quickly. He always had his uniforms pressed and hung neatly in the closet, ready to go. Being a bachelor for so long, he didn't think he could handle a wife or a live-in girlfriend at this stage in his life. He was a fanatic when it came to order and organization, and not having another person there to move things out of place was just fine with him. He knew his mom would love to have a grandchild, but he just didn't see that happening. Max was the only companion he needed. Since he didn't feel like making a pot of coffee, he decided instead to grab a cup at the drive-through on the way to the station.

He walked out of the house and realized it was going to be another beautiful day. They'd had their share of foul weather in the winter months, so when a perfect summer day came along, Officer Butler was not one to take it for granted. He lifted his head and took in a deep breath; the sweet, pungent fragrance of wild Prairie Roses filled the morning air. The landscaping at his modest, two-bedroom home was not the greatest, but some of his neighbors had beautiful flowerbeds. It was always a joy to drive by and take in their scent when the time allowed. His life in North Dakota was so different from where he'd grown up in Detroit. By the time his family had relocated, gangs had been taking over the streets, and his mom was afraid to go anywhere without his father. His dad was a burly man—not overweight—just stocky and intimidating. He always thought his father looked like a bouncer at a nightclub. Officer Butler's career path had been determined early in life, which was due, in part, to his dad being such a tremendous role model. The other determining factor had been watching his best friend being gunned down by a gang as he crossed the street at the wrong intersection.

"Morning, Allen." Officer Butler entered the police station, holding a cup of coffee from the Donut Palace. In the other hand, he had Max's leash as Max followed close behind, happy just to be going somewhere. Bunting Valley had six full time police officers and one detective. Their shifts rotated so at least two officers were on duty at all times. Officer Butler's immediate boss was the Chief of Police, Carl Felder.

Carl, a crusty man, was the only one who had an actual office; the others sat in an open pool of four desks. The desks sat in two rows, completely flush against one another. Each desk had a computer and a phone. File cabinets lined the grey, sterile walls. Since none of the police officers spent much time in the office, it didn't honestly matter that they didn't have a desk to call their own. Only the detective had one, which was the furthest from the doorway he and Max had just entered. He glanced through the wall of windows to see if the boss had arrived. It appeared that since Chief Felder wasn't at his desk; he hadn't come in yet.

"Good morning, Rich." Detective Allen Stephens peered over his reading glasses with the morning newspaper in his hand. He had begun his career as a police officer, but moved into his current position when the previous detective had retired four years earlier. Already in his early sixties, Detective Stephens was thinking about retiring in a year or two himself. He wasn't the most organized person, which was quite evident by the mess on top of his desk. Several papers with brown coffee stains evident on their corners were haphazardly tossed on its surface. He had grey, frizzy hair and an overgrown moustache, which had the remnants of a jelly donut still clinging to it. Even though he didn't look like much, he was a terrific detective with an eye for detail and a photographic memory. He could give you the details of every case he had been involved in, without ever having to refer to his notes.

"How'd things go yesterday at the clinic?" Officer Butler asked as he walked toward the detective.

"Okay, I guess." Detective Stephens dropped the paper, pulled his glasses off, and set them down. "I was there the biggest part of the day; EKG, CT scan, MRI, chest x-rays, blood work . . . you name it, they did it. So now . . . I wait. I just hope they find something. These dizzy spells are really starting to worry me. I'm just worried I might have one when I'm driving and cause an accident. How about you? I heard about the activity at Lake Gerber. I thought there might be some mention of it in the paper, but I didn't find anything."

Officer Butler took a seat at the desk closest to Detective Stephens, pulled out his notepad, and went through the details of the day from start to finish.

"I just find it hard to believe that *no one* you spoke to heard or saw anything. It wasn't as if they were in a crowd of people and got separated. The girl was sitting on the sand—in plain sight, for God's sake."

"The workers at the paddleboat rental station said that they thought they could have rented a paddleboat to whoever it was that took the missing child; but Max didn't turn up anything concrete. I think it may have been wishful thinking on their part."

"How are the parents holding up?"

"I guess as well as can be expected. They spent the majority of the day sitting down by the water, thinking she'd reappear back in the sand where they'd last seen her. Mrs. Taylor seems numb. She keeps saying, 'It's as if she vanished into thin air.' It's kind of eerie. I had a hard time convincing them to leave, but I finally talked them into going home and getting some rest. I promised I would call them as soon as we heard anything."

"I just can't imagine what they are going through. To have your child missing and not know whether she's dead or alive, they must be going crazy."

"Oh, I almost forgot. I found this in the sand." He pulled the charm bracelet from his pocket. "I thought it may belong to our suspect. Maybe we should have a DNA test run to see if we can find a match. In the meantime, I'm going to see if I can locate David Miller. Even if he isn't a suspect, he may have some information that might help. From the way it sounds, both he and his mom were there when she disappeared but left before I had a chance to talk to them."

Detective Stephens grabbed the charm bracelet and took a long look at it. "Why don't you put that bracelet in an evidence bag and hold on to it? I'd hate for it to get lost in the evidence room. If it comes down to it and we need to run a DNA test, we'll send it off then. You know how long stuff like that takes around here. I'm still waiting on the results from my last case, and the man was sentenced to ten years last week."

"Yeah, but didn't he plead guilty to the charges?"

"That's not the point. The point is . . . it takes forever. No sense in having it sitting around in a backlog of evidence over at forensics. Just put it in a bag and hang onto it."

"Okay, if you think that's best."

"Did you talk to the chief about this?"

"No, not yet, I phoned him yesterday, but Mrs. Felder said he was out of town. I asked her to let him know I called regarding a missing child, possibly a kidnapping."

"As the chief, the sooner he knows what's going on, the better."

"I thought the same thing."

Be Careful What You Wish For

"Did anyone call in last night with any more information? Something they may have remembered once they went home?"

"As a matter of fact, we did get one call. An older gentleman called. He said you spoke to him and his grandson, Tommy."

"Oh yeah . . . I remember them. They were the fishermen. Did they remember something else?"

"I would say so. They left a message with the night clerk, but Cecil told them that Tommy had remembered, when they walked to the parking lot getting ready to leave, there was a lady leading a little girl by the hand. Just as they climbed in their car, the lady opened a van door. Tommy never actually saw the little girl's face, or the lady's for that matter, but the little girl did have blonde hair and was barefoot. Cecil said she was parked a few spots over from their vehicle, and it was older model conversion van. Tommy seemed to think it was dark blue or black, he couldn't remember for sure. Any other day, Tommy wouldn't have paid much attention, but the lady seemed agitated because the little girl didn't want to get in the van. He said it was hard not to stare. The lady finally picked the little girl up and *made* her get in the van."

"Did they say anything about a boy with a black t-shirt?" Officer Butler sat back down at one of the desks and powered up the computer.

"No. Like I said, Cecil just talked to the night clerk, but I'm sure we can contact him to see if they can tell us anything else." Detective Stephens took another sip of his coffee.

"Well, first things first, I'm going to try and locate David Miller. Then I'm going to see if I can reach the chief again, that is, if he hasn't arrived by then."

"I'll contact the chief. You just worry about the boy."

Officer Butler ran a report using David Miller as the search criteria, since that's all he had to go on. Four matches came back. The girls had said that the boy had been in their class at school, and since they'd just graduated, that should put him somewhere between seventeen and nineteen years old, which narrowed the search down to one. He wrote the address down on a piece of paper: 8797 Crimson Lane. Unfortunately, Officer Butler knew it well; it was an older trailer park on the other side of town, next to an abandoned warehouse. The police department received calls about once a week reporting that the same

60

couple was disturbing the peace. Every time he went there, they promised to keep it down and settle their disagreements in a more civilized manner.

"I got an address for a David Miller over on Crimson Lane, so I'm going to take off."

"The chief is on his way in, so I should come with you." Detective Stephens stood and gulped down the last of his coffee.

"No, it's okay. This is the first time I've been involved in a missing child case from the beginning. I'd like to stay involved and see it through to the end, if you don't mind. Since I'm just going to be asking some questions, I don't see a need for you to come along. Once we get further into it, I'm sure that will change. I'll take plenty of notes. Besides, I'd like it if you could contact Cecil and see if he has any other information that would be helpful. Maybe ask him exactly where they parked at the lake? Max was tracking the scent, but he lost it in the parking lot. If I'd known where they'd parked, then I could have determined if Max gave me a correct response or if he was barking up the wrong tree . . . no pun intended. Besides, you aren't feeling a hundred percent. I'd hate for you to overdo it." Officer Butler folded the piece of paper with the address on it and shoved it into his pocket.

"Okay, I'll stay here. I'll fill Carl in when he gets here. Let me know what you find out after talking to the Miller boy."

"Will do," he nodded. Officer Butler grabbed Max's leash and passed Chief Felder in the parking lot.

"What's your hurry?" Chief Felder called out as they crossed paths. He had his hands full with a department lap top, a cup of Starbuck's coffee and his briefcase. He liked his coffee dark and rich, and the crap the department provided for free just didn't cut it. He fondly referred to it as colored water, with more water than color.

Max was pulling on the leash, as if he was in a hurry to go somewhere and Rich was having a hard time holding on to him, without spilling his coffee. He finished the coffee from the Donut Palace and refilled his cup with some from the department coffeemaker. "It's about that missing child case I called you about yesterday."

The chief just looked at him with a blank stare.

"I spoke to your wife. Didn't she give you the message?"

61

Be Careful What You Wish For

Chief Felder shook his head. "Yes, yes, I got the message. For some reason, I dreamt that was an episode of Law & Order and wasn't completely sure it was real. Come back in and fill me in on the details."

"There's no time now. I need to go and follow up on a lead. It may be nothing but I want to talk to a teenage boy who was there. Talk to Allen—I filled him in on all the nuts and bolts. Sadly to say, at this point there aren't that many." The chief turned and resumed walking to the office. Officer Butler noticed he was having a hard time juggling everything he was carrying.

Max, still tugging on the leash, was so anxious. "My goodness, Max. What's wrong with you today? Are you running late for an important date with that poodle you fancy?" Officer Butler chuckled as he opened his car door and Max jerked the leash, sending his paper coffee cup to the ground. As he bent over to pick it up, he muttered, "Oh well, I guess I can stop for another."

✑ *Chapter Seven* ✑

The next morning Bea woke up in a foul mood. She leaned over David's sleeping body, and then screamed his name as loud as she could.

He jerked upright and narrowly missed Bea's face. It was as if someone had shot him out of cannon. *"What?"* David squeaked; he was awake.

"Get outside and clean the inside of the van, NOW!"

"What time is it?" David rubbed his eyes.

"It doesn't *matter* what time it is. *I told you to get up and clean the van."*

"It can wait . . . I didn't get much sleep last night and I'm tired."

"No, it cannot wait." Bea jerked the blankets off his body. "Get up, and get out there, *now.* Use your *toothbrush* to scrub that carpet."

"My head is killing me . . . and why would I want to use *my toothbrush?"* David asked as he turned and placed his feet on the old, worn-out carpet.

"I *don't care* about your *head!"* Bea yelled, trying to make it worse . . . "and the *toothbrush* is your *punishment.* Once you are done, you have to brush your teeth with the same toothbrush."

"I will not! That is the most *disgusting* thing *I ever heard."* David pulled on a pair of shorts.

"It will make you think twice about drinking and driving again, won't it? That van better smell as fresh as a daisy when you're finished!"

Once David finished, he brushed his teeth, gagging the entire time. Bea stood and watched, smiling at how well her punishment seemed to be working. She then called a family meeting in the living room.

"Since Maggie was all over the bed last night, I didn't get a good night sleep. I can't count how many times she kicked me in the middle of the night," Bea complained as she stood with her hands on her hips.

Be Careful What You Wish For

Josh whispered to John, "She probably deserved it!" John started laughing.

"There's nothing funny about that. Anyway, I don't want it to happen again tonight, so we're going to make some changes in the sleeping arrangements."

"What kind of changes?" Josh asked.

"For one thing, Maggie needs her own room."

"*Her own room* . . . are you *kidding me?* There are only three bedrooms in this little trailer; and three *small* bedrooms at that. You are not suggesting all four of us sleep in the same room, are you?" Josh looked at his brothers.

"Let's move some furniture around, and then we'll decide who will sleep where."

Pounding headache or not, David could not remain silent. "Don't be *ridiculous!* There's no room to move the furniture around."

"David, after the trick you pulled last night, you'll do what I say."

"What did he do last night?" John asked.

"He did something incredibly stupid, that's what," Bea snapped, and then stopped talking. She stood and stared down the long, skinny hallway. The trailer had three bedrooms, two of them extremely tiny, directly across the hall from each other. The third bedroom, where Bea slept, was at the very end of the hall. "Okay, here's what I'm thinking. Maggie will sleep on the twin bed in the first bedroom on this side of the hallway." Bea pointed to the left. "You, Josh, and David will share the other bedroom—that should work."

Tugging at Bea's shirt tail, Mikey asked, "What about me, Mommy? Where am I supposed to sleep?"

Bea swatted at him as if he were a pesky insect. "I thought you could sleep on the floor in the living room for the time being."

"On the *floor* . . . in the *living room* . . . ?" Mikey repeated it just to be certain he'd heard her correctly.

"Well it's either on the floor, or you can sleep on the couch."

Be Careful What You Wish For

"You can't be serious. Mikey can't sleep by himself. You know he has nightmares." Josh looked directly at Bea.

"Not my problem."

"Mikey, you can sleep with me." Josh put his arm protectively around Mikey's shoulder.

"Well, whatever works—but for now, we need to take one of those twin beds out of Maggie's room. With both beds in there, there won't be enough room for all of her stuff."

"What stuff?" John asked.

"The stuff I plan on buying for her when I get my next disability check."

"You promised you'd give me some money to buy a uniform, so I could play ball on the varsity team at school this year." Josh reminded her.

"Oh shut up, Joshua. Does *everything* have to be about *you?* We have *Maggie* to think about. Her wants and needs come before any of yours." Bea raised her finger and pointed at all the boys.

They walked down the long, skinny hallway to the first bedroom on the left. Even though it was small, it was the second largest bedroom in the trailer. The walls were painted Pepto Bismol pink; and the faded Pink Panther curtains with tiebacks hung in the window. The tiebacks were uneven and one top was fuller than the other. In the small room, there were two twin beds pushed up against each other. This *had been* John and Mikey's room. Mikey had nightmares almost every night, and needed someone to sleep with, so they'd pushed the beds together. The closet was tiny and had accordion doors. One side was off its track and hung cockeyed in its framework—however, no one seemed to notice.

David picked up a twin mattress, moved it out into the hallway and propped it up against the wall. "How is this going to fit in our room?" David asked while returning to grab the box springs.

"I never said it had to *fit* in your room. I just said it *couldn't be* in Maggie's room. However you want to rearrange your room so that all of you boys are comfortable is completely up to you."

Be Careful What You Wish For

"What are you talking about? We can't rearrange that room. We can barely walk in there. As it is, I have to turn sideways to walk around the bed," David snapped.

"Well, it doesn't concern me." Bea flipped her hand up in the air. "You work it out. Take the rest of the bed frame out of Maggie's room. She's feeling cramped already."

"You're one crazy bitch!" David said under his breath as he picked up a piece of the bed frame and took it out into the hallway.

"Don't call me names." Bea slapped David on the back of the head.

David pulled his fist back as if he were going to punch her. "Don't hit me. I have a splitting headache, and you're not making it any better."

"Don't you *ever* raise your hand to me *again!* I took that from one man, and I'm not going to take it from another. Oh, and about the headache—I don't give a shit! As I already explained to Maggie, she's *the most* important child in this family . . . more than the rest of you. The sooner you all learn that, the better off we'll be. Now, get this furniture rearranged so we can walk through the hallway."

"You want the furniture arranged, arrange it yourself. I *told you,* there's *no way* four boys can sleep in that tiny room."

"You'll do as I say. I said to move the furniture. Do it *now!*" Bea turned and walked away.

"Maybe it's time I move out," David yelled after her.

Bea snapped her head back around. "You'll do *no such thing!* I need you around here."

"Need *me* . . . need me for *what?* I told you, I'm not getting involved in any more of your harebrained schemes."

"Regardless of how much you annoy me, I feel much safer with you here than if we were alone. Besides, where would you go?"

"Sometimes I think prison would be nicer. At least I'd be away from *you!*"

Be Careful What You Wish For

"Think all you want, but you know you love me. After all, I *am* your *mother*. There's nothing you can do about it. Now, be a good boy and do as I say. Fix these rooms up, so everyone is happy."

"As long as *you're* alive, *none of us* will be happy!"

"What a horrible thing to say." For a moment, Bea pretended David's words actually hurt her, but then she continued, "As soon as we get the furniture rearranged, we need to go to Miracle Mart and get some toys. It's not acceptable for a cute little girl like Maggie to be stuck playing with Match Box cars." Then she grabbed Maggie's hand and led her down the hallway to the living room. She looked back and saw David standing in the hallway with one hand resting on the mattress propped up against the wall, shaking his head. Once the bedroom arrangements had been ironed out, Bea was in a much better mood. "Put on your shoes, kids, we're going to Miracle Mart to get some toys for Maggie."

"Oh, Mom, why do we *all* have to go?" Mikey and John said in unison. Mikey had large, round wire frame glasses that were too big for his tiny face. They were so dirty that Bea wondered how he saw *anything*. He was chubbier than the other three boys and his skin was white as snow. John had already put a stick of gum in his mouth and was getting ready to blow a bubble.

"Yes, I want all of us to go together. Maggie needs to get to know each and every one of us. In order to do that, we need to spend lots of time together and act like a happy family. If you're good, I might get a little something for each of you."

"Like a new skateboard?" Mikey asked.

"What do I look like . . . Ivana Trump?"

"Ivana . . . *who?*" he wanted to know.

"Never mind . . ." Bea shook her head. "I was thinking along the lines of a candy bar or something."

"Wow, a candy bar . . . can we each get our own, or do we all have to share?" John asked sarcastically and popped his gum.

"What is wrong with you lately, John? You're acting as bad as your older brother. I'm telling you right now, David has tried my patience more times than I can count, and I won't put up with it from you, too. Change your attitude, or else . . ."

John shrugged his shoulders.

"David, take the car seat out and put it in the van. We can't be driving around with Maggie just wearing a seat belt. It's not safe. If you see Mrs. Brown out there, don't say anything to her. She asks way too many questions. Even though I like her, that nosey old biddy should learn *to mind her own business.*"

"So, when the nosey old biddy comes over and asks why I'm putting a car seat into the van, I'm just supposed to ignore her?"

"You can talk to her but don't mention anything about Maggie, you hear me?"

"What do I look like . . . an idiot?" David mumbled.

"What did you say?" When David didn't respond, she slapped him on the back of the head.

David grabbed the car seat and headed out to the van. Bea kept a keen eye on him, peering through the curtains in the living room. The curtains were old and dusty and made Bea sneeze. She'd made them from a bed sheet a few years back, and they had seen better days. *No Mrs. Brown in sight. The old biddy must be sticking her nose in someone else's business today.*

David was back in no time. "Okay, the car seat's in—anything else. . . *Master?*" David seemed to be trying his best to get Bea to blow up at him, but it wasn't working.

"Okay, boys, we have to get to the van quickly. I don't want anyone to see Maggie with us, just yet."

"This is so stupid," David said. "How long are we going to have to do this? Hide from everyone just because you did something foolish and kidnapped someone's kid?"

"I don't know. I'm hoping not too long, but after we get back from Miracle Mart, we shouldn't have to leave the house for a few days, maybe even a week or longer."

"A week, *or longer* . . . have you *lost* your *flipping mind?* I can't stay cooped up in this little trailer for a *day* with you, let alone a *week* or longer! I need to get out of here!"

Be Careful What You Wish For

"You will do no such thing. I might let you out later in the week to mow the lawn, *if* you remain on your best behavior. After last night's fiasco, you should be happy to stay home."

"How many times are you going to throw that in my face? I made a mistake. *Deal* with it."

"Don't start with me, David. I could have left you there, you know?"

"You can't make me stay home simply because of her." David pointed at Maggie.

"Do you think I like this any more than you do? I finally have the perfect little girl. I wish I could tell everyone I know, but you see . . . the difference between you and me is . . . I'm willing to keep my mouth shut for the sake of this family."

"No, you're willing to keep your mouth shut to keep your *ass* out of *jail*. It has *nothing* to do with this family."

"Watch your mouth, David. Think what you want, but remember, we're in this together. In the eyes of the law, you're an adult. You were my accomplice. Whatever happens to me . . . happens to you."

"We'll see about that."

"Oh, is that a *threat?* If so, I'm shaking in my boots." Bea shook her entire body for effect. "Don't even *think* about trying to blackmail *me*."

With nothing left to say, Bea grabbed Maggie and hurried to the van. She put Maggie in the van through the open side door which faced away from Mrs. Brown's trailer. It didn't appear the other neighbors were out yet, either. *Thank goodness Miracle Mart is open 24 hours. I hope we can get there and back before anyone has a chance to notice we are gone.*

The boys all piled in the van; gum popping, feet dragging, clanking, and banging, Bea couldn't believe how loud and disgusting they were.

"Why does it stink in here?" Mikey asked.

"Why don't you ask David?"

Be Careful What You Wish For

"Why does it stink in here, David?" Mikey pushed his glasses up on the bridge of his nose.

"None of your damn business," he bit out.

Bea just shook her head.

The van was silent the rest of the ride; and within minutes, they arrived at Miracle Mart, a small department store, almost three miles from the trailer. They didn't carry a lot of the name brands, but what they did have was hugely discounted. Bea placed Maggie in a cart she found in the parking lot, and the four boys followed her like little puppies.

"Stick with me. I don't want to have to run around looking for you when I'm ready to leave. Do I have to remind you what happened the last time?" Bea looked at Joshua and John.

David huffed. "I did everything you asked me to do, and I'm done. You wished for a stupid girl, and you got one. You *can't hold me prisoner* in that trailer for a week or longer. You *just can't. I won't* do it."

If looks could kill, David would be dead. "This is *not* the *time*, or *place* for this, David." Bea spoke through gritted teeth. "We'll talk about it when we get back home."

"We won't talk about it when we get back home. I'm done talking."

As if David had never even spoken, Bea said, "Okay, everyone, put on a happy face. We're going shopping."

"What a psycho," David mumbled. Bea completely ignored him.

They passed through the front entrance. "Stop!" the door attendant yelled.

Bea froze in her tracks.

"You can't bring her in here." He looked straight at Maggie.

Bea's heart jumped to her throat. She could feel the color running to her face as it turned a dozen shades of red. A million things were going through her head. Her tongue felt as thick as a cotton ball. She couldn't *speak*. She couldn't *breathe*. She felt as if she were going to either pass out or throw up. *Oh no! They must have issued an Amber Alert. Maggie's picture must be posted everywhere. They know.*

Be Careful What You Wish For

Everyone knows. The police are on the way. It's over. Oh my gosh . . . it's over. I've lost my baby girl.

As they all stood there, mouths agape, completely dumbfounded. David finally had the nerve to speak up. "What are you talking about?"

"She's not wearing any shoes. We have a strict policy. No shoes, No shirt, No service." The greeter pointed at Maggie's feet.

Bea, finally feeling the air return to her lungs, took a deep breath.

"Darndest thing," Bea used her most charming southern accent. "She outgrew all her shoes overnight. Can you believe that? We came to our favorite store to get her a new pair. I'm sorry if we're breaking the rules, but I swear, Bobby," she lightly touched the greeter's name tag, "we won't take anything that doesn't belong to us—at least not this time." Bea flashed him a gummy smile.

"Okay, but take this sticker with you. If my manager thinks I let you in here without mentioning it, I'll get in big trouble."

"Sure thing, Bobby . . . you're a gem." Bea fluttered her eyelashes. *Whew! That was close.*

David shook his head.

"What's wrong with you?" Bea asked.

"One of these days your luck will run out, and I hope I'm there to see it."

᥅ *Chapter Eight* ᥅

Officer Butler knocked on the door at 8797 Crimson Lane, but no one answered. He gingerly crossed over the deck or what was left of it. It was mostly rotting lumber and a few 2 x 4's had fallen off and were lying on the ground in splintered pieces. He intended to peek through the front window, but the condensation had accumulated between the two window panes, so it was hard to see. From what he could observe, the small trailer was extremely cluttered and few, if any, improvements had been made since the trailer was built in the seventies. Gold, sculpted carpet covered the living room floor and several rugs were scattered about. He knocked again, but no one seemed to be home, so he decided to try his luck with the next door neighbor.

The neighbor answered the door before he finished knocking.

"Good morning, ma'am. I hope I haven't caught you at a bad time."

"Goodness, no . . . what can I do for you today, Officer?" She nervously put her open palm across her chest.

"I'm Officer Rich Butler, and this is my K9 partner, Max. I'd like to ask you a few questions about your next door neighbors—the Millers."

She was a round, elderly lady with silver hair. She had on a floral house dress with a white apron, and she seemed happy just to have someone to talk to. "I'm Edna Brown . . . you can call me Edna. Come in, come in." She opened the door and stepped back. Mrs. Brown's trailer sat to the left of the Millers'. Although her trailer looked like an older model, it was painted a bright white and had black shutters. Hanging baskets filled with bright red geraniums hung on the deck and the flower beds lining the driveway were immaculate. The flowers were in full bloom and the place looked like a picture from *Better Homes & Gardens* magazine.

"Do you mind if I bring Max in?"

"Not at all, not at all," she said as she stepped back from the door. "I'll put on some tea," she offered.

"You don't need to go to any trouble on my account."

Be Careful What You Wish For

"Oh, it's no trouble. I was just thinking of having a cup myself, so it's no trouble to make two. Make yourself at home. I'll be right back."

Officer Butler shut the door behind him, and then entered the living room and sat down on the sofa. The walls were covered in floral wallpaper, and the carpet, even though it looked brand new, was the old 80's-style shag. The furniture, which was all oversized, made the tiny living room look even smaller. There was a sofa, with a matching chair, and ottoman. Next to the chair, was a dark brown end table with a reading lamp. He assumed this was where Mrs. Brown spent the majority of her time, since piled nearby was a stack of books and magazines in addition to a pair of reading glasses. The coffee table, which sat in front of the sofa, was covered with a white lace doily. On top of the doily, a flower arrangement sat next to the *Holy Bible*. Max found a seat next to the sofa. The aroma of lilac potpourri filled the air and Officer Butler could hear the ticking of a clock. Upon further investigation, he spotted it. It was shaped like a black cat, hanging on the wall directly next to the doorway Mrs. Brown had disappeared through. With each second, the cat's tail and gemstone eyes went back and forth. He smiled as he remembered his grandma having one just like it when he was a child.

He could hear Mrs. Brown opening cupboards and gathering things in the kitchen. The tea kettle whistled and within minutes, she was back in the living room. She brought a tray with her, which held a small teapot, two mugs, sugar and cream, and some pound cake. "I hope you like pound cake. I was thinking of baking some banana bread to use up the bananas that are turning brown, but I never got around to it. I don't have a dog, so I'm sorry I don't have a treat for your friend."

"Pound cake is just fine, and Max sticks to a strict diet. Thank you for thinking of him, though. Let me tell you how beautiful your flower beds are. Do you take care of them yourself?"

"Yes, yes, I do. I've had a green thumb my entire life and love working in the soil. Something about rich brown earth in my hands, it just makes me feel alive. I get so excited each spring when the flowers start popping their little heads out. I forget what all I planted, so each one is a surprise." Mrs. Brown poured Officer Butler a cup of tea and then offered him cream and sugar, but he declined both. "Okay." She took a deep breath. "What can I tell you about the Millers?"

73

Be Careful What You Wish For

Officer Butler pulled his small notepad from his breast pocket and began, "How long have you lived next door to them?"

"Several years; let's see—my Howard—God rest his soul—died in December, 1999." She stared out into space. "I bought this trailer with the life insurance money and moved here early the next year. When I moved in, the Millers were already living next door. It was Bea, David, Joshua, and John. John was just a baby, maybe one or two years old. Mikey didn't come along until after that, perhaps three or four years later."

"What about Mr. Miller?"

"Oh, he died a long time ago. From what I heard, he was killed in a motorcycle accident—on his way to the hospital to see Bea. It was the day John was born, that the accident happened—it's such a sad story. I've only heard bits and pieces, and every time it came up in conversation, it seemed Bea still had a hard time with it—after so long, I just stopped asking."

"You said there are four boys, correct?" He took a bite of his pound cake.

"Yes, David is the oldest, followed by Joshua, John, and then Mikey,"

The exact names that had been on the charm bracelet . . . "Well, if Mr. Miller died when John was a baby, where did Mikey come from? Did Mrs. Miller remarry?"

"Oh, heavens no. This is a good story—sad, but good. I don't like to gossip, but since I heard it directly from Bea, I guess it wouldn't be considered gossip. I didn't even know about Mikey until spring that year. During our rough winters in these parts, we hibernate around here, staying indoors a better part of the winter, trying to keep warm. I don't see much of my neighbors from late October until the spring thaw." Mrs. Brown wiped her hands on the front of her apron. "Perhaps it would be better if I went back and started from the beginning."

"Please do," he suggested, trying to keep track of the story.

"Okay," Mrs. Brown spoke softly as she took a sip of tea. "Bea's sister, Elizabeth, had adopted Mikey. Elizabeth never married but wanted to have children. She finally decided when she turned forty she was tired of waiting so she started the adoption process. It had taken her four years

74

before she found Mikey; but from what I understand, it was love at first sight. Elizabeth was smitten, and Mikey was spoiled rotten, which is the way it should be. Before Elizabeth adopted Mikey, she and Bea had a falling out and had lost touch, but Elizabeth wanted Mikey to get to know his only aunt and his three cousins. Tragically, Elizabeth died when Mikey was just a few months old. Breast cancer . . . *tsk, tsk* . . . such a shame. Anyway, since Bea was her only living relative, she spelled out, rather explicitly in her will, that Bea should get custody of Mikey. Bea brought him home—in late October, I believe—and I didn't officially meet him until April or May the following year. By then he was already walking. Who am I kidding? That boy was running! He learned to walk really early, around eight or nine months old, I believe."

"When was this, again?" Office Butler queried as he tried to write the pertinent facts down in his notepad.

"I think maybe six or seven years ago. At my age, the years have a way of all running together, you know?" She smiled sweetly at Officer Butler.

"So you think Elizabeth died seven years ago in 2003, and the first time you saw Mikey was six years ago, in the spring of 2004?"

"That sounds about right."

"Do you know where Elizabeth and Mikey lived before she died?"

"From what Bea said, they lived nearby. I'm not sure what nearby means, but I assumed it was pretty close."

"Did you ever meet Elizabeth?"

"No. Like I said, I never heard anything about it until the spring when I saw Bea outside with Mikey and she came over and explained it all to me."

Officer Butler nodded his head. "So, what can you tell me about David, the oldest one?"

"Not much, really. He's very quiet. I think he assumed the role of man of the house when Mr. Miller died. He seems to help out a lot. I've seen him mowing the lawn many times . . . he wears a lot of black clothing. The young kids today are so into that look. I just can't understand it myself. They look like death warmed over."

Officer Butler chuckled. "What about the other two—John and Joshua, you said?" he asked, referring to his notes.

"I don't really know much about them. I think Joshua plays baseball. From what I've heard, he's pretty good. I've seen his name in the local paper before."

"Is there anything else you think I should know?"

"Nothing that I can think of right off the top of my head," she responded, and then took a sip of her tea.

"Would you consider them good neighbors?"

"I guess, relatively speaking . . . don't really see much of them. I do wish, however, they would keep their yard and trailer in better shape; but, I understand it's hard for Bea with all those kids and no adults to help her."

"Thank you for taking the time to talk to me and especially, thank you for the tea and pound cake. As a bachelor, I don't get many homemade baked goods, but I sure do appreciate it when I get them."

"Oh, it was my pleasure. Can I ask why you need to know about the Millers? Does it have anything to do with the intruder?" she asked him as they both rose to their feet.

"What intruder?" He was intrigued.

"Some time ago, Bea shot and killed an intruder. It was in broad daylight. Not much was said about it. It wasn't on the news, and I looked in the paper for a month, but never did find anything. Have they reopened the investigation?"

"Hmmm . . . that's the first I've heard about that. How long ago was that?"

"Probably three or four years ago now . . . I was standing out on my deck when they wheeled him out in a body bag. Bea was really shook up."

"I can imagine. Thanks for letting me know."

"If it's not the intruder, are they in some sort of trouble?"

"No, no trouble. There was something that happened yesterday down at Lake Gerber, and I believe they were there. I'd like to question

76

them to see if they remember seeing or hearing anything . . . nothing major."

"Lake Gerber . . . what happened at Lake Gerber?" Officer Butler could tell Mrs. Brown loved to hear about everyone else's business.

"Oh, just some activity where the police were called out . . . an alleged kidnapping."

"Do you think the Millers kidnapped someone?" Mrs. Brown put her hand over her mouth.

"No, not at all . . . since I don't have any concrete facts, I really can't get into it, but I know they were there and may have seen something that might help us find the missing girl."

"Oh, I see, is there anything else I can do?"

"Yes, as a matter of fact, there is. Do me an enormous favor and don't mention to the Millers that you and I had this conversation, and please," he said handing Mrs. Brown his card, "give us a call if you see or notice anything unusual going on next door, okay?"

"Will do," she said as she peered at the business card he'd handed to her.

Max and Officer Butler headed toward the door. "Thanks again, ma'am." He waved to Mrs. Brown standing in her doorway once he'd climbed into his patrol car. He sat for a moment looking at the trailer the Millers lived in. Weeds stood knee high in the flower beds, and the once gravel covered driveway was now reduced to nothing but dirt. The siding on the trailer was filthy and pieces of the skirting were bent and missing. The last window on the left was broken and taped together with silver duct tape. The screen door was not latched and, depending on the direction and strength of the wind, it was obvious it would blow wide open. It was in sharp contrast to Mrs. Brown's trailer. He backed out of Mrs. Brown's driveway and headed back to the police station to see if he could find anything on Mikey's adoption when he was a few months old, as well as the subsequent death of his adoptive mom, Elizabeth. He thought he would look to see if he could find out anything on the intruder Mrs. Brown had mentioned while he was investigating the Millers.

He picked up his phone and dialed the number for the station to talk to Detective Stephens, but when he didn't pick up, Officer Butler decided against leaving a voicemail message. After all, he was on his way back to the station, so he'd be able to talk with him when he got there. Driving down the street, he saw a mom and dad pushing a little girl in a stroller, and his thoughts drifted to the Taylor's. He wondered how they were doing. He wasn't a religious man, but in times like these, he couldn't help but mutter a prayer, "Please watch over Maggie Taylor. Keep her safe, and give Abby and Tim a little peace knowing that this is in your capable hands."

ᥩ *Chapter Nine* ᥭ

The van turned onto Crimson Lane coming back from Miracle Mart. "Oh shit. That old biddy is looking out the screen door. We can't possibly carry Maggie in there with her watching."

"How about we all get out and go in . . . and leave Maggie in the van for a few minutes? Then, once the old biddy shuts her door, we can go back out and get her?" David suggested.

"That's a great idea! Everyone just climb out of the van like you normally would. Don't do anything out of the ordinary to call attention to yourself."

Bea and the boys climbed out, carrying the purchases they had just made at Miracle Mart. When Maggie saw no one was unbuckling her, she screamed.

Mrs. Brown walked out onto her small front porch. "Good morning, Bea. You're out awfully early today."

"Yes. We wanted to get over to Miracle Mart for the early bird specials. John needed some new shoes."

"Did I hear a scream a moment ago?"

"Yes, you did." Bea threw her hands up in front of her. "There's been a bee flying around our van for the last two days, and it finally stung Mikey. I told him to leave it alone, but you know little boys. Their curiosity always gets the best of them."

Maggie screamed again.

"Mikey, stop screaming . . . I told you I'd doctor you up once we get in the house." Bea smiled as she swatted Mikey on the head with a thud, much harder than she intended. The van doors shut, Bea waved at Mrs. Brown, and the five of them went into the trailer.

Bea continued to watch Mrs. Brown out the kitchen window. She crouched in the kitchen so she could keep an eye on the van, as well as Mrs. Brown. Mrs. Brown was fiddling with the hanging flower baskets she had on her porch. She grabbed the watering can and filled it with water and gave the plants a good, long drink. Bea swore she could see the van jerking, but hoped it was just her imagination. Regardless, Mrs.

79

Brown was too busy with her flowers to notice. She took her time, plucking off all the dead blooms and sticking her finger in the dirt to make sure she had watered them all sufficiently. *I can see the water dripping from the bottom of the containers, so obviously you've given them enough water. For the love of Pete, go back in the house!*

Finally, Mrs. Brown finished, put down the watering can, and went back inside the trailer. As soon as Bea heard the bang of her front door, she sent John out to rescue Maggie. Once Maggie was safe and sound inside their trailer, Bea felt she could relax. Bea took a towel and doused the moisture off of Maggie's head. "Much longer in that hot van and she would have been a goner for sure," Bea laughed.

David shook his head.

"Okay, sunshine. What would you like to do now?"

"Ride the pink pony."

Bea smiled. "I'm afraid the pink pony is sleeping. How about we open your new toys and play with them?"

"No. Take me home."

"You are home, sweetie."

"No. This is not home."

"Yes, it is. Your mommy and daddy gave you to me. You live here with me, John, David, Josh, and Mikey now. We're your new family. We'll love you and take care of you and make sure nothing bad happens to you."

"Want to go home now," Maggie said again.

"I told you, sweetheart. You are home."

"No. Don't like this home. It stinks." Maggie reached up and pinched her nose shut.

Bea snickered. "You'll get used to it. Now, let's open up your new toys and play. I haven't played with girl toys in a really long time, and I'm looking forward to it."

"Don't want to play. Want to go home," Maggie whimpered, and was almost crying now.

Be Careful What You Wish For

"Maggie, sweetie, this *is* your home. You live here now." Bea tried to explain it in childlike terms.

"Take me home . . . *now!*" Maggie screamed.

Something inside of Bea snapped. "I'm going to say this again. *This* is your home. You ask me one more time, and I'll tape your mouth shut."

Maggie jumped up and ran across the room to Joshua, who was sitting Indian style on the floor.

Joshua caught Maggie in his arms. "What in the world is wrong with you?" He looked at Bea. "C'mon, Maggie, I'll play with you." Maggie put her head on his shoulder.

Maggie loosened her grip on Josh and climbed down. Josh began tearing the boxes apart and removing the tags from the toys Maggie had picked out at Miracle Mart. She plopped down on the floor next to him. "Don't open that one." Maggie pointed to one of the boxes.

"Why not?" Josh asked.

"Surprise for Maddie." Maggie's little face was so sad.

Josh looked at Maggie. "Who is Maddie?"

"Maddie is my sister." Maggie sounded disgusted as if Joshua should know who Maddie was.

Bea watched from where she was sitting on the couch across the room. The furniture in the living room was decidedly old—Early American style tweed, with gathered ruffles by the floor. In addition to the two pieces of furniture, there was a green plastic, outdoor lawn chair. There was no television set. Bea felt watching TV was like communicating with the devil. She climbed down on the floor and crawled over to where Josh and Maggie were sitting. Maggie quickly scrambled back onto Josh's lap when she saw Bea coming toward her.

"I'm sorry, Maggie. Is it okay if I play with you?"

Maggie looked at Josh, and then back at Bea. "Nope." She shook her head as her beautiful hair, now dirty and tacky, moved around.

David leaned back onto the two back legs of the green lawn chair and started laughing. "I guess she told you!" David righted his chair on all fours, "High five, Maggie." He held up his hand up for Maggie to slap.

Bea was angry. "Well, if she doesn't want to play with me, she's not playing with any of us." Bea bent over and began grabbing and gathering up all the toys.

"You're the one who wished for a little girl." David had a smug grin. "Be careful what you wish for; you just might get it."

With that, Bea stood up, slapped David on the back of the head, and left the room.

Officer Butler arrived back at the police station and told Detective Stephens everything Mrs. Brown had said about the Millers. Referring to his notepad, he relayed the story about Bea's sister, Elizabeth, and Mikey's adoption. Officer Butler had a gut feeling there was more to the "Mikey story" than Mrs. Brown had been told. It didn't make sense why a woman, who had been feuding with her only sister just a few months before, decided to give complete custody to her when she died.

Detective Stephens suggested they run an inquiry in the death database to see if they could find a death certificate on file for Elizabeth. Even without a last name, if they knew the cause of death and her age, they should be able to find it. Mrs. Brown felt certain it was about seven years ago. They had enough information to at least start. If nothing turned up, the two of them could try another route. Officer Butler had a feeling there was no such person, dead or alive.

"My gut is telling me there is no such person." Detective Stephens scratched his head.

"I was just thinking the *same thing!* By the way, what did Carl say about the trace?"

"He thought it was a good idea, and we sent someone over to their house this morning. I called to let them know what was going on."

"Who did you talk to?"

"Mrs. Taylor."

"How did she sound this morning?"

"Not good. It sounded as if she were crying when we were talking."

Officer Butler shook his head as he looked down at his notepad. "Anyway, there was another thing I found interesting. According to Mrs. Brown, some years back Bea Miller shot and killed an intruder in her home. Mrs. Brown said it was never reported on the news or in the newspaper. While I'm looking at the database, can you see if you can find anything out about the shooting?"

Officer Butler opened the Department of Vital Statistics database on the police computer. Not exactly sure where to start, he clicked on the DEATH LINK and answered the questions in front of him as best he could. He decided to try seven years ago first. He hit the *Enter* button. The screen flashed *Searching* for what seemed like an eternity. Finally, the result came back: *No Match.* He decided to try again using the same criteria but a different year. He hit the *Enter* button and the results came back the same: again—*No Match.* He keyed in another year and hit the *Enter* button for the third time, with the same outcome. It was the first time he was ever pleased *not* to find something.

"I'm not getting anything over here and I feel as if I'm wasting my time. I could sit all day and enter city names and years, and still not find it. I'm just going to call the Bureau of Health Services and tell them what I know, see if they can help me." Officer Butler picked up the phone and dialed the number the police used to bypass the customer service representatives.

"Smith here." The phone had only rung twice, when an angry voice came over the line.

"Hello, Mr. Smith. This is Officer Rich Butler calling from the Bunting Valley Police Department. We're working on a missing child case and I was hoping you might be able to help us. I'm trying to find out information regarding a death somewhere around seven years ago. At least we think it was seven years ago; also, a possible adoption about the same year. Can you help me?"

"Tell me what you got, and I'll see if I can help," Smith grumbled. Officer Butler could hear him as he shuffled papers around on his desk.

"Well, all we know is that her name was Elizabeth, and that she allegedly died of breast cancer. I think she was around forty-four or

83

forty-five years of age. She lived in Bunting Valley or close to it. She adopted a baby boy, and then died a few months later. We think she died about seven years ago, in 2003, but it could have been 2002 or even 2004. An elderly woman provided the information, and she wasn't quite sure of the exact year."

"That should be enough to get me started. As soon as I find something, I'll fax it over."

"That would be great. How long do you think it'll take?"

"Well, considering it's about lunchtime, I'm guessing a few hours . . . if not today, then probably, first thing in the morning."

"Mr. Smith, we're in a bind here. The child has been missing for over twenty-four hours, and I'm sure you know the more time that passes the less likely it is that we'll find her alive."

"I understand the importance, but you aren't the only person requesting information. I'll get to it when I get to it."

"If you could move this up on your priority list, I'd greatly appreciate it. We're talking about a missing child here. I think this should take precedence over any other calls you've received today."

"You have no idea what kind of calls I've received today. *Everyone* wants something from me, and everyone thinks their request is more important than the last," Mr. Smith vented.

"Do you have children Mr. Smith?"

"Yes. He's five years old and my ex up and took him to Florida. I've seen the kid three times. The only time I hear from them is when my child support check is late. Any other questions?" Mr. Smith huffed on the other end of the line.

"I'm sorry to hear that but just imagine what the parents are going through. They are distraught. Their beautiful baby girl is missing. Can you please put yourself in their shoes and realize the sense of urgency here and move it up on your list? Please, I'm begging you?"

"Fine," Smith sighed. "I'll skip lunch and get right on it. What's your fax number?"

Officer Butler told him the fax number and then added, "Thank you so much."

"Don't thank me. I haven't done anything yet." *Click,* the phone went dead.

"I just found something interesting," Detective Stephens said as Officer Butler placed the receiver back on its cradle.

"What's that?"

"The neighbor was right. Four years ago there *was* a shooting at the Millers'. It says here it was self-defense. A man knocked on the door and then shoved his way in. Mrs. Miller was at home alone at the time, and she was able to get to her handgun and shoot him. It seems pretty cut and dry. The case was closed."

"Does it say who the man was?"

"No, it just says 'an unidentified white male.' There are photos of Mrs. Miller. She was pretty beaten up. The odd thing I found in the file was a newspaper article. Listen to this, 'It started out as a routine trip to the supermarket, but then the unthinkable happened. When the mother stepped around the corner to grab a box of cereal, someone swooped in and took the two-month-old baby boy, right out of her shopping cart.'"

"When was that?"

"In the fall, of 2003 . . ."

"Did they ever find him?"

"This article doesn't really say, but it was at the Greenfield Stop-N-Save."

"That's odd. I wonder why that article about a kidnapped baby boy was in the same file as the shooting of an intruder at the Miller house. What does Mrs. Miller have to do with a baby being kidnapped from the Stop-N-Save?" A light bulb went off in Officer Butler's head.

Detective Stephens seemed to be thinking the same thing. "Oh my gosh . . . the adopted boy . . . they are one and the same! The Greenfield Stop-N-Save is only about forty miles from here."

"I'm on my way." Officer Butler grabbed his keys.

"Let me hit the restroom and I'll be right out."

"I'd rather you wait here. What if someone from the Bureau calls? Besides, I was hoping you could keep an eye on Max for me."

"Okay, but next time, I'm coming whether you like it or not."

"I know, I know, but this has been very educational for me. I like being personally involved."

"Keep me posted on what you find out."

"Will do . . . fill Carl in, he should know what's going on. And let me know if the trace picks up anything."

"Okay. I will." Detective Stephens glanced as his watch as he sat back down.

Officer Butler literally ran from the police station. This new bit of information had given him hope. He was certain this kidnapped baby boy was Mikey. It had to be. It was like a giant puzzle and all the pieces were beginning to fit. As soon as he climbed in his car, his cell phone began ringing. "Good afternoon, Officer Butler here."

"Hello. This is Abby Taylor. I just spoke to Detective Stephens, and he gave me your number. We hadn't heard from you, and Tim and I are on pins and needles. Has anything happened?"

"Oh, Mrs. Taylor, I've been meaning to call you. I think I may have a lead."

"You found her?"

"No, we haven't found her. We did find *something* interesting, however. I'm on my way to Greenfield right now to talk with their police department regarding a missing boy."

"A missing boy . . . ? What does that have to do with Maggie?"

"We are hoping *a lot*. I can't really go into the details just yet since I'm not certain; however, as soon as I finish meeting with them, I'll call you."

"In the meantime, isn't there something we can do? Print off flyers . . . ? Talk to the news media? Beg the kidnappers to give our baby back? We feel absolutely helpless sitting here."

"I'm sure you do, but if we scare them, they may take off—or worse yet, harm her, which is exactly what we *don't* want them to do. I have a feeling they're still close by. You and Mr. Taylor just sit tight and stay close to home. If they call asking for ransom, you need to be there to

86

answer the phone so the trace will kick in. I'm hoping I'll have something for you in a few hours."

Shortly after the phone call ended, Officer Butler turned off Highway 415 to Route 62. He was about two miles from the Greenfield Police Department. He hoped when he got there, they'd recall the case and have some information that would prove helpful. He parked on the south side of the building, and his cell phone began ringing again. "Yes?" he answered and noticed the telephone's caller ID identified the call coming from the police station.

"I just got a call from Mr. Smith over at the Bureau. What a nice man," Detective Stephens said sarcastically. "He found no death record of our Elizabeth from breast cancer. He checked all three years. He also ran a search on the entire state of North Dakota, and nothing came back. He also found nothing on an adoption. He didn't seem very pleased when I told him we were happy he didn't find anything. He said something about us sending him on a wild goose chase and wasting his time, and then he hung up the phone."

"Thanks for the call. That *is* good news."

"Wait . . . one more thing."

"What?"

"You're not going to believe this, but one—*David Miller*—was arrested last night in Bakersfield."

"Arrested . . . for *what?*"

"DUI."

"Are they still holding him?"

"No. Bea Miller bailed him out and took him home around three a.m."

"Interesting . . . at least we know they're still in the area. Thanks for the information." Officer Butler pushed the button to end the call, and placed his phone back in his pocket. He climbed out of his car and entered the police department through the front doors.

The Greenfield Police Department was much larger than Bunting Valley's department building. A security guard greeted him as soon as he entered through the front door. Once he had produced his ID and badge, he was cleared to bypass the metal detector with his gun still in its holster. Officer Butler had only been to the Greenfield Police Department once before, and that was to pick up Max. It was hard to believe that it had been almost two years ago.

He stopped at the front desk and explained why he was there. The young lady dressed in an officer's uniform ushered him straight back to the desk of Detective McClure.

Detective McClure was the complete opposite of Detective Stephens; sharply dressed, both his hair and beard were meticulous. His desk was exceptionally organized and he had family photos on the credenza directly behind his chair. Officer Butler extended his hand. "I'm Officer Rich Butler from the Bunting Valley Police Department." Detective McClure stood and shook his hand. "I'm here to ask some questions regarding a boy who was kidnapped about seven years ago from the Stop-N-Save." Officer Butler sat down in the guest chair and arranged it at an angle in front of Detective McClure's desk.

Detective McClure sat down, spun around in his chair, pulled out a file drawer, and within seconds, the file folder was open on his desk. "This case has been haunting me for years. I remember it as if it were yesterday. What can I tell you?" the detective asked.

Officer Butler, not one for beating around the bush, got right to the point. "Yesterday, a child was allegedly abducted from Lake Gerber in Bunting Valley."

"Yes, I'm familiar with Lake Gerber." The detective nodded. "I've been there many times with my family."

"The missing child is a three-year-old, female Caucasian, approximately three feet tall. She was allegedly taken from the sand near the beach while her parents were sitting ten to fifteen feet away. No one saw anything. No one heard anything. One minute she was there, and the next minute, she was gone . . . *vanished*, into thin air. The parents called 911. I was first to arrive on the scene with my K9 partner, Max. Max tracked around several times, and finally came to a stop in the parking lot, at which time we believe that the alleged kidnapper placed the missing child in a dark-colored, conversion van and fled the scene. Two other patrol cars were dispatched, and the entrance and exit gates were barricaded. We personally searched every single vehicle from that point forward, but there was no sign of the missing child. We believe that the alleged kidnapper had left the area before we arrived."

"Are there any leads?" Detective McClure folded his hands and placed them on top of the file folder.

"Only two; and I'm not sure they're related in any way to the alleged kidnapping. There was a boy in his late teens spotted on the beach wearing a black t-shirt. Two young females identified him as David Miller from their class at school. I'm not certain he has anything to do with the missing girl. One thing I *can* say he's guilty of is overdressing for the beach." Officer Butler chuckled at his joke. "The attendants at the paddleboat station said that a young man matching the description of this boy rented a paddleboat and asked for a life jacket for his baby sister. They reported they never saw the little sister, and Max didn't pick up any scent of her at—or around—the paddleboat station. The second thing," Officer Butler continued, "is a charm bracelet I found at the scene." He pulled an evidence bag from his pocket, opened it, and dumped the bracelet into the palm of the detective's outstretched hand.

Detective McClure looked at the charm bracelet and handed it back to him. "I still don't understand what all this has to do with the missing boy."

"I paid a visit to the Miller's, hoping to talk to David Miller—the boy in the black t-shirt—but no one was home. I went next door and had an enlightening conversation with their elderly neighbor, Mrs. Brown. Mrs. Brown informed me how her neighbor, Bea Miller, had been willed a baby boy by her sister, Elizabeth. The sister, Elizabeth, allegedly adopted the child at birth. When she contracted breast cancer and ultimately passed away when he was only a few months old, she left the child to her sister. Mrs. Brown hadn't seen the boy they call Mikey until late spring when he was around eight or nine months old. If this story is true, that would put him at about two months old when the baby boy was kidnapped from the Stop-N-Save in 2003. We had the Bureau run a search to see if we could locate the death certificate for Elizabeth, but the search came back empty. I think this neighbor of Mrs. Brown's is collecting kids. She already has four boys, and I have a hunch that she now has our missing girl. I'd stake my reputation on it."

Detective McClure seemed a bit skeptical at first; but the more Officer Butler talked, the more intrigued he appeared.

Be Careful What You Wish For

"What can you tell me about the missing boy?" Officer Butler asked.

"Well, it seems as if you've done your homework. An infant was snatched from a shopping cart in the Stop-N-Save over on Perkins. It was the year that we had that snowstorm just before Halloween, you remember, in 2003." Officer Butler nodded and the detective continued. "His mom, let's see, what was her name?" Detective Stephens referred to the file folder. "Ah yes, Nancy Novak. How could I forget? Anyway, she was grocery shopping. She left the infant in her cart, and then she stepped around the corner of the aisle, to grab a box of cereal. When she returned, he was gone. He was wearing a yellow snowsuit, and bundled, from head to toe. I have a picture of him right here." Detective McClure turned the file folder around, so Officer Butler could see it. "He was a cute little guy. The mother and father went on the news and pleaded for the safe return of their baby. It's funny, but the situation she described back then sounds eerily similar to the one you're describing now about the missing girl. The mother didn't see anything. She didn't hear anything, and neither did anyone else in the store. I believe she described it as if he'd *vanished into thin air*."

"What did you do?"

"We searched for quite a while—a year or longer—in every dumpster, trash can, trash bag, and landfill. We put up missing child posters. His picture was even on milk cartons. Nothing ever came of it. We never found him and eventually his parents moved away. They said there were too many terrible memories in this town. Can't say as I blame them, this case has given me nightmares for years. I keep wondering if there's something else I could have done—something else I could have asked—something that I may have missed. The case has pretty much gone cold. Who am I kidding? It was cold from the start."

"Were there ever any leads?"

"Just one . . . someone thought they saw a dark van pulling out of the parking lot at the Stop-N-Save around the same time the kidnapper would have been fleeing with the child. Of course, since they didn't think anything of it, they didn't bother to get the license plate number or even the actual make and model of the van. The person who came forward was worried they didn't see enough, and they didn't want to frame the wrong person."

90

"Didn't the grocery store have security cameras or tapes you could seize?"

"Funny you should ask. They do have a security system, but the assistant manager, who opened the store that day, forgot to turn them on. Can you believe that? Of all the days it could have happened, the one day we need to *see* the tapes—there aren't any."

"Do you think he was involved? It sounds very suspicious, like you said, of all days he forgot to turn on the cameras."

"We did suspect him at first; however, after I talked to the store manager, apparently the guy was extremely forgetful and had forgotten on other days to turn the cameras on, as well. I believe he no longer works at the store. He was just a kid fresh out of community college trying to get his feet wet in the working world."

"So where does the case stand now?"

"You're looking at it. A file folder with a picture and a couple of notes . . . that's all there is to it. I've waited a long time for this. If you could find the missing girl, that would be terrific; and if the missing girl could lead us to the missing boy—that would be the icing on the cake!" Detective McClure closed the folder and placed it back in his file drawer. Officer Butler noticed, however, that he placed it in the very front, probably hoping he would need it again real soon.

ᒉᔎ *Chapter Ten* ᔍᒑ

B y the time Officer Butler got in his car and headed back to Bunting Valley, his stomach had begun growling. He looked at the dashboard clock; it was already after six p.m.—later than he thought. *No wonder I'm so hungry.* The day had flown by—however, he felt they'd made some real progress. As promised, he called the Taylors.

"Hello," Abby said breathlessly, as if she had just finished running a marathon. It was obvious she'd been waiting for the call.

"Good evening, Mrs. Taylor. Sorry to bother you so late. I hope I'm not interrupting dinner."

"No. I don't have much of an appetite and neither does Tim. Madeline went to her Grandma's. It was just too hard with her constant questions. I'm going to have Tim pick up the other phone so he can hear our conversation if that's okay with you."

"That's fine." When Officer Butler heard the click and assumed Tim was listening, he began. "I've spent the last few hours with a detective over in Greenfield. It seems there was a baby boy kidnapped some years back from the Greenfield Stop-N-Save."

"I still don't understand what this has to do with Maggie." Abby sounded desolate.

"Just bear with me for a moment. The day Maggie went missing, we believe there was a family at Lake Gerber about the same time you folks were. Two girls who were sitting a short distance from your family on the beach identified a boy from their recent graduating class as one of that family's members. You—Abby, also mentioned noticing the same boy—the one wearing the black t-shirt. I ran a trace on him and found out where he lives. I went to see him, but no one was home. I ended up talking to a neighbor, an elderly lady who was full of information. She told me all about the family living next door to her. As it turns out, there are four boys in the family. As the story was told to the neighbor, the youngest one was turned over to them six or seven years ago, when his adoptive mother died of breast cancer."

92

Be Careful What You Wish For

"Turned over to them? What exactly does that mean?" Abby asked.

"When his mother died, she allegedly left a Last Will and Testament stating her family should get custody; or, more specifically, her only sister. The circumstances surrounding her death tossed up red flags everywhere, so we decided to dig a little deeper. As it turns out, there's no record of her death or the adoption anywhere, which leads us to believe that the family didn't gain custody of the boy the way it was reported to the neighbor. I've been at the Greenfield Police Department for the last few hours, discussing the disappearance of an infant boy— and the similarities between his abduction, and Maggie's. As it turns out, they're alike in many ways."

"How so . . . ?"

"Well, the boy was taken from the Stop-N-Save in broad daylight while his mom was in close proximity. After he had turned up missing, people were questioned, but no one saw or heard anything. He was never found. It was as if he'd vanished into thin air. Likewise, Maggie was taken in broad daylight while you and your husband were just a few feet away. As you know, we talked to several people and no one saw or heard anything. I believe *you* said that it was as if Maggie had vanished into thin air."

"That's *all* you have?" Abby sounded disappointed.

"No, there's more. When Max and I were down by the beach, I found a charm bracelet in the sand precisely where you told me that Maggie had been sitting. The charm bracelet had five charms. Four of them had the names of boys engraved on them. The last charm—a princess crown, was still blank."

It appeared Abby was speechless, as she waited to hear more. Officer Butler then heard her as she began to sob, and assumed Abby was valiantly attempting to come to grips with all of this.

Tim finally spoke up, "As you can imagine, my wife is having a hard time. Please continue, Officer Butler."

"That's not all. We did get a call from an older gentleman who thinks he saw a woman leading a little blonde girl matching Maggie's description to a dark van in the parking lot at Lake Gerber. The only eye witness at the Stop-N-Save thought they saw a dark colored van leaving the parking lot around the approximate time the kidnapper would have been fleeing with the infant boy."

"That was several years ago. Do you really think they'd still have the same van?" Tim felt it was highly unlikely.

"It's possible, since the witness at Lake Gerber said it was a dark, older model van. Statistics state consumers are prone to purchase the same make of vehicle if they have good luck with their latest one. This could be a different van, but the same consumer."

"You think they have Maggie?" Tim finally asked since Officer Butler had not said so.

"My gut is telling me *yes*. I'm almost positive."

"Where do they live?"

"I'm afraid I can't tell you that."

"Fine, but what are you waiting for? *Go get her!*"

"Not so fast. First thing tomorrow morning, I'm going to go back and pay them a visit. Hopefully, the van will be in the driveway, and I'll get a chance to talk to her; or the boy with the black t-shirt. If we could catch them red handed, we will be able to lock her up and throw away the key."

"Why tomorrow? Why can't you go now?" Abby sounded desperate.

"It's almost seven p.m., Mrs. Taylor. While I understand your urgency, everything we have is just circumstantial at this point. We want to make sure we get something concrete so we can send this woman away for a long, long time. We all need a good night's sleep. Besides, if we rush in and catch her off guard, she may do something stupid like hold Maggie hostage, which is not what we want. I promise you, first thing in the morning I will be knocking on their door. It's almost over, Mrs. Taylor. I can feel it in my bones."

"What if they know we're on to them? They might leave in the middle of the night?"

"They have no reason to believe we're on to them, so I doubt they will leave. Besides, I plan on having someone watch the residence all night, just in case."

"What if they hurt her? You said they have four boys. I just don't like the sound of it. What if they sexually abuse her or something?"

"I don't think that's likely. The neighbor didn't indicate any signs of child abuse going on. If the woman is smart, she won't touch those kids. All she would need to do is one stupid thing like that and it will call attention to them; about that time, Child and Family Services will be all over her like whiskers on a catfish."

"Are you sure you shouldn't go tonight? I just have this horrible feeling that the kidnapper isn't as nice and pleasant as the next-door neighbor led you to believe. I just want my baby back safe and sound."

"I know Mrs. Taylor. Trust me . . . *I know.* First thing tomorrow I'll be back over there knocking on her door."

"Okay. We'll wait to hear from you tomorrow. Thank you so much for calling. Have a good evening."

"You do the same," he said, though he knew Maggie's parents wouldn't have a good evening, until she had been returned to them, safe and sound.

Detective Stephens was still at the police station, waiting for Officer Butler to return and pick up Max. He told him all about the information that he'd gotten about the abduction of the infant at the Stop-N-Save.

"The only eye witness seems to think the alleged kidnapper was driving a dark van. It's just *too* coincidental that Cecil told us the same story. I think when I finally meet up with Bea Miller, she will be the owner of a dark van."

"You don't have to wait until you meet up with her. I did a personal and criminal background check on her, and it shows that she drives a 1995, dark blue, Chevy conversion van."

"*You're kidding me!* What else does it show?"

"Her last known address was in Seattle, Washington. She spent some time in jail in 1980 for shoplifting . . . besides that, not much. She's managed to keep her nose clean for quite some time."

"So, her shoplifting has escalated to kidnapping?"

"Yep, appears so. What about the missing boy?" Detective Stephens scratched his head. "Did anything ever turn up on him?"

"Absolutely nothing . . . their detective showed me a photograph and a couple of notes. They looked for him for quite a while—years in fact, but finally gave up."

"So where does it stand now?"

"I believe he said it's a cold case."

"Hopefully we will be able to shed some light on it soon. Those poor parents are probably going crazy not knowing."

"I can only imagine. Oh, I spoke to Mr. and Mrs. Taylor and she voiced her concern about the Millers leaving with Maggie in the middle of the night. I told her we would have someone sit and watch their residence, just to make sure they didn't."

"I'll go."

"Are you sure?"

"Yeah, I'm sure. I've been sitting here doing nothing all day. I don't have a wife, or family to worry about, so I'll be fine."

"I don't have a wife or family either."

"No, but you have Max. Just go home and get some rest. Tomorrow's another day. I've been on numerous stakeouts. I know what to look for."

"Okay, if you're sure. Please don't hesitate to call if you need something."

Officer Butler could hardly wait for his alarm clock to go off. He didn't want to be too early, yet he didn't want to wait long enough to give them the chance to leave. At precisely 7:30 a.m., he pulled into the driveway at 8797 Crimson Lane, right behind an older model, dark blue Chevy conversion van. He climbed out of the patrol car and walked up to the door of the Miller's trailer. A bubble gum chewing boy, who appeared to be around twelve years old, peeked through the curtain and ran to answer the door.

"Hello, young man, is your mom at home?" Officer Butler used his most gentle voice.

Be Careful What You Wish For

"Yep, she sure is." John opened the door, so Officer Butler could enter.

"Mom," John yelled. "There's a policeman here to see you."

While waiting for Bea, Officer Butler had a chance to glance around the small living room. He'd looked through the window yesterday when he was here; however, standing inside the little trailer now, he realized it was even smaller than it looked. The mobile home also had a distinct odor, but he couldn't quite figure out what it was. There were some toys scattered about, which he would undoubtedly say, belonged to a girl. Not having any children of his own, it was hard for him to know for sure, but they didn't look like anything he would have played with as a child. Not only were there toys, but there were empty boxes and a pair of pink *Dora the Explorer* sandals. It was obvious the toys and shoes were new and had recently been opened.

Bea walked down the long, skinny hallway to the front door. When Officer Butler finally saw her, she looked as if she was walking the plank, and the closer she got, the paler she became.

"Good morning, Officer. May I help you with something?"

"Yes, ma'am . . . sorry to bother you and your family so early, but my name is Officer Rich Butler, and I have a few questions for you."

"Honestly, we were just getting ready to go out."

"Either you can answer my questions here and now, or we'll bring you down to the station and you can answer them there. The choice is yours."

"What's this about?" Bea asked. "Does it have to do with David's arrest? I thought I paid for everything, and he was free to go."

"No, ma'am . . . it has nothing to do with David and his arrest."

Bea pushed a piece of hair behind her ear. "Have my boys done something wrong? You know, I've been a single parent for years. At times, the boys tend to get out of hand. I try to keep an eye on them, and for the most part, they're good boys. Without a male role model, sometimes they get into a little mischief. What did they do now? Don't tell me, Mrs. Brown phoned in a complaint again about loud music? That lady, she means well, but sometimes I wish she'd come over here first to see if we can settle a disagreement, before contacting the police. I remember one time . . ."

"No," Officer Butler interrupted before Bea had a chance to say more. "This visit isn't about your boys; however, I would like to talk to David if he is around."

"David? I don't think he's here."

"Yes he is." The bubble gum chewing boy was twisting gum around his finger.

"John, don't interrupt me when I'm talking. Where are your *manners?* And how many times have I told you to keep the gum in your mouth!" Bea said sternly.

"But he's here. He's still in bed." John pointed toward the hallway.

"What I meant to say is he's here, but he's in the backyard mowing, so he's not available to talk right now. Once he starts the lawn mower, I never call him away for fear he won't go back and finish. He's a teenage boy. I'm sure you can understand." Bea gave a nervous giggle.

Mowing, at 7:30 in the morning? Officer Butler listened intently to see if he could hear the roar of a lawn mower coming from the backyard. He couldn't, and he could tell from the way Bea was babbling, she was hiding something.

"Ma'am, were you and your family down at Lake Gerber two days ago, on July seventeenth?" Officer Butler asked.

"Why, yes we were. The boys wanted to go swimming, so I agreed to take them."

"What time did you arrive?"

"We got there about eleven o'clock. We grabbed a late breakfast on our way."

"What did you do while you were there?"

"I sat on the beach and watched the boys swim. John just loves that water slide."

"Did you see a little girl while you were there?"

"Of course, I did. There were lots of children there, boys and girls."

"What about this one?" Officer Butler pulled the picture of Maggie from his breast pocket.

"No—I don't recognize her. There were so many, it's hard to remember. They were all over the place. Some were playing in the sand; some were playing in the water."

"She was wearing a blue bathing suit. I understand she has the most beautiful blue eyes. If you'd seen her, I'm sure you would remember her."

"I'm certain I didn't see her. I don't disagree that she's a cute little girl."

John walked over to sneak a peek at the photograph, and Bea quickly handed it back to Officer Butler.

"When you went to Lake Gerber, did you take the van parked out front?"

"Yes, I did. It's the only vehicle I have. I would love to get a new one but, unfortunately, it's not in the budget."

"What about this?" Officer Butler pulled the charm bracelet from his pocket. Bea's reaction was just what he hoped for; shock, disbelief. "Have you seen this before?"

"No, I haven't. It looks like a charm bracelet. I thought those went out of style years ago." Bea shook her head.

"Mom . . . isn't that..." John started as Bea placed her hand over his mouth.

"When will he learn to stop interrupting?" Bea said slapping John on the back of his head.

Officer Butler rolled his eyes. "Mrs. Miller, if I may ask; how many children do you have?"

"I have four—four boys to be exact."

Officer Butler purposely glanced at the girl toys scattered all over the floor hoping Bea would admit to having a girl. When she didn't respond, he raised his eyebrows and said, "I see. Well, I won't keep you any longer. Thank you for your time. Oh, and please tell David I'll be back to talk with him at another time when he's not so busy—mowing the lawn." He opened the door and stepped outside.

"I'll let him know, Officer." Bea moved over to hold the screen door for him.

Officer Butler walked out and headed toward the patrol car. He hesitated in the driveway, turned, and then walked to the backyard. The grass was about a foot high; it hadn't been mowed in weeks. No lawn mower. No David. Mrs. Brown was out pulling weeds, so Officer Butler thought he'd stop by and say hello. He left his patrol car in the Miller driveway and walked across the grass.

"Hello again, Officer . . ." Mrs. Brown tilted her head up, so she could see him from under the wide brim of her sun hat. "Did you get all your questions answered?"

"Hmmm?"

"The Millers . . . did they tell you everything you needed to know?

"Oh, yes, they did. Tell me something. Have you seen a little girl at the Miller's?"

"No. I've lived next to them for years, and I've never seen a girl."

"What about recently, in the last couple of days?"

"No, I haven't seen a girl . . . just Bea and the four boys."

"Since my visit yesterday morning, has anything strange happened next door?"

"There is something. I don't know if it's strange or not, but it seemed odd to me."

"What?"

"Yesterday, shortly after you left, they pulled in their driveway. I was standing just inside my door when I saw them, so I came out to say hello. I was talking to Bea, and I heard a scream."

"A scream . . . ?"

"Yes, a scream. Bea claimed that a bee had been buzzing around the van for a few days, and it finally stung Mikey. I found it odd a bee could survive a few hours in a hot car; much less, a few days in this heat. Then I heard the same scream again, and Bea claimed it was Mikey, but I was watching, and I didn't see Mikey scream. The whole thing was odd to me. It left me with a funny feeling."

"What happened after that?"

"They all went inside, and I watered my hanging baskets. That's about it."

"And you are absolutely positive there wasn't a girl?"

"Nope . . . it was just Bea, and the four boys."

"Thanks for the information."

᥉᥅ *Chapter Eleven* ᥅ᥲ

B ea was pacing back and forth in the trailer trying to figure out what her next move should be. Mrs. Brown was still out pulling weeds, so she decided to walk over and have a chat with her. Maybe she would be able to shed some light on what the police officer was thinking.

Bea snuck up behind her. "Good morning, Mrs. Brown."

Mrs. Brown nearly dropped her gardening spade. "Oh, Bea, you startled me."

"Sorry . . . I didn't mean to scare you. Your flowers are beautiful, as always."

"Thank you."

"I was just wondering what the police officer was talking to you about."

"Not much really. He was admiring my flowers, too."

"Is that all?"

"Pretty much . . . oh, and he asked if I've ever seen a girl at your house. Isn't that funny?"

Bea laughed nervously. "Yes, that *is* funny. What did you tell him?"

"I told him that I had never seen a girl over there—just you and the four boys, and that I've lived next door to you for years."

Bea stood watching Mrs. Brown pull weeds. *What a fine mess I've gotten into. Why did I lie to him? Maybe I can get David to take the fall for me.*

"Was there anything else?" Mrs. Brown stared up at her.

"No . . . I guess not. Have a good day." Bea waved as she walked away.

"You too . . ."

Be Careful What You Wish For

Bea went back into the trailer and hurriedly marched to David's room. She reached over and slapped him across the face, trying to wake him.

David blinked and put his hand up to protect his face. "Owww. What are you doing?" David yelled.

"Shut up," Bea snapped as she shut the bedroom door. "We're in trouble. An officer was just here and I think he knows I lied to him. Worse yet, I think he knows that I have Maggie."

"No shit, *Sherlock*. I could have told you that." David rolled his eyes as he sat up.

"Now is not the time to place blame, David. This is serious. We have to think of a plan—a way out of this mess."

"Don't look at me." David threw his hands up. "You're on your own. I told you from the beginning this wasn't a good idea, but you wouldn't listen to me. Now you've got your balls in a vice, and I'm just sitting back, waiting for the fireworks." David smiled as he leaned back and intertwined his fingers behind his head.

"You don't have to be so crass . . . and *besides*, that officer asked about you, too, so you'd better not think for a second that this is all on me."

David felt as if someone splashed him in the face with cold water. He sat straight up and looked at Bea. "He asked about me? What did you tell him?"

"That you were out mowing the lawn."

"You stupid *bitch* . . . why did you tell him *that?* You could have said I was sleeping, or I wasn't at home; but mowing the lawn? At seven-thirty in the morning . . . ?"

"I was scared. I didn't know what to say. He just kept asking questions, and looking around at all of Maggie's toys. Then he pulled my charm bracelet out of his pocket, and I almost swallowed my tongue."

"Serves you right . . . I knew eventually your luck would run out."

"It hasn't run out yet, but we need to get out of here. I'm sure Mrs. Brown is watching, so how do we get Maggie out of the trailer without her seeing?"

"I know. Why don't you kill her, cut her into a million tiny pieces, and flush her down the toilet?" David offered sarcastically.

"Don't be ridiculous, David. I don't have a knife that sharp. Besides, I want to get out of this mess with our family intact—*all of us.*"

"I was just kidding." David shook his head in disbelief.

A moment later when David was not coming up with any feasible ideas, Bea spoke, "I know! We can carry her out in the same bag we used at the lake. It worked then, it'll work now." Bea opened the bedroom door. "Go get the bag from the van and tell your brothers to pack up some things. We're leaving and we won't be back."

"Where are we going?"

"I don't know yet. We just have to get as far away as possible."

Three patrol cars, in addition to Officer Butler, were parked in the empty lot directly across from the entrance to the trailer park. The lot had an abandoned warehouse that, at one time, manufactured macaroni. When the macaroni company was purchased by a big conglomerate, all the employees were laid off, and the entire operation went up for sale. No one bought it, so it still stood empty with weeds growing up through the cracks in the parking lot. It was the perfect spot to sit and wait. Detective Stephens and Chief Felder sat in one car, and Officers Wolfe and Rife were in the other two. Sitting on the side of the building out of view, Officer Butler had a pair of binoculars and could see the front of the Miller trailer.

Bea reacted just the way he had predicted. When he showed her the charm bracelet, even though she'd denied owning it, her eyes had told him a different story. As soon as he'd backed out of the Miller driveway, he phoned Detective Stephens and told him what had happened. Now, all they had to do was watch and wait for her to come out of the trailer with Maggie. They suspected she was probably beginning to panic and wasn't sure what to do now.

Be Careful What You Wish For

Exactly one hour and ten minutes later, the entire Miller family walked out the front door at 8797 Crimson Lane. When he looked through the binoculars and saw the Millers leaving, Officer Butler was filled with anticipation. *Hmmm . . . I don't see a little girl—but that young boy must be Mikey.*

His police radio came to life as Detective Stephens broadcast, "The suspect is coming out of the trailer with four boys. One is wearing a black t-shirt, carrying a red bag of some sort. The other three are dragging, what appears to be, suitcases. Mrs. Miller has her arms full with what looks like blankets and pillows. There's no sign of a little girl."

Is it just me, or is that red bag actually moving? Officer Butler wondered, peering intently through the binoculars.

As soon as the van door slammed shut, David unzipped the bag and helped Maggie into her car seat. Bea turned the key in the ignition, and the van sputtered and died. "Come on, don't fail me now." Bea pounded on the dashboard with the palm of her hand. She turned the key again. The van tried to start, but the motor turned over briefly, and *again*, it died.

"Why don't you pump the gas pedal a few times?" David suggested from the back.

"Why don't you shut up, and *mind your own damn business?*" she snapped. "I've started this van a million times, David. I know what I'm doing. Sometimes it just takes a few tries." Bea turned the key and this time the engine hesitated, caught, and started. "See? I told you I knew what I was doing."

"If you knew what you were doing, it would have started the first time." Apparently, David just couldn't leave well enough alone.

"Since when did *you* become such an expert, David? I swear I have half a mind to kick your ass out of this van, and let you fend for yourself. I'm so sick of your sarcasm and negativity." Bea put the van in reverse and backed out of the driveway. "If you only knew how good you have it you wouldn't give me such a hard time." Bea looked one last time at the trailer as she pulled down the street.

Be Careful What You Wish For

She remembered back to when she first rented it, right after Henry, the love of her life, had been killed in that horrible accident. She, David, Joshua, and John started a brand new life, and things were going well for them. There were so many happy memories. Then, there was the mix-up with Mikey. He ruined everything. Things would be much better now that she had her little girl. Bea could find them another place to live, in a different city, in a different state. At this point, it didn't actually matter, as long as she had Maggie, and they were together.

Bea put on her signal and turned out onto the main road. Within seconds, she was surrounded on all sides. She pulled into the parking lot of the warehouse. **"STEP OUT OF THE VAN. STEP AWAY FROM THE VEHICLE WITH YOUR HANDS UP!"** shouted a man through the police loudspeaker.

Bea opened her door and climbed out. She slammed the door and turned around facing the van. "What is going on? What have I done?" Bea acted totally surprised.

Detective Stephens, with Chief Felder following not far behind him, came over and slid the van door back. There, securely fastened in her car seat, was Maggie Taylor and she looked exactly like her photo. Besides being completely fascinated by all the flashing lights, she looked healthy and happy.

"Drop the act, Mrs. Miller. No one is buying it," Officer Butler said. "You are being arrested for the alleged kidnapping of a two-month-old baby boy from the Stop-N-Save Supermarket in Greenfield seven years ago, as well as the alleged kidnapping of a three-year-old girl from Lake Gerber two days ago." Officer Butler swooped in and pulled her arms behind her back, snapping on the handcuffs as he spoke. "You have the right to remain silent. Anything you say *can* and *will* be used against you in a court of law. You have the right to speak to an attorney. If you cannot afford an attorney, one will be appointed to you. Do you understand these rights as they have been explained to you?"

"This is just a misunderstanding. I can explain," Bea said.

"Explain it to the judge." Officer Butler led Bea over to a patrol car and placed her in the backseat. Four boys piled out of the van. David was wearing a black t-shirt.

"You must be David," Officer Butler said as soon as he saw him.

Be Careful What You Wish For

"Yes I am, Sir."

"I've been looking forward to having a talk with you."

"Really . . . about what, Sir?" he spoke softly.

"Oh, I'm sure there are lots of things you can tell me, aren't there?"

David seemed genuinely nervous about how much he should tell the police. Officer Butler glanced over at Bea, and he could see that she was yelling something through the glass of the patrol car; however, no one could hear what she was saying. Whatever it was, she kept screaming it repeatedly, beating her head against the window.

David hung his head, and then finally, he looked at Officer Butler. It appeared someone opened the levee, and the words began to flow. Once he started talking, he couldn't stop. "Bea's a complete psycho. She took Mikey from the grocery store several years back. She wanted a girl and thought *he* was a girl. He was dressed in a yellow snowsuit and she couldn't tell. She brought *her* home, and then was surprised when *she* turned out to be a *he*." For a moment, he stopped to catch his breath before he continued.

"At first Bea didn't want him. She talked about getting rid of him, but she wanted me to do it, and I couldn't. I told her if she harmed him, I'd go to the police. She already had the name Michelle picked out so the name turned to Michael, and we kept him. However, that wasn't enough. She wouldn't stop. She just kept talking about a girl and going somewhere to find one. She concocted the plan to take one from Lake Gerber. 'There will be no mistaking a girl for a boy on the beach when all they have on is a swimsuit,' she'd said. So we went to Lake Gerber and watched all the little kids playing. Finally, Bea picked out Maggie and we took her. I'm truly sorry, but I had to do what I was told. You don't know how she is."

"What about the other kids? Were they kidnapped, too?" Officer Butler asked.

"No, just Mikey and Maggie . . . I'm sorry to say, the rest of us are *related* to *it*." He looked at Bea's face in the patrol car window. She appeared to be furious.

Handcuffs were put on David, and he was placed in a different car.

"Thanks for the information, son. If you testify against Bea, I'm sure the judge will go easy on you."

Officer Butler walked over to where Chief Felder was standing, holding onto Maggie's hand. He kneeled down, so his size wouldn't be intimidating to the little girl. "Hi, Maggie, I'm Officer Butler. We've been looking for you. Are you okay?"

"Yes. Just waiting to ride the pink pony," Maggie replied, matter-of-factly.

Officer Wolfe took the car seat out of the van and installed it in the back seat of Officer Butler's patrol car. Max, who usually rode in the back, seemed happy to give up his seat to sit in front next to his partner. Officer Wolfe walked back over to where Officer Butler stood with Maggie.

"Rich, I'm almost positive I searched this vehicle the other day over at the lake. I remember those boys. I don't know how I missed the girl."

"Don't worry about it. It turned out okay in the end."

"I know, but what if it hadn't? Maybe it's time I retire and let someone else with a better set of eyes take over."

Officer Butler didn't know what to say, so he patted Officer Wolfe on the back and said nothing. Finally, after several minutes, he spoke, "I'm going to take Maggie to the hospital to get her checked out. As soon as the Taylors show up, I'll leave there and go over to the county jail where they are taking Bea and David Miller. I'd like to be present when they start questioning her."

Once back in his patrol car, Officer Butler found the Taylor's number and wasted no time phoning them.

"Do you have my baby?" Abby Taylor asked before he even had a chance to identify himself.

"Yes, Mrs. Taylor. She's right here. I'm on my way to the hospital. Meet me there."

"The hospital . . . ? Is she okay?"

"She seems fine. It's standard procedure to get a kidnap victim examined, just to be on the safe side."

Be Careful What You Wish For

"Which hospital . . . ?"

"Lake South . . . "

"We're on our way."

Officer Butler looked at his recent call list and dialed the number for the detective in Greenfield, who answered on the first ring. Officer Butler explained to him how the oldest Miller boy had confessed that Bea had taken a child from the Stop-N-Save almost seven years prior. Although there was no way to be one hundred percent certain at this point, he was pretty sure the boy was the same one; alive and well. Detective McClure was beyond ecstatic. He almost hung up before Officer Butler had a chance to tell him they would be taking the boy to Lake South Hospital, just as a precaution, to make sure he was okay.

Officer Butler stood just outside the curtain where they had taken Maggie. Moments later, the Taylors arrived, and Abby's eyes were red and swollen. It appeared she had been crying nonstop for the last couple of days. They opened the curtain to go in while the medical staff examined her.

"Mommy!" Maggie shrieked.

As he smiled, he could only imagine the hugs and kisses that were going on behind the closed curtain. Tim Taylor came out with an outstretched hand. "Thank you so much! I have a feeling Abby isn't going to let her out of her sight for days."

"You're very welcome. I'm glad it all worked out. I'm going to take off now since you seem to have things under control. Please call the station if there is anything else we can do for you." Office Butler shook Tim's hand, turned and left the emergency room. Never one *not* to give thanks where it was deserved, Officer Butler looked up to the heavens and said, "*Thank you* for taking care of her."

✎ *Chapter Twelve* ✎

Bea and David were taken to the Federal Building in Jamestown, a major city not far from Bunting Valley. Separated, Bea was already in an interrogation room by the time Officer Butler arrived. Detective Randy Baker was assigned to interrogate her. Officer Butler had heard good things about Detective Baker and his expertise in psychological manipulation. Officer Butler stood in a dark room on the opposite side of the one-way mirror, watching and listening.

"I'm not going to say anything until my attorney gets here." Bea was sitting at a table with her legs crossed, nervously shaking her foot up and down.

"Nervous, Mrs. Miller . . . ?" Detective Baker asked.

"Why should I be nervous? I haven't done anything wrong. Once I explain everything, you'll see what a horrible mistake you've made."

"Tell me, how many children do you have?"

"I have five children," Bea proudly announced.

"How many of those children are actually yours?"

"They are *all* mine." Bea slammed the palm of her hand hard against the table.

"Come on, Mrs. Miller. There is no reason to continue with the charade. You will only end up hurting yourself in the end."

"I'm not saying anything else until my attorney gets here. Stop trying to trick me into admitting something, and stop asking me questions. I love those children dearly. Well, all except Mikey. He was a mistake since *day one*."

"What, *exactly*, does *that* mean? A mistake since day one . . . ? You mean, the day he was born, or the day you *took him* from the grocery store?"

"I'm not answering that. Where are my children now? When do I get to see them?"

"Well, Maggie has been returned to her family and . . ."

Be Careful What You Wish For

Bea covered her mouth. "My baby girl . . . you took my *baby girl?* Those people didn't deserve to have her. I found her in the sand at Lake Gerber. They weren't even watching her. She could have drowned."

Detective Baker stared at her incredulously, as he rose to answer a light knock on the door. An older gentleman dressed in a suit and carrying a briefcase entered. "Hello Mrs. Miller. My name is James Monroe. I've been appointed to represent you." He turned to look at Detective Baker. "I need a moment alone with my client, in a room where we will not be watched or recorded." James Monroe had been a fixture in the criminal court system for years. He usually didn't have high profile cases since those clients had enough financial means to obtain their own legal counsel, so when he heard about Bea Miller; he was thrilled to be a part of it.

Bea stood, and she and Mr. Monroe left the room. They were given a small conference room just down the corridor. "Boy, what I wouldn't give to be a fly on the wall in there," Officer Butler said when the detective returned.

"Why don't we go back into the interrogation room and you can tell me all you know about this case," Detective Baker said to him as they entered the interrogation room and waited for Bea and Mr. Monroe to return. The detective pulled out a spiral notebook which Officer Butler assumed was to take notes.

Officer Butler turned the chair around backwards and straddled it. "Well, we know she abducted Maggie Taylor from Lake Gerber two days ago on the seventeenth. When we surrounded her vehicle, Maggie was found securely buckled in a car seat near the rear of the van. Her face was a little flushed, but I think that's because the van didn't have air conditioning, or it just hadn't gotten up to temperature yet. She's at the hospital now getting checked out just as a precaution; but I would venture to say, she's no worse for wear."

"Well I guess that's a blessing. So many times I've seen cases where the child is found, but is so physically and emotionally abused that they never recover. I've been told it's almost impossible to get over something like that. Is there anything else?"

"Yes, her oldest son, David, told me that she took the youngest boy from the Stop-N-Save in Greenfield almost seven years ago. His name is Michael, but they call him Mikey. Having done a little research on my own, there was a child abducted from the Stop-N-Save seven years ago this October. He was never found. As far as the other boys, David seems to think they're her biological children."

"Have you had any conversations with Bea Miller?"

"Yes. I went to her residence this morning. I asked her if she had been at Lake Gerber on the seventeenth, and she answered in the affirmative. At that time, she didn't admit to taking Maggie, but there were new toys and boxes strewn about the living room. The toys I saw would be considered something a little girl might play with—dolls and things of that nature. I also saw a pair of pink shoes."

"This is good stuff. Anything else you can think of?" Detective Baker scribbled in his notebook as Officer Butler spoke.

"My K9 partner, Max, found a charm bracelet in the sand where Maggie was last seen. It had five charms on it. Each of the four boys had a charm, and then there was one—a princess crown—that had been left blank, almost as if she were waiting to see what the little girl's name would be before she went to the trouble of having it engraved."

"Where's the bracelet now?"

"It's over in Bunting Valley. I'll bring it with me the next time I'm out this way. I showed it to Mrs. Miller when I paid her a visit. She denied owning it."

Detective Baker shook his head as he continued to write in his notebook.

"Furthermore, Mrs. Miller drives an older model Chevy conversion van. The van was parked in her driveway when I arrived at the residence this morning. It was also the same van that we surrounded shortly after she pulled out of the trailer park. There was an older gentleman at Lake Gerber the day Maggie was abducted who stated his grandson saw a woman leading a little barefoot, blonde girl to a dark-colored van in the parking lot. Also, seven years ago, a dark van was seen leaving the parking lot at the Stop-N-Save; it was about the same time the perpetrator would have been fleeing the scene with the baby boy."

"Pretty good work, Rich. I've ordered a search warrant, so we can go back to her residence to gather any evidence. When it comes,

112

which should be soon, if you don't mind going back and looking through her stuff . . . that would be helpful."

"Absolutely . . . I'll contact Chief Felder and Detective Stephens. They will probably want to meet me there. Oh, by the way, I did mention to David Miller that I would see to it that judge goes easy on him if he cooperates and helps build a case against his mother."

Moments later the detective's phone rang. "Great. Thanks for calling." He disconnected the call. "The search warrant has been signed by the judge. No sense in you hanging out here. I'm not sure how long they'll be in that room. Bea Miller has a lot of explaining to do."

"Yes, provided she tells the truth. I've never seen *anyone* who can sit and tell a bold-faced lie—when she knows she's been caught red-handed—like she can."

"Seems she has a screw loose somewhere . . . as if there's some kind of disconnect in her brain between what's right and what's wrong. I see it all the time. It's almost as if she believes she is telling the truth." The detective closed his notebook and Officer Butler stood and left.

One hour later, Officer Butler, Chief Felder, and Detective Stephens were at the Miller trailer on Crimson Lane. The warrant gave them permission to search the property—and the van, which had been seized at the scene. Anything outside those two areas would not be admissible in court.

The trailer was a mess and had some sort of odor. Officer Butler had noticed it earlier and couldn't quite put his finger on it. The living room walls were paneled and there were no knick-knacks of any kind. The furniture, all covered with slip covers, appeared to match as the claw legs were exposed. Cereal bowls were left sitting on the kitchen table as flies buzzed about, helping themselves to the leftovers stuck on the dirty dishes in the sink from the night before. The kitchen cabinets were old and needed a fresh coat of white paint. Several of the cabinet doors were missing handles and weren't properly aligned, so they hung crookedly on the cabinets. The rest of the trailer wasn't much better; stained and worn out carpet, some areas so threadbare that you could see the padding beneath it. The bedrooms were in a shambles—beds unmade, closets and

113

drawers ransacked. It was hard to believe five people had been living in this small, rundown excuse for a home.

After finishing a quick walkthrough, Officer Butler said, "I'll check the bedroom at the end of the hall. I'm assuming it's the master bedroom, even though it's not much bigger than the other two." He put on a pair of latex gloves and entered the dimly lit room. He searched for a light switch and found one, but when he switched it on, nothing happened. He pulled back the heavy drapes, which let in a little natural light, and then turned on a lamp on the nightstand. It had no shade and the bulb was covered with dust. Looking around the room, the task of searching it seemed to be overwhelming. *Where do I even begin?* Officer Butler slid the closet door back and started on the top shelf. Buried under a blanket, he found a portable fireproof safe. *I can't imagine she would have anything worth putting in a safe.* He pulled it off the shelf, cleared a spot, and placed it on the bed. It needed a key. "Chief, can you come here for a moment?"

Chief Felder entered the room as Officer Butler stood looking at the safe. "I found this safe."

"I'm surprised she didn't take it with her."

"It was under a blanket on the top shelf in the closet. I'm sure she was in a hurry and missed it. It appears I need a key to open it."

Chief Felder shrugged. "You can look around the room and see if you can find where she might have hidden it, or just bust it open. I have one of these at home and the key is not that unique. You could probably pry it open with a butter knife."

Officer Butler and Chief Felder began opening drawers to find the majority of the contents were already pulled out, either left lying on the floor, or assumed to be packed up and taken. Taped inside the top drawer of the dresser was a small envelope. Inside the envelope was a little, flat key. Officer Butler removed the key and placed it inside the lock on the safe. *Perfect fit . . .* he turned the key and heard the lock mechanism turn over as it unlatched. He pushed the top back to find the safe was full of papers, a few photos and an old, worn out book.

The photos were taken many years prior. One was a worn and faded photo of a man and woman. The back said Mama and Papa. There was another with a woman and a baby. Officer Butler flipped it over to find *Aunt Benita and Beatrice* scribbled in childlike printing. The third photo was a wedding photo. The lady looked like a younger version of Bea Miller. Standing next to the man was an Elvis impersonator. There was a marriage license. BEATRICE G. NOSLEN and HENRY P. MILLER; it was dated October 10, 1989. The seal was from the state of Nevada. There was a birth certificate for DAVID JAMES MILLER, born September 3, 1991. It listed Henry P. Miller as the father. There was a hospital ID band from Mercy West Hospital. It read: BABY BOY LOGAN, DOB 06/12/98. They also found a death certificate for HENRY P. MILLER. He died June 13, 1998. Cause of death: Asphyxiation. There was a title for the Chevrolet Conversion Van, purchased at a dealership near Seattle, Washington in November of 1997. Officer Butler removed the book and ran his finger over the gold etching on the top. **JOURNAL,** it stated in bold letters. The cover was brown with black binding. As he flipped through the pages, the handwriting changed several times throughout. He looked at Chief Felder and they took a seat on the bed. He opened and read the entry just inside the front cover.

My life has been a continuous downward spiral since the day I was born. I decided it might be a good idea to detail the journey, which will explain the person I have become. If all goes well, I hope to give this journal to my only child, David, when he becomes an adult at the age of 21. When he reads it, if he does, it will help him understand I am not perfect, but I would do anything to please and protect the ones I love. My favorite aunt, Benita Noslen, whom I fondly refer to as Aunt Nita, retold the beginning entries to me; and, I wrote them down—the best I could recall—some years later. Aunt Nita came into my life when I needed her most and departed at the worst possible moment; when I was still young and vulnerable.

"I think we hit the jackpot. This just seems too good to be true." Officer Butler scratched his head. "We may have all we need right here in this journal . . . a confession, and possibly a motive for all of this. It can't get much better than this. Notice she said *David* was her *only* child. I wonder if that means she wrote that when he was an only child, or if he's her only biological child?"

"Good question." Chief Felder grabbed the journal and flipped through it.

The three men continued to search for a while longer, collecting little, if any, evidence: an empty box for a baby doll, and a box for a pair of *Dora the Explorer* shoes. Their main find was the safe and all of its

115

contents. They left the Miller trailer a few hours later on their way back to the Federal Building.

When they arrived back at the Federal Building, Bea and her attorney were once again in the interrogation room with Detective Baker. Officer Butler and Chief Felder stood and watched for a few minutes and then Chief Felder lightly tapped on the door. Detective Baker stepped outside and shut the door.

"How's it going so far?" Officer Butler asked.

"She went before the judge about an hour ago and bail was set at two million dollars, one million for each of the minors we know she kidnapped. I'm sure she doesn't have that type of money, so she's not going anywhere. It is scheduled to go before the Grand Jury next week. At that time, we'll need to call in a couple of witnesses, if we can."

"How long do you think all this will take?" Officer Butler glanced at the chief.

"Hard to say exactly but we're luckier than most. The justice system typically moves very slowly, but in North Dakota, criminal cases take about a day. Even the bigger criminal cases take no more than a week. The State has picked a prosecutor—a young man by the name of Gregory Hildebrand.

Officer Butler was thwarted. "A young man . . . I wonder why they didn't pick someone who has been around the block a few times?"

"Mr. Hildebrand is really good. He may be a young man, but he's been practicing law for six years. He graduated early at the top of his class. He's tried several cases and his win-loss ratio is spectacular."

"Why haven't I ever heard of him?"

"This will be his first high profile case as the lead prosecutor, but he has assisted on a few. Trust me, Rich . . . he knows what he's doing."

"I trust your judgment, Randy, but I'd just hate for us to lose on something small like an inadequate prosecutor."

"He was given the case file and I'm sure he'll have a lot of questions, so I'll contact him tomorrow. By the way, how was the search? Turn up anything?"

"Yes. We found a few things that we assume belonged to Maggie Taylor. We also found a safe that had a lot of documents, photos and a journal."

"A *journal* . . . what type of journal?"

"It appears to be similar to a diary. We only read the inscription written on the inside cover. It sounded as if it were something she may have added as an afterthought to the other entries."

"How big is it?" Detective Baker cleared his throat.

"Pretty big . . . I rifled through it and the last entry was July 17, 2010—the day Maggie Taylor went missing."

"You're kidding me! Where is it now?"

"We checked it in as evidence along with a few other items."

"I'm going to go get it. I can't wait to see the look on her face when I show it to her." Detective Baker looked like a kid in a candy store.

"How's David holding up?" Officer Butler was concerned.

"I don't really know. He was taken to a different location about forty-five minutes ago."

When Detective Baker walked away, Chief Felder put his hand on Officer Butler's shoulder. "Rich, you've done such a fine job with this case so far. If you don't have any objections, I'd like you to devote all your time to it . . . see it all the way through from trial to sentencing. Help round up witnesses, do the legwork, and offer your assistance and help wherever you can. You know, Detective Stephens will be retiring within a year or two. If all goes well, I'd like to recommend you for the job."

Officer Butler remained speechless for a few moments before he finally spoke, "Carl, you don't know how much this means to me. Ever since I was in high school back in Detroit and my best friend was shot and killed in front of me, I was determined to do something with my life to make a difference. Shortly after he died, my family transferred here when my dad's job relocated him. I went to college and studied law enforcement knowing this was what I was meant to do. Before I got involved in this case, I had been content to be part of a K9 unit, handing out speeding tickets, helping maintain order, and the like. However, something has changed. I'm interested in knowing what happens after the arrest. I want to learn all I can about how the criminal mind works."

"Glad to hear it. In the interim, I'll let Officer Wolfe man the K9 unit and take care of Max. If you need any help, or have any questions, you know where we are."

"You know he mentioned retiring earlier today in the parking lot over at the warehouse."

"I know. He does that every time he thinks he did something wrong. If I could count how many times he has 'retired' since I've been chief—well, let's just say I'd have to take my shoes off to help me keep track." Chief Felder chuckled and patted Officer Butler on the back, and then turned and left.

Detective Baker returned with the journal and entered the interrogation room. "Does this look familiar, Mrs. Miller?"

Bea did not respond. She looked dumbfounded, the same look she had when Officer Butler asked her about the charm bracelet earlier that morning.

"Let's read the first entry, shall we?"

Bea quickly reached across the table in an attempt to snatch the journal from him. Detective Baker backed his chair up, beyond her reach, and began reading.

August 17, 1965

The day I was born, I was told, was an unseasonably cold and rainy day for August. Aunt Nita said she received a call informing her that Mama was in labor early in the morning, around 6 a.m. Knowing Papa the way I do, I'm sure he didn't make it easy on Mama. Aunt Nita claimed Papa never wanted any children, so when he found out Mama was pregnant, he told her—in no uncertain terms—I had better be a boy, or she was going to pay dearly. Since Papa had no trouble beating and abusing me, it makes me sad to imagine how he treated Mama.

When they finally got to the hospital, things progressed relatively quickly; and in a few short hours, I made my screaming debut into the world. Mama named me Beatrice Grace, which I've been told means "Bringer of Joy". Having lived with Papa as long as I did, I can understand why Mama needed a little joy in her life. Aunt Nita said that

118

from the moment Mama saw me, it had been love at first sight. I had a perfectly shaped head with plump lips, soft gray eyes, and a tuft of dark hair on the top of my head . . . Papa said I looked like a troll.

Aunt Nita thought I could have been a poster child for what a healthy newborn should look like; pink and chubby, weighing eight pounds and nine ounces. Mama, however, wasn't as lucky with her health. She'd had bronchitis when she entered the hospital and it had turned into pneumonia. Aunt Nita said she had been sick for months, but Papa wouldn't let her go to the doctor because he didn't want to waste money on her. He got so angry when she coughed and drowned out the sound of the television set. He had to get up and walk all the way across the room to turn up the volume.

Sadly, three days after I was born, Mama died at the age of 27. I wish I could have known her. Aunt Nita tells me she was a wonderful woman. I'm not sure if that's true, or it's just what Aunt Nita thinks I need to hear. Regardless, I still feel as if she is watching over me, and helping me, when things get tough. I know they say most people can first recall things that happened to them when they were around three or four years old. I don't know if that's true, but sometimes when I smell baby powder, I picture Mama's face—and she is wearing a hospital gown. I think she must have smelled like baby powder.

As you can imagine, Papa was none too pleased. First off, he didn't want any children, and secondly, he sure didn't want me—a girl. Now that Mama had passed, he was stuck taking care of me all by himself. That's when he called Aunt Nita and she moved in with us.

Officer Butler stood captivated as he noticed a tear running down Bea's face. She sat and listened, powerless to stop the rehashing of her horrific childhood for all to hear. She leaned over and put her head down on the table.

"Is this really necessary? Can't you see you are upsetting my client?" Mr. Monroe asked.

The detective's only response was to continue reading.

I asked Aunt Nita how Papa and Mama met. She didn't know many of the details, but she did know it was on a blind date when Papa was 25 and Mama was 22. Aunt Nita explained to me a blind date had nothing to do with not being able to see. Then why did they call it that?

They courted for a short while, about six months, and then they were married.

Aunt Nita did tell me when Edward and Marcy were dating that Edward was very good to her. Those were their names–Edward and Marcy. Papa already had a good job at a scrap yard, and his own home, although very small, was where we lived until I turned eight years old. He came home from work every night, sweaty and hungry, and as long as Mama had dinner on the table, he was bearable. Some things never change.

All-in-all, I wouldn't say Papa is an ugly man. He just doesn't have, what I would call, memorable looks. There's nothing about him that would make someone look twice, except his hairy knuckles. His knuckles are so hairy, when he scolds me and shakes a finger in my face; I imagine he is a monkey. The pictures I have seen of him early on showed him with his hair slicked back with some type of hair gel, and he had long sideburns. I think he was channeling Elvis or something.

As long as I can remember, he has been a smoker. I wished on so many occasions that he would die from lung cancer, but I guess you don't always get what you wish for. His brand was Camel, unfiltered, and to this day, I can still smell the nasty stench he left everywhere he went from those horrible cigarettes. I often fantasized how amazing it would be if his hairy knuckles would catch fire from a burning ember, but . . . that never happened either.

I've seen a few pictures of Mama, too. She had long, straight hair, parted down the middle and tucked behind her ears. If it weren't for her buck teeth, she would have been quite beautiful. When I look in a mirror, I can see her eyes staring back at me.

Aunt Nita was two years younger than Papa. From the beginning, as she tells it, I absolutely adored her. She was a lovely woman with a heart of gold. She had light brown hair that fell in loose curls framing her face. I remember how her bright green eyes twinkled, each time she laughed, and oh, how Aunt Nita loved to laugh. Despite never having any children of her own, she was very protective of me, just like you would imagine a mother should be.

Detective Baker stopped a moment. "Where's your aunt now?"

Bea, with her head still on the table, never moved.

Be Careful What You Wish For

"Never mind . . . if she's still alive, we'll find her."

Detective Baker looked towards the one-way mirror. Officer Butler assumed he was signaling him, so he pulled the notepad out of his breast pocket, and wrote down Benita Noslen. The first of what he was sure was to be a long list of witnesses.

Detective Baker looked back at the journal and resumed reading.

Papa gave Aunt Nita $75 a week to pay for all the things I needed. He told her he had given Mama $75 a week and she never asked for more, so he didn't expect her to need more either. He told her I didn't need anything special, just the necessities. Regardless of what Papa said, Aunt Nita spoiled me rotten. She loved to sit and rock me. She would hum Brahms Lullaby and make up her own words. Aunt Nita had a lovely voice. I don't know how many times she rocked me to sleep singing that song, or some version of it. I felt safe in her arms. Whatever was lacking in my relationship with Papa, Aunt Nita made up for it a hundred times over.

July 9, 1966

Aunt Nita told me a month before my first birthday that she asked Papa what we were going to do to celebrate. According to Aunt Nita, Papa still blamed me for Mama's death and he got angry each time Aunt Nita brought up my birthday. Papa told her I didn't deserve to celebrate living, when others had died because of me. Of course, Aunt Nita said she always came to my defense, telling Papa he was being ridiculous. But, that didn't matter. Papa hated me and wouldn't change his mind. He told her many times he didn't want me to forget the misery I had caused the day I was born. As I got older, I remember him telling me, too.

Detective Baker stopped reading for a moment and looked at Bea. Her shoulders were shaking from the silent sobs. Mr. Monroe's face was beet red, and he looked as if he were about to blow a gasket. Still, Detective Baker continued reading.

August 17, 1966

Aunt Nita told me she went against Papa's wishes and while he was at work, we celebrated my birthday–just she and I. She said she took pictures and sang Happy Birthday, as I tried to blow out a single candle on a cupcake. There were no presents. She was afraid Papa would see the wrapping paper and get mad. But she did tell me she promised to protect me, love me, and make sure Papa never hurt me. I guess, at the time, it seemed like a nice thing to say, but now that I look back on it, not even Aunt Nita had that kind of power.

February 9, 1967

Aunt Nita told me the day I was playing with Papa's truck keys, and he was late for work because of it, that he grabbed me by the arm, scooped me up, and hit me so hard, I was black and blue for days. He just kept hitting me with his balled up hairy fist. The more I screamed, the more he liked it. I think he was thinking about Mama and how she died, and he was finally able to punish me for killing her. Aunt Nita said if she hadn't stepped in when she did, she honestly thinks Papa would have killed me. He considered me a nuisance, and that his life would have been much better if I had never been born. I learned early on that I was not living in a house where I was welcome, nor did I belong.

ᏬᏛ *Chapter Thirteen* ᏬᏛ

D etective Baker slammed the book shut, which caused Bea to jump. She lifted her head up, face wet with tears. "Please don't read anymore. I wrote those entries for David. They are painful memories that I have spent a *lifetime* trying to forget."

"We've read enough for now. I'll let you and your legal counsel return to the conference room you were in before. I'm sure you have new things to discuss." He stuffed the journal under his arm and exited the room. Officer Butler was standing outside the room, just where he left him.

"Rich, this is good stuff," Detective Baker said, shaking the journal. "See if you can track down her aunt. What was her name . . . Nita?"

"Already planned on it . . . I'll start right now. Oh, by the way, I'm here as long as you need me. Chief Felder reassigned me so that I could remain involved in this case until the end. So, whatever you need done, just let me know."

"Glad to hear it. Why don't you go ahead and take the journal? You can read through it, to see if it mentions any other people that we can try to track down for witnesses, if we need them. I wonder where her dad is . . . he sounds like a real piece of work." Detective Baker chuckled. "I would love to get *him* on the witness stand."

"What about the chain of custody? Are you sure it's all right if I take the journal with me? I don't want to do anything that might make it inadmissible in court. Perhaps it would better if we turned it over to the prosecuting attorney's office."

"It's fine. I told them when I borrowed it that we might hold on to it for a few days . . . just as long as it's back before the trial begins. It was seized under a search warrant, so it will be admissible no matter what."

Officer Butler grabbed the journal and went in search of a database to locate Benita Noslen. The main police station near the Federal Building was *huge* in comparison to Bunting Valley. There was an open bullpen with several rows of desks. Many were occupied as phones rang, drawers and doors slammed, and people talked. Officer Butler stood there for a moment, looking around in amazement at the flurry of activity. Finally, someone noticed him. "May I help you?" a beautiful, young brunette asked as she approached him.

"Yes. I'm Officer Rich Butler from the Bunting Valley Police Department. I need access to a database to track down a possible witness."

"Sure, right this way." He followed behind the young lady, past a copy machine and a room that had vending machines and several tables with chairs. "If you want a cup of coffee, it's in the break room." She pointed as they walked by. Finally, arriving at an empty desk with a phone and computer, she said, "You can sit here. If you need to make a call, dial "eight" first to get an outside line. The phone number is displayed on the phone in case someone needs to call you back." Right before she turned to leave, she stuck out her hand and said, "By the way, I'm Jodi."

"Nice to meet you, Jodi, and thanks for the tour," he replied, and then shook her hand.

"That was just the nickel tour. Stick around and I'll give you the quarter version later." Jodi smiled a perfect smile. "Is there anything else?"

"Yes, I have one more question. Do I need a password to log in?"

"Yes. Just use MASTER, in all caps."

"Oh, and one more thing. . ."

"You said you only had *one* question, so I'm afraid this one will cost you."

Officer Butler grinned, hoping the price was a date with Jodi. "Where's the restroom?"

"Next to the break room," she smiled. "You can't miss it." Jodi turned and walked away, while Officer Butler watched her hips sway back and forth until she was out of sight. He shook his head and powered up the computer.

Luckily, Benita Noslen was a unique enough name that there weren't that many listed. Doing the math, Officer Butler assumed she was between 70 to 75 years old, if she were still alive. This narrowed it down to one—living in Phoenix, Arizona. He dialed the number listed, and an elderly woman answered the phone.

"May I speak to Benita?"

"This is she."

"This is Officer Rich Butler from the Bunting Valley Police Department. I'm working on a felony case, and your name came up as a possible character witness."

"A character witness . . ." the voice queried, "for whom?"

"Beatrice Miller." It sounded as if Benita had dropped the phone. "Are you still there?"

"Yes . . . yes, I'm sorry. I just lost my grip on the telephone. Beatrice Miller, you say? Would this be the same Beatrice as Beatrice Noslen?"

"One and the same . . ."

"Oh my . . . what has she done?"

"Kidnapping for starters," Officer Butler responded while he tapped the eraser end of a pencil on the desk.

"How did you get my name?"

"We found it in a journal she had written."

"You said you were from Bunting Valley?"

"Yes, that's correct."

"Please remind me. Where exactly is Bunting Valley?"

"North Dakota . . . about an hour west of Fargo," he informed her.

"My health isn't what it used to be. I don't know if I can travel. I'll have to check with my doctor. Can I have your phone number and I'll get back to you?"

"Absolutely . . . any costs incurred in getting you here, Ms. Noslen, will be reimbursed."

"It's Mrs. Adams, now. I married after I left Beatrice, although I'm a widow now."

"When did you leave her?" Officer Butler started jotting down notes.

"She was six years old. Hardest thing I ever did was walking out on that little girl. I still remember the look in her eyes."

"I won't keep you any longer. Get back to me after you talk to your doctor. I'll find out when, and if, we will need you to appear. My guess is it will probably sometime next week when it goes before the Grand Jury." Officer Butler rattled off the phone number before hanging up the phone.

When he opened the journal, he paused for a moment. Throughout this entire ordeal, all he felt for Bea Miller was disgust and repulsion; but now, as he sat looking at her journal, he felt something he hadn't felt before: *empathy*. Part of him didn't want to hear anymore, but it was like a train wreck and he couldn't look away.

September 13, 1970

I started kindergarten, the fall I turned five years old. From the very first day, I remember loving school. Just getting away from a house where I wasn't allowed to be me, to a place full of colors and laughter was the absolute best. I remember the first day of school; my teacher, Mrs. Schindle, had a celebration for all the kids who'd had a birthday during the summer. She had wrapped gifts for us, and we had a party. The gifts were nothing big, like a coloring book and crayons, a set of jacks, or a Match Box car for the boys— but to me, they were so much more. They were the only gifts I had ever gotten for my birthday. Sure, Aunt Nita did things for me, but I never had a present wrapped in beautiful wrapping paper with a big floppy bow. I hated to tear it. There were brightly colored balloons and we played games and sang songs. I never knew this is what people did on their birthdays. Besides the few cupcakes I had shared with Aunt Nita over the years, I thought birthdays were supposed to be sad occasions. I remember asking my friend, Shelley, who she killed the day she was born.

I made friends easily back then. I had invitations at least once a month for a sleepover or a party at someone's house. Aunt Nita never let me go for fear Papa would get angry. So, to make up for it, Aunt Nita and I often went to the salon together to have our nails done when she knew the other girls in my class were at a party, having fun. I was the daughter she always wished for, but was never lucky enough to have.

126

Be Careful What You Wish For

November 23, 1970

When I started school, Aunt Nita got a job working at a flower shop. Papa didn't care, as long as the house was clean, the laundry done, and supper was on the table when he walked in the door. When Papa suggested he no longer needed to give Aunt Nita $75 a week, since she was earning her own money at the flower shop, they had a terrible argument. She quickly told him little girls are expensive, and the older I got, the more expensive I would become. I saw Papa raise his hairy hand and shake his finger in Aunt Nita's face. "This girl is not going to be expensive. As soon as she's old enough, she'll earn everything she wants, just like I did," he said. I wondered what he meant when he said that, and soon I would find out.

August 15, 1971

The private birthday celebrations with Aunt Nita continued without Papa finding out. However, the year I turned six, it all came crashing down. I asked Aunt Nita if I could invite Shelley over for birthday cake this year. I know I shouldn't have said it so loud, but I didn't stop to think what I was doing, and . . . I didn't realize Papa was as near as he was. Aunt Nita quickly tried to shush me but she was too late. As long as I live, I will never forget what happened then. Papa walked into the room wearing a stained white sleeveless t-shirt, a lit Camel in one hand, and scratching his big Buddha belly with the other. He looked at Aunt Nita and asked her what I was talking about. I didn't want Aunt Nita to get in trouble, so I told him I'd like to invite my friend, Shelley, from school over for my party. He reminded me of why we don't celebrate my birthday and what happened when I was born. He called me an evil little girl who had killed her own mother.

He turned to Aunt Nita to get her side of the story. She quickly told him we may have celebrated my birthday a time or two—nothing big, just a cupcake and a song. Papa was livid. He screamed at Aunt Nita. "You bitch! You deliberately disobeyed me! I told you no birthday celebrations, EVER! I gave you one simple rule, and you couldn't follow it." He lifted his hand and slapped Aunt Nita across the face. Standing nearby, I cringed at the sound; it was almost as if he had slapped me. He continued to yell at her. "Get out! If I can't trust you, you cannot live under my roof. Get your things and get out of my house!"

Aunt Nita tried to reason with him, but he wouldn't hear of it. He had been betrayed, and he wanted her out. I stood by and watched her as *she packed up a few of her things. I felt like it was my entire fault. I began to believe what Papa had said; I am an evil little girl. I begged her not to go, but she had no choice. I begged her to take me with her but she couldn't. Before she left, she knelt down so she could look me straight in the eye. I'll never forget the last words she said to me. "You be a good girl, Beatrice. Don't make him mad if you can help it." She gave me a hug and then she was gone. The only person who ever loved me walked away, and I never saw her again. I was only six years old. I had already lost Mama, and now I had lost Aunt Nita. This left me all alone with Papa and no one to protect me. My life as I knew it was about to change.*

Officer Butler was horrified. Every aspect of Bea's childhood was documented in the script of a child. He recalled Benita saying she left when Bea was six years old. He could only imagine how scared Bea must have been. She never got to celebrate her birthday. Officer Butler could not even begin to comprehend what it would be like growing up in a household like that. His parents, still happily married after forty-five years, adored him.

August 19, 1971

Four days after Aunt Nita left, Papa came home from work early, and I didn't have dinner ready. I didn't know how to cook, but I had watched Aunt Nita make scrambled eggs, so that's what we had been eating for the last three nights. As soon as I heard the bang of the car door, I remember I almost peed my pants. Papa was going to be mad and I knew he would hit me.

I apologized for not having his supper ready, before he even had a chance to speak. I promised I would have some eggs ready in a couple of minutes. But he surprised me. He wasn't angry at all. As a matter of fact, he promised to take me out for a hamburger.

I hadn't been out to eat in a long time. Every once in a while Aunt Nita would take me out to eat, and a hamburger sounded so good, my mouth started to water. But, before Papa would get me a hamburger, he wanted me to do something for him. Being only six years old, I honestly didn't know what I could do for him; however, I listened as he told me to prove to him that I could go into a store, see something I wanted, hide it under my clothes, and walk out without being caught.

I immediately told him that sounded like stealing, and my teacher always said stealing was wrong. He assured me it was only wrong if you got caught, which I didn't understand. I thought stealing was stealing; what difference did it make if you got caught or not? But he asked me to trust him, and since this was the first time he actually talked to me, instead of talking at me, I decided to listen to what he had to say.

He told me if you see something you want, take it. Don't wait for someone to buy it for you. Don't wait to save enough money. Just take it. It won't hurt anybody, and you'll get what you want. You'll be happy, and the store will be happy that their customer is happy. The way Papa explained it to me, it made perfect sense.

I had never stolen anything before, and didn't know what would happen if I got caught. Would they throw me in jail? Would they cut off my hands? Papa assured me, if I did exactly as he told me, that I wouldn't get caught. I could hear Aunt Nita's words—'don't make him mad if you can help it,' as Papa explained to me what we were going to do. If I did what Papa asked, he would be proud of me and maybe . . . just maybe, he would love me.

Officer Butler could not believe what he was reading. Edward had taught Bea how to steal when she was six years old, and she had been doing it ever since. *All she wanted was for him to love her, and to be proud of her.*

He sat up straight and entered a new name into the database. EDWARD NOSLEN. Born in 1935 and died in 2006. A link for an obituary came up.

NOSLEN, EDWARD, passed September 9, 2006. Unable to find any next of kin, the body was cremated and the ashes scattered in the rose garden near the center of town.

He leaned back in his chair, waiting for Benita to call back. Startled when the phone on his desk started ringing, he picked it up to find Benita Adams on the other end. She informed him that her doctor had given her permission to travel. Officer Butler told her that he would get back to her once they'd had a chance to determine when they would need her.

"I still can't believe Beatrice kidnapped someone," she uttered. "Are you certain?"

"Yes ma'am. I'm afraid so. She was caught red-handed with the boy and girl in her van."

"She kidnapped two kids? I find it hard to believe we are talking about the same person. The Beatrice I know was such a good little girl. I wonder what happened after I left."

"Oh, I don't think you'd believe it if I told you. Let's just say she didn't have someone looking out for her best interests."

"Are you talking about Edward, my brother? I know he lost his temper quite easily, but what did he do? Was he in on the kidnapping with her?"

"No, all indications are, either she acted alone, or had the help of her oldest son, David."

"Beatrice has a son?"

"As far as we know, yes, she has at least one son, maybe three."

"How can you not know how many kids she has?" she asked Officer Butler curiously, before they hung up.

"It's rather complicated. We'll talk about it when you come into town. I'll be in touch." They said their goodbyes, and he hung up the phone and took out his notepad to jot down some ideas. He wanted to document the abuse Bea Miller had suffered at the hands of her father. Officer Butler glanced back through the journal to find the entry of the first time she had recorded being physically abused. It was February 9, 1967—when Edward had found her sitting, playing with his truck keys. These basic observations would help with the trial. The only question was—would they help Bea Miller, *or* the *prosecution?* At this point, Officer Butler wasn't a hundred percent positive which side he was on.

ᴄ✍ᴑ *Chapter Fourteen* ᴑ✎ᴄ

James Monroe led Bea down the corridor back to the small conference room they'd been in earlier. As soon as the door shut and they sat down, the conversation began. "Why didn't you tell me about the journal?"

"I forgot, okay?"

"You forgot? How could you forget something like that?"

"Well, maybe I didn't forget, but I was as surprised as you when that detective showed it to me. Where did he get it?"

"Have you forgotten why we're here? You kidnapped two children. They searched your house. Where do you think they got it?" James Monroe disbelievingly shook his head.

Bea reached up and ran her hands through her hair, pulling and tugging on it. "Everything is happening so fast. This isn't the way it was supposed to go. This wasn't part of the plan."

Mr. Monroe, afraid that Bea was going to have a nervous breakdown, spoke calmly. "You have to be completely honest with me, Bea; remember that I'm on your side. Tell me what else is in that journal that might hurt us."

Bea started to laugh. The more she tried to stop, the less control she seemed to have, and the harder she laughed. She laughed so hard that tears ran down her cheeks.

James Monroe sat and stared at her. She almost looked possessed. "What in the *hell* is so funny?"

"You asked me what else is in the journal. The better question is what's *not* in the journal?"

"What are you saying?"

"I'm saying *everything* is in there—all my thoughts and feelings, the way Papa treated me the time I was arrested for shoplifting, when I ran away before he killed me. I wrote about the day I was raped and when I had an abortion. I told about the day I met and married Henry, as well as the day he died. I told how David, Joshua, John, and Mikey came into my life. The journal is a detailed account of my entire life."

"What you mentioned so far doesn't sound that bad. It might actually help us."

"You don't understand. That's just the tip of the iceberg. It's *all* there in black and white—my own private hell."

"Why don't you tell me some of it so we can determine our game plan from here?"

"Tell you some? You make it sound like an innocent bedtime story."

"That's not what I meant. I know how difficult this must be for you."

"You have *no idea* how difficult this is for me." Bea huffed and leaned back, crossing her arms.

"Calm down, Bea. Getting upset isn't going to solve anything. Just tell me some of it, the best you can recollect, okay?"

"Well, you already know how the story begins because that horrible detective read it out loud to us."

"Yes." James Monroe rested his elbows on the table and cupped his chin with one hand.

"It got worse . . . when I was six years old. Papa threw Aunt Nita out because he found out that we had been privately celebrating my birthday. That was the one rule he gave Aunt Nita when she moved in, 'No birthday celebrations . . . *ever*.' Do you remember how I said that he blamed me for killing my mother? Since Aunt Nita broke the cardinal rule, he no longer trusted her, so he kicked her out. I can still see her in my memories, packing up her things. I stood there feeling so responsible for what was happening. I begged her to take me with her, but she couldn't. Papa would have never allowed it. He didn't want me, but he sure as hell wasn't going to let me go, either. Soon after Aunt Nita left, Papa taught me how to steal."

"Steal? You mean shoplift?"

"Yes. He taught me how to walk into a store and take things. He told me to hide them under my clothes and walk out, without paying for

132

them. Obviously he was an excellent teacher because I'm very good at it. The first thing I tried to steal was a steak, and it didn't go so well."

"What happened?"

"I did everything Papa said to do, but when I went to stuff the steak under my clothes, it was really cold against my naked skin and I screamed. Not a loud scream, mind you . . . I just remember jumping up and down, and saying, 'It's cold, Papa, it's cold.' He got *mad*. When we got out to the car, Papa slapped me so hard, my nose started dripping blood. It was awful."

"What did you do?" James Monroe hardly blinked as he listened to the story.

"I cried. He stopped and got himself a hamburger, and it smelled *unbelievably delicious*. But since I was evil, I didn't deserve one. I went to bed hungry that night, which was the first of many. The next morning, I got up for school, and I had two black eyes. When Papa saw me, he laughed and laughed. Can you believe that? He gave me two black eyes, and he thought it was funny. I told him I couldn't go to school with two black eyes but he assured me I could. He told me if anyone asked what happened, I was to tell them it was none of their damn business."

"Oh no, you didn't, did you?"

"I sure did. I told my homeroom teacher, and she sent me to the principal's office. Some lady from Child Protective Services came. She started asking questions, and finally I lied and told her I fell in the bathtub. As I look back on it, it was my first experience with an agency that was there to protect me, and all I was worried about was protecting Papa. Anyway, I don't think she believed me, but she did give me a business card with her name on it and told me to call her if I ever fell in the bathtub again. When I got home, I told Papa what had happened, and he hugged me and told me that he was proud of me. For the first time, I felt Papa didn't hate me, but I didn't know why."

"Wow, that's quite a story, but since it didn't go so well, I guess that was the end of that?"

"Are you kidding me? Three weeks later when Papa came home from work, I had just finished frying him a steak for dinner. When he walked into the house, the aroma hit him, and the first thing he said was, 'Steak? Where did that come from?' I told him how I walked to the grocery store after the school bus dropped me off. I remember talking to myself the whole way there trying to convince myself I could do it. I was so scared, but it meant so much to Papa, I just had to try. So when I got to the store, I pretended to shop, looking at the gum and candy, then I went over and looked at the cookies and chips. Finally, I went back to the meat section, took a real tasty-looking steak, and stuck it under my shirt."

"Didn't it fall out?"

"No. Papa taught me to tuck the bottom into the waist band of my pants to keep it from falling out. Worked like a charm. I bought a pack of gum for a dime and walked out with a three dollar steak under my shirt. When Papa got home from work, he was so excited. I told him it was much easier than I thought it would be. He kept asking me to tell him how it went, over and over again. I actually felt loved that night, but it didn't last for long."

James Monroe was mesmerized. "What do you mean it didn't last long? What happened then?"

"Well, we ate like royalty that night. Papa told me if I kept at it, we could work as a team, traveling across the country, living high on the hog, and never paying a dime for any of it. Finally, Papa had a reason to tolerate my existence."

"So that was the beginning?"

"Yes, that was the beginning of my life; and I guess my sitting here, in this room at the Federal Building is the end."

"Not so fast. I'm sure there's more."

"A week or so after I stole the steak, Papa and I went into a store and he told me he needed a new pair of sunglasses. He left me alone near the sunglass display while he flirted with one of the sales clerks. I never truly understood how he did it, but he always managed to say just the right thing. Anyway, I didn't know what kind of glasses he wanted so I picked a pair I thought he would like. I pulled the tags off and left the store with the sunglasses on my face. When I got outside, Papa was waiting for me. He told me the glasses were ugly, and that he wasn't pleased. When we got home, he jerked me out of the car by my hair, dragged me into the house, and into my room. I remember trying to be brave and not cry, but it hurt—*terribly*. He picked me up and threw me

134

onto my bed. I remember how hard he slammed the door and I waited, thinking he was going to come back and beat me, but he didn't. I cried myself to sleep that night as my stomach moaned, telling me it was hungry." Bea had a faraway look on her face, almost as if she were there now, laying on the bed waiting.

"Did you ever put up a fight when Edward tried to abuse you?"

"No. Not really. But I do remember the time I got mad and called him a mean man. I think I even told him I hated him." Bea put her hand up over her mouth, still sorry for what she said so many years ago. "I was almost eight years old. The bus dropped me off at the corner, and while I was walking home, I saw something colorful in a bush on the side of the road. I went over to get a closer look and there, sitting on a branch, was a parrot. It was green, yellow, and red—and the most beautiful bird I ever saw. I reached over to grab it, and it didn't try to fly away or bite me. I figured it had escaped through an open window or something. I mean seriously, why would a parrot be outside? I looked around to see if someone might be looking for it, but when I didn't see anyone, I decided to take it home to see if Papa would let me keep it. I had never had a pet before, and it would be nice to have something that would love me, no matter what. I held on to the parrot with both hands, careful not to squish it, and hurried home, so excited to show Papa. Papa was sitting on the front stoop, already home from work. He said that they had let him come home early because the shredding machine wasn't working properly. He said that they didn't want him to get hurt before they were able to get it fixed."

"So Edward still worked at the scrap yard?"

"Yes. That was the only job I ever recollect him having. Anyway, I hid the bird behind my back, and Papa seemed to be in a good mood, so I slowly brought it out to show him. I told him I had found it, down the street in a bush, and I asked if I could keep it. Papa grabbed the bird from my hand and twisted its head off and threw it at me." Bea's eyes were wide open as she made a twisting motion with her hands.

"What did you do?"

"I screamed. That was the *worst* thing he ever did to me, and that was when I yelled at him. I called him a mean man, and I told him I hated him. He slapped me so hard that I fell to the ground. I jumped up, ran to my room, and slammed the door. My shirt had blood on it, blood

135

from the beautiful bird Papa so brutally killed for *no reason at all*. I was so mad that I didn't come out of my room all night. I remember lying in bed listening to my stomach growl." Bea had tears spilling over the rims of her eyes. "My stomach didn't understand."

"Do you know where Edward is now?"

"Yes, I know exactly where he is."

James Monroe obviously waited for Bea to continue and when she didn't, he said, "And where would that be?"

"He's burning in Hell where he belongs."

⤳ *Chapter Fifteen* ⤳

So many times over the years, Officer Butler had heard stories and read newspaper articles of child abuse, but when you didn't know the victim, it just didn't register what they went through. Reading it here, and knowing the woman Bea Miller had become, it just broke his heart. Her father had taken an innocent child who trusted him more than anything, and molded her into what he wanted. He taught her to lie, cheat, and steal; and, when things didn't go according to his plan, he beat her and made her go to bed without any food. *She must have lived every day of her life in fear of what this man might do to her.* He skimmed through the next several journal entries and felt sick to his stomach. Officer Butler stood and walked back to the interrogation area where Detective Baker was sitting alone. He rapped lightly on the door, and Detective Baker stepped out into the hall.

"I got a hold of Benita, Bea's Aunt. She lives in Phoenix. She's not in the best of health. She is, however, willing to come in and testify. We just need to contact her and let her know when we need her. I also found out that Bea's father, Edward Noslen is dead. He died in 2006."

"That's too bad. He would have been quite a character on the witness stand. Have you had a chance to read any more of the journal?"

"Yes, I read several more entries. What a horrible childhood she had . . . just *horrible!* I can't fathom what she went through. I'm actually surprised she turned out as well as she did."

"Try not to turn sympathetic, Rich. I know it's hard, but she's a criminal—a cold-blooded, heartless criminal. If you start to feel sorry for her, it will change the way you think about the job we have to do. She kidnapped two kids. Lord only knows what else she did."

Officer Butler nodded his head, pretending to be in agreement.

"I haven't gotten much more out of her. Every time she starts to answer a question, her attorney jumps in and interrupts. Right now they are down the hall in the conference room. After I read a few lines of the journal, Mr. Monroe decided he needed to have another chat with his client."

Be Careful What You Wish For

"I guess he has her best interests at heart. I think I'm going to head out. If it's okay, I'll take the journal with me and read some more. I want to get over to Bunting Valley and get that bracelet out of evidence for you before I forget."

"Okay. See you back here in the morning, then?"

"Absolutely, I'll be here."

The whole ride back to Bunting Valley, Officer Butler thought of Bea and what she had gone through. Because he was an only child, sometimes his parents doted on him too much and refused to accept the fact that he was a grown man and capable of taking care of himself. Just last month his mom had brought him a pot of chicken soup when he told her he was battling a summer cold. Bea Miller never had the luxury of growing up in a household full of love. He couldn't believe Detective Baker was so hardened that he'd lost his ability to care. *I hope I never get like that. I think having emotions will help me do my job better, not stand in my way.*

Without consciously thinking about it, Officer Butler's patrol car headed towards the police department. As soon as he got there, he grabbed the charm bracelet and placed it in his car so he'd have it tomorrow when he went back to the Federal Building. Max and Officer Wolfe were still there, handling some last-minute details. Max, full of unconditional love, was happy to see his ex-partner.

"Hey Max! How's my favorite boy doing?" he said as he rubbed Max behind the ears. Max wagged his tail a mile a minute in response.

Officer Butler spoke with Officer Wolfe and made arrangements to get him Max's things. He hated to give Max up, but he knew he couldn't run the K9 unit and devote all his attention to the Miller case at the same time.

Once he returned home, Officer Butler settled down for the evening, after he made a light dinner. He opened the journal to read some more. As he sat in his La-Z-Boy recliner, he noticed the tone of the writing changed, and he realized it was now in the present tense. He made another note in his notepad: Bea started writing in the journal when she was eight years old.

Be Careful What You Wish For

May 21, 1973

You are never going to believe what happened tonight. When Papa fell asleep in front of the TV, which he does every night, I decided to sneak into his room, which is forbidden. I'm only allowed in there, to gather the dirty bed linens, and he stands in the doorway to watch me, even then. But tonight, he was snoring so loudly, I thought the roof was going to blow off; so, I knew it was safe.

I quietly opened up dresser drawers and looked to see what I could find. I found a photo of him and Mama, and also one of me and Aunt Nita. I looked like I was only a couple of years old in the one with Aunt Nita. She looked exactly the way I remember, with sparkling eyes, filled with love. I took both pictures, so I would have something to remember them by. The best thing I found, however, was a pillowcase that had money hidden in it.

I took the pillowcase and tip-toed past the still snoring Papa, into my room where I stashed the money inside a pair of balled up socks and put it, along with the pictures, in my book bag. I decided to count it later. I thought if it belonged to Papa, he would be mad as a hornet when it turned up missing. He taught me how to steal, but I bet he never thought I would steal from him. Be careful what you wish for Papa, you just might get it.

June 6, 1973

Today is the day we moved from our small house into an RV. The RV was bought used, but I guess it's nice. It has a small kitchen and toilet. It has one bed and the kitchen table folds over to make another one. Papa said it would be easier if we didn't have a permanent address; that way, no one could find us. He packed up what he felt was necessary, which wasn't much of anything for me. Some clothes mostly. Thank goodness, I carried the things I felt were important, in my book bag with me. I still had the pictures and the money I had found in the pillowcase. I tried to count it once but gave up after I got to $2,000, and there was still more.

He came and picked me up at school today and told me I would never have to go back. He claimed life's lessons were more valuable than book lessons, so school was no longer necessary. He quit his job at the scrap yard, and everything I pocketed would be pawned or traded.

Be Careful What You Wish For

Papa drove for an awfully long time, and then we stopped in a small city just outside Dallas. He had a new idea on how we could make some fast cash. He stood me on a street corner with a sign that said, **HOMELESS AND PENNILESS. PLEASE HELP.** *I couldn't believe it, but people just stopped and gave me money. Fives, tens, twenties, spare change. Papa didn't care, money was money. We were making well over $1,000 a week, and Papa was happy.*

September 6, 1973

Standing on the street corner is going well, but Papa had the bright idea that I could make more money if it looked as if I were handicapped. So, he took a wheelchair from some man that had only one leg. The man had left it sit outside of a bathroom stall at the public restrooms, and Papa took it. I actually felt sorry for the man; but Papa laughed when he talked about the one-legged man and how he must have felt when he finished his business, and then found his wheelchair gone. It was then I realized Papa was heartless. I had seen it in his eyes before, but I always tried to look past it and see the good in him. Lately, it's getting harder and harder to see the good, mostly because the bad is always there.

Officer Butler was becoming sleepy; so, he marked his spot, closed the journal, and stared at the cover of Bea's journal for a while. The corners of the cover were frayed and the binding was coming loose. The etching on the pages had been gold at some point, but it had flaked off and looked dull in the lamp light. Some of the pages looked as if they'd gotten wet since they were rippled around the edges. He could picture Bea hanging on to the journal as if it were a lifeline, sneaking to write down her thoughts and fears, hoping her father wouldn't find it. He continued to inspect the tome. There was still a sticker on the back of it in the lower-left corner which read *Five and Dime*. The price was *twenty-one cents*. He imagined it was one of the things she stole at some point, knowing that her father would never buy her such a luxury item. He climbed into bed and drifted off to sleep; *dreaming of children, birthday cakes, and birds. The children's laughter turned into screams as a big faceless, monster laughed maniacally while he sliced into a birthday cake, which oozed blood all over the table.*

After a fitful night's rest, he couldn't wait to get downtown to the Federal Building. From what he'd read so far in the journal, Bea's life consisted of just her and her father. No friends. No family. Knowing

140

Detective Baker didn't have the need to talk to Bea again today; he looked in the bullpen and found him seated there, behind his desk.

"Good morning, Detective. Here's the charm bracelet I promised you," he said as he handed over the bag.

"Thanks . . . and please . . . call me Randy. We will be working some long hours together, and there's no need for such formality." He held the evidence bag up, so he could get a good look. "I'm going to send it off to forensics for DNA testing just to make sure it's hers. This would be a great piece of evidence to show the Grand Jury. Just to let you know, the DNA results came back on Mikey and he *is* the little boy who was kidnapped from the Stop-N-Save."

"I figured he was. Speaking of the Grand Jury, any idea when that might be?"

"Yes, as a matter of fact, I do. It's scheduled for next Thursday."

"That soon? . . . Wow."

"I told you, we don't mess around in North Dakota." Detective Baker smiled.

"Did you want me to get Benita Adams in town for it?"

"That depends. Did you find anyone else in the journal that might be more worthwhile? I don't want to screw around with this, Rich. We need someone—or *several* someones—who will have the most impact. I want to leave the jury with their mouths hanging wide open, so there's no doubt in their mind that we are dealing with a very sick person here—one who needs to be punished."

"I read some of the journal last night before I went to sleep. So far, it just talks about Bea and her father. Have you thought any more about David? He should know more than anyone."

"Yes, I was thinking about him and what you told him, about going easy on him if he's willing to testify. I'm sure the judge would be willing to accept a deal if he cooperates."

"I'm sure he'll cooperate. The look on his face when we spoke the first time, I think he hates Bea about as much as her father hated her. I'm sure he'll talk."

141

"Good. Why don't you go and pay him a visit today? See what he has to say."

"Will do . . . anything else?"

"Read some more of the journal. See if it mentions someone else. We need as much ammunition as we can get."

Officer Butler stopped for a quick bite to eat on his way over to visit David. They had moved him, and he was now being held in a small city jail about five miles from where Bea was. If all went well with David, he didn't know when he'd get to break for lunch, and he was already hungry. He took the journal in with him, so he had something to read while he ate.

March 15, 1974

Today I saw a woman who looked just like Aunt Nita. It's been so long since I've seen her, but I swear it was her. She was with a man about her age. They were walking arm-in-arm, and she stopped to put money in my basket.

I mentioned it to Papa and he called me an idiot. "Why in the world would she be here of all places?" he said. I don't care what Papa thinks. I know it was her. She smiled at me. I wonder if she recognized me. If so, Aunt Nita, please come back and get me. I'll be good this time, so you don't have to go away.

March 16, 1974

While I was asleep last night, Papa drove the RV to another city. Now we are near Albuquerque, New Mexico. It is terribly hot here. I asked him why we had to move, and he said we overstayed our welcome, whatever that means. I think he was afraid that the lady I saw was Aunt Nita, and she'd cause trouble for him. Oh well, I guess she won't come back for me any time soon.

July 23, 1975

Papa and I are actually getting along, and he hasn't hit me for a few weeks. The last time he did, I deserved it. I had put a beautiful diamond necklace in my pocket, and when I got outside, it was gone. I don't know if I dropped it or what happened, but he called me a stupid bitch and punched me in the nose. Blood gushed everywhere. I know he broke my nose, again. I got two black eyes and Papa actually thought I did better on the street corner with the wheelchair and the black eyes. He even suggested he beat me more often. Then he threw his head back and laughed. I hope he was only kidding, but with Papa you never know.

November 28, 1975

Many of the stores tend to ramp up their security around the holidays, so I take to pilfering on the street corner more often than not. It's an easy way to earn a few hundred dollars.

Today is Friday, the day after Thanksgiving and that day they call Black Friday. We've been near Denver for a couple of months now, and the weather is downright frigid. I sat on the corner all day—in my wheelchair, in the blustery weather, freezing my ass off. Papa told me when we were done for the day that he would treat us to a real nice, hot meal. With the holidays so close at hand, people seem to feel more charitable, and business is good. When business is good, Papa is happy, and when Papa is happy, everything is so much better.

January 7, 1976

Today I thought I was dying. I went to the bathroom, and there was blood all over my panties. I grabbed as much toilet paper as I could and stuffed it in my underwear and ran to tell Papa. I thought sure he would rush me to the hospital to see if there was any hope. Instead, he leaned back and said, "This is exactly why I didn't want a girl." He explained to me that I had gotten my monthly curse. Because I was a girl, I was cursed and would bleed every month as a reminder that I am evil. Again he reminded me how I killed my mother and now I was paying for it. I didn't understand what he was talking about, and I didn't like "the curse" at all. The next stop we made, Papa climbed on the RV and pulled a box of sanitary napkins from under his coat. "Use these for the curse," he yelled throwing the box at me. He told me he was ashamed of me. Papa was ashamed of me, and I didn't even do anything.

Officer Butler was mortified. Every chance he got, Edward reminded Bea of how she killed her mother; and now, something entirely natural was happening to her body and Edward turned it into something evil and sadistic. *I wish he was still alive. I would love to give him a piece of my mind,* Officer Butler thought as he shoved a forkful of the bacon omelet into his mouth.

Be Careful What You Wish For

October 22, 1978

I haven't written in a while. Living in an RV, Papa is so close, I don't dare let him know I am keeping a journal. If he knew, I'm sure he would take it. But something happened today that I have to write about.

Papa and I were sitting in a restaurant, and Papa got up and started talking to a man at a nearby table. They kept pointing at me while they talked. I didn't know what was going on but before long, Papa came over and showed me a $100 dollar bill. He told me the gentleman had given it to him. I was curious how Papa could talk a total stranger into giving him $100. I knew Papa was good, but I couldn't wait to hear of his latest swindle.

Papa said the stranger had told him how beautiful he thought I was. He asked Papa if I was his wife. I always looked older than my actual age—but seriously, I'm only 13 years old. When Papa told him I was his daughter, the man became extremely interested. He asked Papa if I were still a virgin. Papa told him as far as he knew, I was. Then the man offered $50 to have sex with me. Papa was so proud that he managed to get the price up to $100. "Now," Papa said, "All you have to do is go to a motel room with the nice man for an hour." He held the $100 dollar bill up between his two index fingers and snapped it tight.

As I write this, I don't know why it was such a shock to me. Papa would sell me to the devil if he thought he could make some money. He coaxed me into leaving with the man. He told me it wouldn't be that bad, and he would give me ten of the hundred bucks he made. He told me he didn't understand why I was so apprehensive. Really, Papa? I thought parents were supposed to protect their children, not push them into the arms of a total stranger.

I'm not happy to say that I left with the man, and as Papa so eloquently put it when I returned, this was the day I became a woman. I don't feel any different. I don't look any different. I just feel dirty. I had never seen a totally naked man before, and I realize now, I wasn't missing much. I insisted he leave the lights off, hoping it would make it easier to deal with what was happening, but he refused. He took his good old time, making sure to get his money's worth, touching and groping me all over my body. At some point, I just shut down. I felt as if I were floating out of my body. I tried to think of sometime in my short life when I was truly happy. I remembered Aunt Nita, and how she'd rocked me to sleep, singing lullabies. She had a beautiful voice. Oh, how I wish she were here now. I could just hear her yelling at Papa for what he did . . . "How could you, Edward? She's just a child!" I hummed Brahms lullaby— and just as I got to the end, he finished what he paid for and then kissed me on the forehead. I realized later I didn't even know his name. Papa, once again, told me how proud he was.

Officer Butler shook his head. *Not only lying, cheating and stealing, but prostitution. Is there anything this man won't do for money?* He suddenly lost his appetite. Officer Butler shoved his plate back, closed the journal, and left the restaurant.

They moved David to another location. They thought he might be more forthcoming with information if he knew his mother wasn't nearby. It was a small jail, compared to where Bea was being held. Since David wasn't considered a dangerous felon, he was brought to an open, exercise area outdoors to see his visitor. David seemed happy to see Officer Butler.

"Oh my gosh . . . when they told me I had a visitor, I thought it was going to be my mom. She's the last person I want to see right now," David, who wore an orange jumpsuit, said as he took a seat on the picnic table directly across from Officer Butler.

"Why did you think your mom would come see you? She's in jail."

"You don't know my mom. She is the luckiest person. She can worm her way out of anything."

"Well, I believe her luck has finally run out."

This bit of news, apparently made David happy as he smiled . . . a big, broad grin which showed off his dimples. "How is she, anyway?"

"I guess as well as can be expected. I haven't talked directly to her, but I saw her. The state appointed her an attorney, and he won't let her say much. We obtained a search warrant and went back to the trailer and found a few things. One was a journal. Did you know that your mother has kept a journal since she was a young girl?"

"I've seen her writing it in before. She said it was her version of a therapist."

"Have you ever read any of the entries?"

Be Careful What You Wish For

"No. I never really cared to. I lived it. I didn't need to read about it." David tapped his fingers nervously on the picnic table.

"Has your mom ever mentioned family members?" Officer Butler pulled out his notepad just in case David mentioned something he needed to write down.

"Not really. She just told us over and over again how lucky we had it compared to her upbringing. She's always been something of a drama queen, so I'm sure it wasn't all that bad."

Officer Butler shook his head. "I'm afraid it was worse than you could imagine. Her father was a horrible man; and she's been both physically and psychologically abused since she was a small child—if her entries in the journal are true. She was raped at the age of thirteen."

David opened his eyes wide and looked at Officer Butler. "Really . . . ? I always assumed she was exaggerating."

"I'm afraid not. Tell me, did she ever physically harm you or your brothers?"

"Not horribly . . . I mean there was the occasional slap on the back of the head. Then there were the punishments she came up with, which always went beyond extreme."

"What do you mean by beyond extreme?"

"Once she made Mikey sleep in a cage for a week."

"*What?*"

David, tired of sitting on the picnic table, stood up, shoved his hands in his pockets and paced nervously. "One day she was cleaning and doing some laundry. When she entered my two younger brothers' room, the smell of urine almost knocked her over. Upon closer investigation, she said she could tell someone had been wetting the bed. She said it was still wet from the night before, and there were several other dried stains. Needless to say, she was beyond livid. I remember that as soon as we got home from school, she called Mikey and John into their room to talk to them. John was always protective of Mikey. Mikey had some issues and constantly had bad dreams. Anyway, John admitted it was Mikey, so Mom decided if Mikey was going to act like an animal, then she would treat him like one. She made him sleep in a cage for a week."

146

Be Careful What You Wish For

"What type of cage?"

"We had an old rabbit cage. Mom took it out and cleaned it up. She told him it was plenty big enough, so she put a blanket in it and made Mikey sleep in it."

"How did that go over?"

"Not good. I remember hearing him cry at night. My brother, John, got a pillow and a blanket and lay on the floor next to the cage and held his hand. It was a horrible thing to do to Mikey . . . but Mom was . . . *proud*. After a week, she let him out, and he never wet the bed again."

"Can you tell me anything else?"

"Yeah . . . once she caught me and my friends smoking in the van, and she made us all eat a cigarette. She was a horrible mother."

Officer Butler chuckled. "That's awful, but it *is* pretty funny. Have you had a cigarette since?"

"No . . . it cured me, that's for sure. She went ballistic because she said her father smoked and she had always hated it. Then one time she went shopping and two of my brothers went with her. She told them they had twenty minutes. When the twenty minutes were up, she went out to the van and left. She drove all the way home and then planned on making them have to walk home almost two and a half miles. When she told me her plan, she had a creepy sneer on her face. I made her go back and get them."

"How did you do that?"

"I threatened to go get them myself. I didn't even have a driver's license, but I *would have* done it. So, she finally relented and went. She was always trying to think of the perfect punishment; some special thing which would teach us the perfect lesson. I don't know why she was so hell bent on it; if anyone needed to be taught a lesson, it was her."

Officer Butler blinked his eyes. "Can you tell me what happened the day Mikey was kidnapped?"

"Actually, it started a couple of days before he was kidnapped. Mom kept saying she was so depressed, and she wished she had a little girl. I pretty much ignored her, but she wouldn't let up. So finally, just to humor her, I asked her how she planned on getting one since she wasn't dating anyone and I was old enough at that point to know that you have to have sex in order to have a baby."

"What did she say?"

"She told me point blank—she could just take one. She said she knew exactly how she would do it, and all she wanted me to do was pretend when she brought the girl home, that she was my sister." David shrugged his shoulders. "It seemed easy enough, so I agreed. I was willing to do *anything* pretty much, to get her to shut up. I actually thought she'd forget about it. A couple of days later when the school bus dropped me off, I heard mom yelling for me. I thought something horrible had happened so I ran home. She told me that she'd done a really bad thing, and she needed me to fix it. I still had no idea what she was talking about, but then she told me she had gone to a grocery store over in Greenfield, and took a baby from someone's shopping cart. When she got the baby home, she discovered it wasn't a girl at all, but a boy. She asked me to get rid of him."

"Did she tell you how?"

"She didn't really care. She suggested I put him in a dumpster or throw him in a lake."

"What did you do?"

"Of course I refused. I told her I would not pay for her mistake. She was mad at first; but, in a nutshell, that's how we got Mikey."

Officer Butler shook his head. "Unbelievable."

"See, I told you she was horrible."

"After you read the journal, I think you'll have a whole new outlook."

"I don't think so. The thing about mom that really irritates me is she never feels guilty. She never has any remorse. I took a CD once from Music Mart. I still feel guilty about it to this day. I just don't understand her. She doesn't care if someone ends up hurt, or dead for that matter. If she wanted something, come hell or high water, that's what we did."

"It's very sad, but at some point, your mom turned off her emotions. Once you turn them off, I'm not certain you can ever turn them back on again. But, I digress. The reason I'm here is . . . next week the case goes before the Grand Jury. This is the portion of the process

148

where the Grand Jury decides if there's enough evidence to warrant a trial. The prosecution gets to call in expert witnesses and present evidence. It would mean a lot to the case if you would be willing to testify and tell the story of how Mikey was kidnapped."

"Will she be there?"

"No. She's not present for this part of it. But you won't appear in person either. Since you're incarcerated, you'll appear via video monitor."

"Okay, I'll do it. I just don't want to see her, if I can help it."

"I can't promise that you will never see her, but at least you won't be seeing her for a while. You might feel different once things have settled down a bit, and you've had a chance to think things through."

"I doubt it, Officer Butler. I hate her. I seriously do. I hate who she is. I hate what she's done. I hate the life she made Mikey live. She is a horrible, horrible person, and whatever happens to her, she deserves it. I'm just sorry it took so long for her to get her due."

"I'm sorry you feel that way, but like I said, once you read the journal, you might feel differently about her."

David shrugged. "Any idea when I might get out of here? I'm old enough to take care of my brothers and I know I could take better care of them than she ever did."

"I'm working on that now. Hopefully, it won't be too long. In the interim, they are in foster care, but you should have no trouble getting them back once you get out."

ᥱᔍ Chapter Sixteen ᥰᦂ

The hours and days seemed to drag on while they waited for the federal Grand Jury. Officer Butler met with Detective Baker and Prosecutor Hildebrand several times to go over the evidence, and also with the possible witnesses they had lined up so far. As soon as he met Gregory Hildebrand, he was impressed. Officer Butler guessed him to be in his early thirties. He was so full of pent up energy that he couldn't seem to sit still. Pacing back and forth, Officer Butler and Detective Baker told him everything they knew. Officer Butler referred to his notes several times to make sure his statements were factual. Officer Butler suggested they contact Detective McClure from Greenfield. The detective knew firsthand about the events that had occurred the day Mikey went missing. Being a police detective, his testimony would hold a lot of merit, too. Between that and David's story, those two testimonies might be all they need to convince the jury— especially now. The DNA results had positively identified Mikey as the infant who was kidnapped seven years prior, from the Stop-N-Save. They also were able to prove that the charm bracelet did, in fact, belong to Bea Miller.

Nine jurors were picked to hear the evidence. It was decided Benita Adams wouldn't be needed for this round of witnesses; but, if and when it went before a judge and jury, she would be called at that time. When Officer Butler phoned her with the news, he also told her about John and Joshua. Since she was the only living relative as far as they knew, they asked if she'd be willing to take care of them.

"I'm too old for that now. If you had asked me thirty years ago, I would have jumped at the chance," Benita said. "I was never lucky enough to have children of my own. That's why Beatrice meant so much to me."

"I understand. Those boys have been through enough, and I'd hate for you to say 'yes' and then decide it was a mistake. When you come into town, if you'd like to meet them, I'm sure we could arrange it."

"That would be nice, but let me think about it."

Be Careful What You Wish For

With nothing but time to kill, Officer Butler asked Detective Baker if he could pay Bea a visit.

"I'd like to say yes, but her attorney has asked that we stay away from her unless he's present. I think he's afraid she might admit to something. Besides, he's been spending an inordinate amount of time with her," Detective Baker said.

It had been a couple of days since Officer Butler had read anything out of Bea's journal. Things had been progressing relatively quickly, but now he had a few moments. He opened the journal and decided to read some more. He hoped to find another witness or two.

November 23, 1978

I didn't get my monthly curse, and I haven't been feeling well. Things that I used to love to eat now make me feel like I'm going to throw up. When I told Papa, he dropped his fork and said, "Shit!"

He grabbed the yellow pages and looked something up. I couldn't see what it was, but before long, we were in a clinic, and I was taken to the back where I could hear other girls crying and screaming. Soon afterwards, I realized why. They put my feet in these silver circles and spread my legs. A man in a white coat stuck something up inside of me. It all happened so fast, but it hurt badly, and it felt like a vacuum. I didn't scream, but I wanted to. When Papa and I left, I had a hard time walking. We never discussed it, but I bled for seven days. I guess there was something horribly wrong with me and that man in the white coat fixed it. Papa must care about me after all.

September 1, 1980

I celebrated my 15th birthday a few weeks ago. Of course, when I say "celebrate", I mean I turned another year older, and there was no mention of it, whatsoever. Papa still blames me for Mama's death and I think he always will. I wish so badly I could have a normal life, in a normal house, in a normal neighborhood. I miss having friends. I miss going to school. I often think of running away, but I don't know where I'd go. Knowing Papa the way I do, I know he'd find me anyway and beat the living daylights out of me.

October 12, 1980

We have been parked in the same spot going on two weeks now. Some of the people from nearby stores and shops refer to us as "the RV people." I had a hard time sleeping, so I snuck out of the RV when Papa started snoring. Around two o'clock in the morning, from what Papa tells me, two uniformed police officers knocked on the door and startled Papa awake. He was not prepared for the words he heard next, "Mr. Noslen, we have your daughter, Beatrice, at the juvenile county jail. You need to come with us." Papa pulled on a pair of pants and left with the officers, explaining that he didn't even know I was gone.

When Papa arrived and saw me, I could tell he was angry. I was so happy to see him. I ran to him crying as I threw my arms around his neck. His arms remained motionless, hanging at his sides. I whispered in his ear, "Papa, I did a bad thing. I got caught. I need you to pay my bail, so I can come home."

He reached up and took hold of my elbows, removing my arms from around his neck. He looked at me with his beady, empty eyes and turned and walked away. He just left me there—his own daughter. No words . . . just a look that made my blood freeze.

October 17, 1980

I'm back home now. I didn't have my journal with me in jail, but I sat there for five days, wondering what was going on. Where was Papa? When I asked questions, no one seemed to know. I was told he had moved the RV and they couldn't find him. I kept wondering if he hated me so much—that he'd be willing to leave without me. I met with a counselor several times while I was in there but never said anything. I think they were hoping I would open up and spill my deepest, darkest secrets so they could cure me. I learned early on there is no cure for evil. At least that's what Papa tells me.

When Papa finally stopped by to pick me up, he rushed to give me a hug. He looked so happy, and I foolishly thought he had forgiven me. Boy . . . was I wrong!

He asked what he needed to do to take me home. After explaining the details, and handing over a fistful of paperwork, Papa paid $300, and we left. He led me from the building and threw the paperwork in the first trash can he passed. As soon as we got out of earshot, he grabbed my hair and said, "I thought I trained you better than that. I can't believe you got caught. We had such a good thing going. Now you have a strike on your record. They have your fingerprints on file. Do you know how I felt being told you were in jail, *and I had no idea you were even missing? I'm* very *angry, and you're going to pay for disappointing me."*

As soon as we got out to the parking lot where the RV was parked, he jerked me with such force, that I felt—and heard—something in my arm pop. But that didn't stop him. He balled up his hairy fist and hit me time and time again. I fell to the ground as he shouted, "Get up and get in the RV, you worthless piece of shit!"

However, what came next was even worse. When we got in the RV, Papa jerked my pants down, pinned me down on top of the table, which was still made up for my bed, and shoved my legs open. I was completely helpless with what I was sure was a broken arm. Next he jammed his penis roughly inside me. It hurt so badly. When that man paid to have sex with me, he took his time, but Papa didn't care about time . . . he was angry. His eyes were full of hatred, and he needed to punish me.

Officer Butler felt as if he was reading a cheap novel. He could not believe it. *Just when I thought things couldn't get any worse,* Edward *rapes her; Beatrice . . . his own daughter. The only person in her world committed a violent act against her; incest . . . rape.* As far as Officer Butler was concerned, these were the worst crimes of all. At least, now he knew how Bea was arrested for shoplifting; the only thing that had come back on her criminal background check.

Officer Butler closed the journal and picked up the phone. He dialed the Taylor house to check on Maggie, and see how everything was. Abby assured him everything was back to normal. Maggie and Maddie were—once again—quarreling with each other. It was almost as if Maggie had never been gone. Abby did say she kept talking about a pink pony and wondered if he knew what she was referring to. Officer Butler relayed that Maggie mentioned the pink pony to him, as well, but he had no idea what it meant.

On the court docket, to appear before the Grand Jury at three p.m. on Thursday afternoon, was State of North Dakota vs. Beatrice Miller. It was now two o'clock. There would be no judge and just the prosecuting attorney would be present. Officer Butler was somewhat nervous, hoping he had done his job well enough for it to go to the next step and be heard before a judge and a jury. He and Detective Baker got together, just to go over what they needed to present, hoping it was enough, but not too much. They needed to save something for the actual trial, if it went that far.

Detective McClure, from the Greenfield Police Department, was the first to speak. His testimony needed to show reasonable suspicion. Officer Butler could tell he was nervous, as he cleared his throat loudly several times throughout.

"I've tried to put this case out of my mind, but it always has a way of creeping back into my subconscious, especially late at night when I can't sleep. I remember the details as if it were yesterday," Detective McClure stated.

"Do you remember the date?" Mr. Hildebrand asked.

"Yes. It was October 17, 2003. The call came into the station, shortly after ten a.m. The dispatch operator told me there was a hysterical woman was on the phone, and when I picked it up, Nancy Novak just kept saying the same thing, over and over again."

"And what was that?"

"'Someone took my baby! Someone took my baby!' I told her to calm down and I finally managed to get out of her where she was. She was at the Stop-N-Save, which is about six miles from the station. I jumped into my patrol car and arrived there in approximately twelve minutes. I found her right away, as she was the only one sobbing in a crowd of people. Her hands were shaking as she held a tissue and wiped away her tears."

"And, then what happened?"

"I approached her, and she told me what happened. She kept hyperventilating, so she was having difficulty speaking to me. She finally explained that she had arrived around nine thirty to do some grocery shopping. She had dressed Charlie in his new snowsuit because it was so cold out. She walked in and grabbed a cart—one with an attached infant seat. They went up and down each aisle, and she kept talking to Charlie, the way she always did. At the end of the cereal aisle, she was busy talking to him and forgot to grab a box of cereal so when she rounded the corner, she stopped the cart, turned around, and she went back to grab it. When she returned, Charlie was gone."

"Where did he go?"

"Someone took him."

"She left him unattended in the cart—and someone took him?"

"Yes. That is correct."

"Did anyone see anything?" Gregory Hildebrand stood tall with his suit jacket, slightly open, and his hands on his hips.

"Not that I'm aware of. We asked around, and no one claimed to have seen anything. It was as if he had vanished into thin air."

"How do you know that Mrs. Miller's six-year-old child Mikey and the boy named Charlie are one and the same infant who was taken that day from the Stop-N-Save?"

"A DNA test was run; and the test determined that these boys are, in fact, the same child."

Officer Butler sat back and watched the gasps from the jury. He felt as if he was watching a movie, it was so perfect. He almost looked around for the cue cards that would tell the jury the moment to gasp, but then he realized this was not a movie—it was real life.

"Thank you. There are no further questions."

The next witness called was David Miller, whose face came across a screen mounted in the corner. David was sitting behind a table with a microphone directly in front of him.

"Good afternoon, David," Mr. Hildebrand said.

David nodded.

"Please tell the Grand Jury who you are."

"I'm David Miller, Beatrice Miller's oldest son."

"What was Beatrice Miller like as a mother?"

"She was awful . . . horrible . . . nasty . . . dreadful . . ." David seemed to grope for words.

Mr. Hildebrand chuckled. "What made her so awful and horrible, David? Did she abuse you?"

"Physically, no . . . except for the times when she'd hit me on the back of the head; as far as mentally . . . yes, she did."

Be Careful What You Wish For

"Today, I need you to tell the jury about the day Charlie was kidnapped?"

"Who's Charlie?" David asked. The jury chuckled.

"I'm sorry, David. Charlie is the same boy, whom you call *Mikey*. Can you tell us about the day that Mikey was kidnapped?"

David clasped his hands in front of him on the table. "Mom kept telling me how depressed she was, and how having a little girl would change everything. I tried to ignore her, but she told me she was going to go to the Stop-N-Save and get one. A few days went by, and I thought she had changed her mind; but when I got off the school bus, she was yelling for me, so I ran all the way home. I thought something horrible had happened. Mom told me that she took a baby wearing a yellow snowsuit from a shopping cart; and when she got it home, she found out it was a boy."

"So, what happened after that?"

"She didn't want a boy, so she asked me to get rid of him, by throwing him in a lake, or in a dumpster or something. I was only twelve years old, so she said I wouldn't get in as much trouble as she would if I got caught."

"What did you do?"

"I refused and told her if she hurt him, in any way, I would call the police. Then she said she would get a pair of scissors and cut off his penis and dress him like a girl. Thank God I talked her out of that one. She already had the name Michelle picked out, so she changed it to Michael."

Officer Butler was shocked at what David was saying. He knew about the kidnapping, but this was the first he'd heard of Bea Miller saying she wanted to mutilate the infant.

"Thank you, David. I have no further questions." Greg Hildebrand sat down, and the video monitor went blank.

The Grand Jury took a quick ten minute recess; and after that, Officer Butler was called to the stand to give his account of the day Maggie Taylor was abducted. A few pieces of evidence were presented: the charm bracelet, a box from a new baby doll confiscated from the Miller trailer, and the journal. The journal was passed around, so the

156

jurors could flip through it. After it was all said and done, the jury agreed there was enough evidence for a trial, and Bea Miller was indicted on two counts of kidnapping. Officer Butler, still sitting in the room, was elated. One hurdle jumped . . . now, several more hurdles to go.

ᑫᔊ *Chapter Seventeen* ᔊᑐ

As soon as James Monroe received word of the Grand Jury decision, he paid Bea a visit. He was allowed to meet with her in her cell, which was a small 10 x 6 cinder block room with a twin bed, a sink, and a toilet. The bed had a mattress about two inches thick, and Bea complained more than once how badly her back hurt. Mr. Monroe was ushered in by an armed guard who carried a metal, folding chair with him. "They indicted you on two counts of kidnapping; one for Mikey, and one for Maggie. Your bond was set at two million dollars, one for each of the children you kidnapped."

"A couple thousand—a couple million—I don't have either, so at this point, it doesn't really matter. I'm not going anywhere."

"We need to talk more about the journal. You mentioned you wrote about when you ran away. Can you tell me more about that?" James Monroe unfolded the chair and took a seat.

"Like I told you earlier, I got caught shoplifting . . . this time; however, he wasn't satisfied with just beating me. He needed to take it to the next level, so he raped me. I will never forget the possessed look in his eyes. It was almost as if he were a different person. So, I decided to run away before Papa killed me. The moment he began to snore, I got up and wrote him a note—it was short and sweet. I told him I was leaving and wouldn't be back, he had taught me everything I needed to know about how to survive on my own. I put the note on the table top and left. My first stop . . . was the hospital."

"The hospital . . . what made you go to the hospital?"

"I knew Papa had broken my arm; it almost made me cry every time I tried to move it. So, I told the nurse I was homeless, and that I'd fallen down a flight of steps. She asked me where my parents were. I told her they had both died in a car accident. I actually saw something in her eyes I had never seen before. I think they call it sympathy." Bea stopped a moment and smiled. "I was given a full exam, and they asked me if I had been raped. I told them no, but my broken arm was confirmed and set in a cast. Other than bumps and bruises, I tried to remain positive and upbeat."

"Why didn't you tell the truth . . . that Edward raped you?"

Be Careful What You Wish For

"I didn't have a father. My parents were killed in a car accident, remember?"

James Monroe shook his head. "Oh yeah . . . I'm having a hard time keeping the story straight."

Bea gave him an annoyed look. "The doctor told me I needed to stay overnight for observation. I didn't like the sound of that, but I was tired, and didn't want a confrontation, so I agreed to stay. The instant they turned down the lights in my room and left, I got up, changed into my street clothes, and walked out of the hospital. First thing I did was check my backpack to make sure the ball of money was still there. I was so glad when it was. Without that money, I don't know what I would have done. I wandered around the city for a while, trying to decide what I should do, or where I should go. I didn't have any friends. I finally decided that I'd buy a one-way bus ticket, and get as far away from Papa as I possibly could. As I stood there looking at the price board, nowhere sounded far enough away from him: Phoenix, Chicago, Cleveland, Miami, Atlanta, San Diego, Boston, Seattle—they were all too close. It took a while, but I decided on Seattle, Washington. I figured Seattle was a half a country away from Papa. That would give me plenty of time to rest and think about what my next move should be."

"What city were you and Edward in when this happened?"

"We were back in Texas, near Austin. I remember leaning my head back against the window and watching the white lines on the highway fly past, one by one. Those lines were my path to freedom. At some point, I drifted off, because the next thing I remember, I opened my eyes and there was a sign that read—E470 to Colorado Springs—which meant we were already in Colorado. The next morning we stopped at a truck stop just outside the Wyoming state line. I remember when I hobbled off the bus, every inch of my body hurt. It was quite early and I could have kicked myself. Out of all the watches and timepieces I had stolen over the years, you would have thought that I would have kept one; but I hadn't, so I had no idea what time it was. I went to the restroom, and tried to clean up the best I could. When I looked in the mirror, I wasn't prepared to see what I saw looking back at me. I looked as if I had been run over by a semi-truck and had lived to tell about it. I didn't want to miss the bus, so I bought a breakfast sandwich and a cup of coffee. I walked as fast as I could to the convenience store and bought some aspirin before I had to get back on the bus. When I climbed back

159

on board, I took the lid off the coffee and held it with both hands. I just closed my eyes and inhaled the aroma, wishing all my troubles away. I always loved coffee, and honestly, I like the smell more than the taste."

"I'm the same way," James Monroe offered. "There are a few things like that—things that smell better than they taste."

"As I sat on that bus, I wondered how Papa had reacted when he saw the note. I imagined that he would be furious with me for leaving, but, at the same time, he was probably happy that I was gone. One thing I knew for sure, at least I wouldn't have to hear him tell me how I killed Mama anymore, no sir-ee. I didn't kill her, you know?" Bea looked at Mr. Monroe. "I was only a baby."

"Yes I know, Bea. I remember that from when the detective read the journal to us."

"Anyway, the bus pulled into Seattle, my new home, at exactly six-seventeen a.m. the next morning. I knew what time it was because the bus driver told us. I tried to stand up and stretch as often as possible, but even so, my muscles continued to get stiffer and stiffer. I gathered my things and limped off the bus, stopping to chat with the bus driver. I asked him if he knew of a place I could stay nearby. The way he looked at me, I know he was wondering what happened. He told me there was a nice, clean motel right around the corner. He said if I showed them my bus ticket, I'd get a discount. So, I rented a room, gave a fake name, and paid in cash. The first thing I did was run a hot bath. I climbed in and sat there, wishing the warm water and soap suds, could cleanse all my problems away. However, when the last of the water went down the drain, there I stood, *still* naked, battered, bruised, and swollen, with a broken arm and more problems than I cared to count."

"Were you scared?"

"Not *scared* actually . . . no. I was glad to be away from Papa. Not having to worry and wonder what I might do or say to make him angry was a terrific feeling. It was also exciting to be on my own."

"So what did you do next?"

"I decided to keep a low profile for a few days to allow the bruises to lighten and the swelling to go down. I figured no one wanted to hire a girl who looked like she just went twenty rounds with Rocky Balboa. Besides, I had a lifetime to work—I was in no hurry. In the meantime, I walked around town, and searched the *help wanted* ads, plotting out what my next step would be. I realized the money I had wouldn't last forever, so I decided *literally*, to take matters into my own hands . . . just to have a buffer in case I didn't find a job right away."

"Oh Bea, no . . . *what* did you do?"

"No matter how many times Papa called me an idiot and told me how stupid and worthless I was, there's one thing I was good at, and he couldn't deny it—stealing things in plain sight while standing there talking to the clerks. My broken arm turned into such a blessing and such a conversation piece. Everyone wanted to know how it happened. I had a great time making up stories, each one more far-fetched than the last. While standing in a jewelry store eyeing a beautiful $4,000 pendant, I told them I was a horse jockey, and my arm had gotten caught on the saddle, and how my horse dragged me three laps before someone could stop him. The sales clerks, with their mouths hanging open, crowded around me as they listened to the details of my story. The way they hung on my every word, I felt like a medicine man with a magic elixir. When I left that jewelry store, the $4,000 pendant was safely tucked inside my sling. I thought of Papa and how proud he would be."

"Did you always try to do things to make Edward proud?"

"Yes, always."

James Monroe stood up, folded the chair, and leaned it up against the wall next to the sink. He started pacing back and forth in front of Bea, who was still seated on the bed. "Tell me more about your Aunt. What was her name?"

"Her name was Benita, but I called her Aunt Nita. Oh, Mr. Monroe, I loved her *so much*. I don't ever remember her scolding or punishing me. I guess she figured Papa punished me enough for the both of them. Aunt Nita and I went on play dates, and she took me to the zoo, and the playground. We'd go to pet stores, and she'd let the puppies lick my face. We'd stop and get ice cream, for no reason at all, just *because*. She took me to see movies, and always insisted I get the biggest tub of popcorn, knowing there was no way I could ever eat it all. She and I used to play this game; I would tell her I loved her, and she would repeat the same thing back to me. Then I would say 'I love you more' and she would tell me she loved me more. One time I remember telling her, 'I

161

love you more because you have only loved me for five years but I have loved you my entire life.' Gosh, I haven't thought about that for years."

Mr. Monroe blinked almost as if he was trying to hold back tears. "The reason I ask is because I heard the prosecution has called her as a witness."

"Really . . . she's still alive?" Bea excitedly clapped her hands.

"Apparently so . . ."

"Will I get to see her?"

"Just when she's on the witness stand," he answered quickly.

"Aunt Nita knows how mean Papa was. She can tell you first-hand how he treated us."

"Yes. I think that's the angle I will take when I get to question her. In the meantime, Bea, I'd like you to talk to a psychologist. The prosecutor has requested that you go on the witness stand; and I am hoping a psychologist will examine you and determine you are not mentally fit to stand trial. I really don't want you on the stand. I think it would be the worst possible thing we could do."

"What are you saying, Mr. Monroe? You think I'm nuts?"

"No, it's not that at all. It's just the all of the abuse, pain, and suffering you've experienced from Edward may have affected you in an adverse way. Having a psychologist examine you and then present his professional opinion in court may be your only way out."

"Papa may have been responsible for many things; the loss of my innocence, my childhood, and my virginity, however, he did *not* make me lose my mind! I am *fine*. I will go on the witness stand and tell them *exactly* why I took those children—because they were better off with me!"

James Monroe stood, shaking his head. "Just think about it, Bea. This may be the only way you ever get to see freedom. If they find you guilty you could be sentenced to twenty or more years. I strongly recommend—let me emphasize the word *strongly* Bea, that you do *not* take the stand . . . *please*."

"They won't do that to me. Besides, when I take the stand and tell them my side of the story, they will understand this has just been a

162

big misunderstanding. I'm a master of manipulation. When I speak, I am so believable I can convince you your shoes are black when they are obviously brown. It's a gift, Mr. Monroe. Trust me—I know what I'm doing."

"Okay, Bea, whatever you say. You will have to go before the judge shortly to register a plea. I recommend pleading, 'Not guilty.'"

"Of course, I'm pleading, 'Not guilty.'"

"Are you saying you didn't kidnap those kids?"

"No, I didn't. I simply removed them from an unpleasant situation."

James Monroe shook his head, "Is there anyone you know of who we could contact as a witness? Someone who might actually have something agreeable to say that can help your case, instead of hurt you . . .?"

Bea sat for a moment with her lips pursed, while she tapped her chin with her index finger. "What about David?"

"*David* . . . you mean your *son*, David?"

"Yeah . . . he would never say anything bad about me. He knows better."

"I'm sorry to tell you, Bea, but the prosecution has already called him as a witness—for their side. Obviously, promising him freedom has gotten him to open up."

"*What?* You mean that little *shit* is going to get off? He *knew* what I was doing when I rescued those kids. He was my accomplice."

"I'm just telling you what I heard. Now, why don't you tell me what happened next, after you arrived in Seattle and took the $4,000 pendant?"

Bea released a tremendous sigh. "I made an agreement, which included living arrangements, with the manager at the motel. It was a cheap motel—twenty dollars a night. He said I could live there for fifteen dollars a night, which was a reduced rate, but I had to clean my own room. I didn't genuinely care and I was grateful for a place to live. It was small, but large enough for me and what little belongings I had with me. Hell, it was probably bigger than the entire RV that Papa and I lived in.

As time went on, I hardly thought of Papa anymore. The day I turned sixteen years old was glorious! It was the first time since I was five years old that I had actually been able to celebrate my birthday. I decided to treat myself to a full makeover. I always wanted jet black hair, so I got my hair dyed and cut. I looked just like Janet on *Three's Company*." Bea giggled. "I took every opportunity to tell anyone who would listen that it was my birthday. Not having heard it for so long, I thought I would never tire of hearing people wish me a Happy Birthday. I treated myself to a nice dinner and the restaurant gave me a free dessert. It was a *perfect* day. It wasn't long after I turned sixteen that *it* happened for the first time."

"What do you mean, *it* happened?"

"I was out walking around the city. I turned a corner, and I could smell the aroma of Camel, unfiltered cigarettes. I remember I panicked because I thought Papa was nearby. I picked up my pace, and tried to outrun the unpleasant odor. When I got back to my room at the motel, I locked the door and pushed everything I could find—that wasn't too heavy for me to move—in front of the door. I thought to myself that if it *was* him . . . there was *no way* I would let him get into my room!"

"Was it him?"

"I don't know. I stayed inside for a couple of days. As hard as I've tried to escape my past, I thought it had found me again; but this time, I was in control."

ᐒ *Chapter Eighteen* ᐒ

Still trying to round up witnesses for the prosecution and still no mention of anyone else in the journal, early the next morning Officer Butler headed out to talk to Mrs. Brown again. Having lived next door to the Miller's for so long, the jury would probably love to hear her version of how Mikey had joined the Miller family. Even if she said no, they could subpoena her, but Officer Butler wanted to avoid that if he could. It always went better when the witness agreed to appear willingly. Knowing the way Mrs. Brown loved talking and telling stories, he figured she would be thrilled to testify.

Mrs. Brown had been following the case on the news and in the paper. She still couldn't believe Bea had kidnapped two children. It just didn't seem possible. She told Officer Butler that Bea was a wonderful neighbor, and she remembered fondly how Bea volunteered to make cookies for her once to take to the senior center.

"Really . . . she doesn't seem like the homemaker type." Officer Butler scratched his head.

"Yes. As a matter of fact, I think it was the first time I met Mikey. I was outside and saw Bea running around after him and I invited her over for a cup of tea. We got to talking and after she told me about Mikey, she asked me what I had been doing all winter, and I told her . . . just like everyone else, I spent a lot of time indoors. When the weather was nice enough, I told her I went over to the senior center. She asked what we did there, and I told her how we played bingo and checkers and games like that. She genuinely seemed interested. I told her once a week we had a potluck luncheon and everyone brought a dish to share. That's when she told me the next time I went, she would give me some cookies to take."

"That was nice of her. Wonder why she would offer such a thing?"

"I think she was happy for me."

"Why was she happy for you?"

"She wanted to know if I had met any nice men. She kind of winked, and elbowed me when she said that." Mrs. Brown blushed.

Be Careful What You Wish For

"What did you tell her?" Officer Butler smiled.

"I told her yes, I had. I had been spending time with a really nice man. He had been a widower for many years. His wife died shortly after giving birth to their only daughter. When I told her his name was Edward, she nearly choked on her tea."

"His name was Edward . . . Edward what?"

"Edward Noslen. He was originally from San Francisco."

"What did Bea say when you told her his name?"

"Nothing much . . . she choked on her tea and then said she had to leave."

"What ever happened to Edward?"

"One day, out of the blue, he told me he was leaving. He told me he had been renting out his house in San Francisco and it had caught on fire. He had to return to supervise the renovations. He didn't know how long he'd be gone."

"What was he like?"

"Edward was a very nice man. I hadn't so much as looked at another man since my Howard passed away, and I was lonely. He was a several inches taller than me and had dark hair. I loved Elvis Presley when I was a young gal, and dark hair always got to me."

"What did he do for a living?"

"Edward was retired, from what I understand. I waited for a while, watching and hoping he would come back, but he never did. The only thing I didn't like about him was those dreadful cigarettes he smoked; but I know I'm not perfect either, so I was willing to overlook it."

Officer Butler left shaking his head. *This case gets more and more interesting every time I talk to someone. So, Mrs. Brown had a thing for Bea's father? I'm sure Bea knew that the Edward Mrs. Brown spoke about was him. How could she not?* He went back to the Federal Building and told Detective Baker about his conversation with Mrs. Brown. Detective Baker, too, found it interesting, how everyone knew everyone; and somehow or other, everyone was intertwined. Detective Baker told him that Bea had registered a plea.

Be Careful What You Wish For

"Which was?" Officer Butler said, already knowing the answer.

"Not guilty. They always plead not guilty no matter how much evidence is stacked against them."

"So, where do we go from here?" Officer Butler had been called as a witness several times, but he was never involved in the legal process from beginning to end. Detective Baker took the time to explain the entire process to him. He then instructed Officer Butler to go home and read more of the journal since it was found in the trailer under a search warrant; certain sections of it could be presented in court to help the jurors reach a verdict of guilty beyond a reasonable doubt, which is what everyone wanted. One way or another, Bea Miller had to be stopped.

It was a little after lunch and Officer Butler felt guilty about going home so early, but Detective Baker had asked him to read more of the journal; so, he told himself, he was—technically—still working. When he left the Federal Building, he decided to make a quick stop in Bunting Valley to check on Max. Max had been a part of his life for almost two years, and he missed having him around. It was funny, but at times, he actually felt Max was still with him. Like at night when it was bedtime. He'd thought he heard—more than once—the pitter-pat of Max's toenails on the tile floor when he followed him into the bedroom. Then, every morning he gave Max the same kind of dog food. When he cracked open the can—the aroma—although it was dog food, sometimes was mouthwatering. Officer Butler thought for sure he could smell dog food in the kitchen, even though he knew it wasn't there. He hoped the case didn't go too much longer, so he could have his best friend back.

Once he finally reached home, it was after three o'clock. He made a bologna sandwich, a bowl of soup, and then settled down to continue reading about Bea's life. As he ate, he skimmed through several pages of entries. He was happy to see Bea went to the hospital after Edward raped her and broke her arm. He then noticed the handwriting for the next entry was different.

Somehow, it looked more sophisticated, and then he realized why. There were over four years between the entries . . . four long years. He could only imagine what kind of trouble Bea had gotten into during that time. He realized Bea was a professional con artist, very skilled at what she did. So good, in fact, he knew, besides the one time she sat in jail for five days for shoplifting, she had never been caught. Now that she was finally away from her father, he assumed most of the drama was over.

January 22, 1985

It's been a while since I've written but I've been pretty busy. I've had several odd jobs here and there to help me get by. Each and every one, however, paid me more than just minimum wage. The restaurant I worked in, I took food from the freezer; at the grocery store, I took a little something extra from the cash register; and at the department store, I took merchandise out of stock. I'm intelligent enough to know never to take enough at one time to raise any red flags, but enough that I can supplement my meager income and still do quite well.

I still haven't made any real friends. I'm extremely leery of men. The only two men I've ever known—one beat me, raped me, and almost killed me; and the other, after paying for an hour of my time, poked and prodded me as if I were a prize cattle. Men are completely useless, and my life is much better without one.

Girls my age are only interested in shopping and going out to discothèques. I have no interest in either. The only shopping I do is shoplifting, and getting all dressed up to go out to a disco seems like such a waste of time and money. Besides, they only go to find a man— and like I said, my life is better without one.

March 28, 1986

It happened again today. I was on my way to work, and as soon as I stepped outside the door of my motel room, I could smell cigarettes. I looked around and found a butt on the sidewalk just down from where I live. It was the exact same kind Papa always smoked. I know he was here. Why is he following me? What is he doing? What does he want?

June 3, 1986

Since the first time I found Camel cigarette butts outside my door, there have been two more incidents. I just can't stand the thought of Papa lurking around, waiting for me, so I decided to move. I packed up what little I had, which wasn't much. Even though I've been on my own for six years now, I've tried not to accumulate a lot of belongings, nothing to weigh me down. The manager of the Midnight Motel put in a good word for me at another sister motel across town. They were willing to offer me the same arrangement; $15 a week and I still have to clean

Be Careful What You Wish For

my own room. I told the manager if anyone came around asking for me; tell them I moved to Alaska. Hopefully, Papa won't find me this time.

September 10, 1988

I turned 23 last month and started a new job today. I am working at a truck stop just off the highway, mostly at the front counter. So far, it's pretty easy. I had to sit through a training class which was terribly B-O-R-I-N-G. It seems like most of the stuff is common sense, but I had to do it anyway. I have a co-worker named Tammy. She's been at the truck stop for six years. I can't imagine doing what she does for six long years. I actually like her. She's older than me and has a couple of kids. Her husband is in the military and only comes home a few times a year. She invited me over to her house sometime for a cookout. I have not been invited to someone's house since I was in elementary school. It feels kind of nice. I forgot what it felt like to have a friend.

Officer Butler stopped and added a name to his witness list. It was the first time Bea had mentioned someone, by name, other than her father. He got up and got a glass of ice water, content that he finally found another possible witness. He closed the journal and flipped on the television set. He needed something to lighten the mood and make him laugh before bedtime. The last time he went straight to bed after reading the journal, he had trouble sleeping. All the shows were reruns, but he stopped to watch *The Office* anyway. Dwight always managed to make him smile, no matter how ridiculous he was.

169

ᏗᏗ *Chapter Nineteen* ᏗᏗ

The following day, James Monroe went back to visit Bea to see if he could get any more information that would help her case. So far, it seemed, besides the shoplifting and stealing—which most kids outgrew—she was living a pretty uneventful existence in Seattle. He was also hoping she may have thought of a witness they could try and locate.

"Good morning, Bea." Mr. Monroe said when the guard slid her cell door back. Bea was lying on the bed reading a book. "Whatcha reading there?"

"Oh, just some book I got from the prison library—something to help pass the time."

"I was hoping today you could tell me about when you met Henry."

Bea got a big grin across her face as she sat up. "Absolutely . . . thinking about Henry always puts a smile on my face."

"I was still working at the truck stop, shadowing Tammy at the register, when the most gorgeous man I ever saw walked through the door. He was tall, dark, and handsome, just like I thought a movie star would be if I ever saw one in person. I remember it as if it were yesterday." Bea closed her eyes, reminiscing. "He was wearing faded jeans, a red t-shirt, rugged work boots, and a black Stetson cowboy hat. His work boots looked brand new—the tan cowhide still appeared soft as velour. He circled around the small store looking for something, but it appeared he couldn't find it. Judging by the look on my face, I think Tammy knew I thought he was cute because she suggested I go and see if I could help him. I was really nervous, but I went over and said, 'Excuse me, sir. Are you finding everything you need?' He turned and looked at me with gorgeous milk chocolate colored eyes, then he smiled and I went weak in the knees. 'Not really,' he said. 'I was looking for a bandage. I cut my hand trying to fix my truck.' He held out his hand, which was wrapped with a blood soaked paper towel, for me to see."

"Oh my . . . !"

Be Careful What You Wish For

"Exactly . . . I took him back to the employee restroom and helped clean up his hand. I told him we had some bandages and tape that he could use. At some point, I told him my name, and he stuck out his good hand and said, 'My name is Miller. Henry Miller.' The way he said it reminded me of that James Bond movie. My name is Bond, James Bond." Bea giggled.

"We laughed and talked while I got him cleaned and bandaged up. He told me he was a long distance truck driver. He purchased a small trucking company after he won $50,000 on a scratch-off lottery ticket. Can you imagine that? Anyway, he started out with one truck, but then he built Miller Trucking into a fleet of six trucks. Only one of the six trucks delivered locally, but Henry said he preferred the long-distance routes because it gave him an opportunity to see all the beauty the United States had to offer. I didn't believe in love at first sight, but when I saw Henry, all that changed."

"Do you remember when that was?"

"Of course I do. It's one of the dates I have stored in here." Bea tapped her hand against her heart. "September 15, 1988. Anyway, every time he was in the area, he made it a point to stop in and see 'the nice young lady that saved his hand from amputation'. I always thought that was a bit of an exaggeration, but whatever it took to get him in there so I could see him, was fine with me. On October 10, 1989 Henry and I got married. It was thirteen months after we met. It was a spur of the moment thing. The day before he had stopped in at the truck stop and asked if I would marry him. Of course, I said 'yes'. He told me to jump in his truck, and we would be in Las Vegas in less than a day. It was a funny ceremony. Henry pulled out all the stops. He rented a wedding dress for me, and we had pictures taken. Elvis Presley was officiating. Henry promised me someday we would re-do our vows and have a real ceremony. I don't need a real ceremony, as long as I had Henry."

"Did you continue to work after you and Henry got married?"

"No, I quit my job at the truck stop, but Henry was traveling the majority of the time. I remember missing him terribly when he was gone. Not too soon after we married, he mentioned he would like us to start a family. I thought having a baby would be nice—then I wouldn't have to spend so much time alone. Henry told me he wanted a son, one to take over Miller Trucking when he grew old and tired of working. What I wondered was how was I supposed to get pregnant when Henry was never home?"

"After you met and married Henry, did you continue to steal?"

"I'd like to say no, Mr. Monroe, but old habits die hard. Even though there was plenty of money, I still shoplifted from time to time. I just couldn't help it. I felt as if it were a skill, something I needed to continue doing so I didn't forget how. I still couldn't believe how lucky I was. Henry was everything I ever imagined a mate should be, and more. Sometimes when I went to bed at night, I was afraid to fall asleep thinking I was going to wake up and find it was all a dream. Henry was the best thing that ever happened to me, and I wanted nothing more than to make him happy."

"Since David is nineteen years old, you must have gotten pregnant pretty quickly, no?"

"Yes. I'm not sure how I did it, but I got pregnant!"

"You never mentioned driving — did you have a car and a driver's license?'

"No, I never had either. To be perfectly honest, I never felt I needed one. I took the bus everywhere I needed to go. It was just a way of life for me. If public transportation wasn't available, I walked. There was never a question about it. But then I got pregnant and with Henry being away so often, he thought it would be a good idea if I had my own car. That way I could drive to my doctor appointments and such."

"But you didn't have a license?"

"No, I didn't. It was something Henry didn't know about me. He just took for granted I did. When we got married, I used a picture ID and I guess he just assumed it was my license. He never asked, and I never told him. So when he recommended the car, I told him I couldn't drive. So then he suggested I go and take a driving course, which I did, and passed with flying colors. When I called Henry with the good news, he came home from work and took me car shopping. I picked out a golden/tan Chevrolet Impala. It was used, but I didn't care. The thing that sold me was when the car salesman said the trunk was deep enough that you could put a trash can in it, standing upright, and still shut the lid. Can you imagine that?"

"When would you have a need to haul around trash cans?"

172

"I didn't know—but just knowing I could, it was enough."

Mr. Monroe shook his head. "So, what happened next, after you found out you were pregnant and you got your driver's license and a car?"

"I just hoped and prayed the baby would be a boy. I loved Henry with all my heart, and he was so excited about the baby. I found out I was pregnant in March of 1991 and David was born on September third that same year. Henry was beyond blissful. He was out making deliveries when David came, but when I called him, he was bawling on the phone. I didn't ever remember Papa crying."

"That's a nice story, Bea. I'm glad something good finally happened in your life."

"Just wait. I didn't tell you the bad part. The only drawback was that there were complications during the delivery. The doctor said my uterus was in horrible condition, and asked if I ever had an abortion. When he said that, I remember almost passing out. That day when Papa took me to that clinic, I'd had an abortion, and he didn't even *tell me*. The doctor insisted my uterus be removed, and he told me I could never have any more children. But now that Henry has his son, I was certain he'd be happy. I decided not to tell him about my uterus. I didn't want to ruin this happy occasion with distressing news. I knew I'd be fine. The best part was that Henry and I wouldn't have to use birth control anymore."

"So, if you had your uterus removed, where did you get Joshua and John?"

"I took them."

"Oh my gosh, Bea . . . you kidnapped them too?"

"No, I removed them from an unpleasant situation."

"Did you write about it in the journal?"

"Yes. I told you that journal is an account of my entire life."

James Monroe placed his head in his hands and then sighed. "Tell me what happened."

"David was barely three months old, and Henry started bugging me to have another baby. He seemed to think it would be nice to have a spare, just in case David didn't want to follow in his footsteps and take over Miller Trucking. What was I supposed to do?"

"Tell him what happened when David was born, and move on with your life?"

"I couldn't do *that*. If I told Henry then, he would be angry that I didn't tell him earlier; and God forbid, I thought he might even leave me, you know, if he found out I wasn't the perfect woman he thought I was. So, I decided I just needed to figure out a way to find a baby boy."

"So what did you do?" James Monroe asked, but Bea could tell he honestly didn't want to know.

"I decided to take the bull by the horns. When Henry was on the road, he always called me right before bedtime. The next time he called, I told him I was pregnant and due on February fourteenth, Valentine's Day. Henry was ecstatic. He told me he was the luckiest man in the whole wide world. It was actually quite easy to fool him. While he was away, I carried on like normal, but when he was home, which wasn't very often, it was a little bit tricky. I had to pad my belly to make myself look as if I had a baby growing inside of me. I also gained a few pounds, just to make it look more believable. It was kind of nice eating for two."

"And Henry was never suspicious?"

"Not that I'm aware of. He told me over and over again how beautiful I looked when I was pregnant. I thought of Papa, and wished I could tell him how I was conning Henry. Papa would have been so proud."

"So, cut to the chase. Where did you get Joshua?"

"In New Orleans . . ."

"New Orleans? How did that happen?"

"Well, in early February, I told Henry I received a phone call from my Aunt Benita. I told him that she'd said that Papa was very ill, and had been asking for me. Of course, Henry was taken by surprise because I never even told him I had any family. I explained to him that we had been estranged for many years, but if Papa was asking for me, it was a good sign; and I wanted to go and make peace with him. Henry told me he didn't care if I went, but I should check with my doctor before I traveled. He reminded me, our main priority was supposed to be the baby. Henry offered to go see Papa with me, and I just about swallowed my tongue. It was easy to convince him otherwise after I explained to him that he didn't know any of them, and he would probably just get in the way. I also told him taking time off work so close to when the baby was due wasn't a good idea, especially if he wanted to take time off later, after the baby came. Any delivery Miller Trucking didn't make meant less money for us. I knew that would get to him. Henry was a proud man and providing for his family was more important to him than almost anything."

"What does all this have to do with New Orleans?"

"I'm getting to that part. David and I packed up and headed for New Orleans. I'm not sure why I picked New Orleans, but it seemed as good a place as any. As we sat on the plane, David looked out the window, and I thought of Papa. His words came back into my mind as if he were sitting right beside me; *if you see something you want, take it.* I had ten days to find a baby I wanted, and then I had to take it. I could not believe how beautiful New Orleans was. The old, historic buildings and townhouses, with their courtyards and sculptured gardens were breathtaking. The weather was in the sixties, which, I was told, was typical for that time of year. The mornings were chilly, but as the day progressed, it warmed up quite nicely. It was actually good because I could wear gloves and not look out of place".

"Gloves?" Mr. Monroe asked. "What's so important about wearing gloves?"

"I'll get to that part, just wait. As David and I played in the hotel pool, I decided our best bet was to spend a lot of time hanging out where lots of children were; playgrounds, parks, zoos, shopping areas, and those types of places. After all, I just need to get lucky once."

"How long were in you New Orleans?"

"Long enough to get the job done!" Bea laughed. "Every morning we had been going to the city park to feed to birds. David got such a kick out of them. When they saw us with a bag of bread crumbs, it didn't take long for every bird within what seemed like a five mile radius to find us. A young nanny was at the park every morning as well, pushing a baby stroller and keeping an eye on twin girls. The girls appeared to be identical since I couldn't tell them apart. A day or two later, I finally got up my nerve and spoke to her. She told me her name was Yvonne, and the twin girls were Erica and Monica. I waited patiently for her to show me what was in the stroller. I couldn't believe it. She peeled the blankets back, and there, wrapped up like a present, was *Timothy*. When I looked at him, he was the most perfect, baby boy I had ever seen. I just had to know how old he was. 'He's two weeks old today,' Yvonne said. I knew I'd found what I wanted, I just had to wait until I had an opportunity to take him."

"Did you continue to talk to Henry throughout this whole ordeal?"

"Oh yes. I talked to him every night on the phone before bedtime."

"Didn't he ask what you were doing?"

"Of course he did. I told him Papa was not doing well, and the doctor said it could be any time now. I also told him I wanted to stay until the end, unless he wanted me to come back home. He told me to stay, but to take care of myself and our baby. I assured him I would be careful, and our baby was on my mind always."

"Then what happened?"

"David and I continued to go to the park every morning. Yvonne and I would sit and talk while the children played. I told her my name was Robin, and David's name was TJ."

"So you didn't tell her the truth?"

"Of course, not, silly! You *never* give your *real name!* I shared some sob story about how my husband left me, and that TJ and I were on our own. Yvonne told me she worked for a nice family as a live-in nanny. Both of them were partners in a law firm, and had returned to work as soon as they could, after Timothy was born. Yvonne told me she had worked for the Johnson's since before the twins were born, and absolutely loved it. I needed to give Yvonne plenty of time to get comfortable with me, which paid off in a really big way!"

"Oh no . . . you took the baby?"

"You're getting ahead of me, Mr. Monroe. Just wait. One day, not long after that, Monica and Erica were whining and begging Yvonne to take them on the swings. The swings were all the way across the park, and Yvonne made up some stupid excuse that she had to keep an eye on

Timothy and couldn't do it. Of course, I offered to help her out by attending to Timothy's needs while she took the twins on the swing set. It was perfect. I watched them walk away. Yvonne held hands with the girls, and they all swung their arms really, really high, giggling and laughing. As soon as she was out of sight, careful not to leave any fingerprints, wearing my gloves, I grabbed Timothy, blanket and all. I could only imagine the look on her face when she returned to find us gone; serves her right, for trusting a total stranger with the baby."

"How did you tell Henry?"

"I had planned it out perfectly. As soon as I left the park, David, Timothy, and I boarded a plane, and we touched down in Seattle a little over six hours later. When I got home, I called Henry, who was still out on the road, and told him Papa had passed away, and I was on my way home. I knew he wouldn't be home for a few days, so I had plenty of time. I also shared with him that I had delivered a healthy baby boy. Since Timothy was already three weeks old, I told Henry he was a little big but healthy as a horse. Henry said he couldn't wait to get home to see his son."

"And Henry didn't question it?"

"No. I told him that it all happened real fast, and everything went fine. We decided to name him Joshua."

"And you are certain you wrote all of this in the journal."

"Yep... every last detail of it."

"I usually don't swear in front of my clients, but *SHIT!*" James Monroe dropped his head and rubbed his face. "You know what this means? They know all of it. I don't see any way out of this."

"Relax, Mr. Monroe. I told you, once I explain everything they will understand, and it will be fine."

"How are you possibly going to explain taking a baby from a park in New Orleans?"

"Simple . . . his mom and dad cared more about their careers than they did him. Once again, I just removed him from an unpleasant situation." Bea leaned back on the bed and smiled.

"You are unbelievable."

"I know."

"Trust me, Bea, that *wasn't* a compliment."

"I'm tired of talking today. Why don't you come back another day and I will tell you how I removed John from an unpleasant situation?"

Mr. Monroe stood to leave. "I can hardly wait."

☙ *Chapter Twenty* ❧

Officer Butler had been reading through the journal when his jaw dropped. He immediately grabbed the phone to called Detective Baker. "Randy, you are not going to believe this!"

"What's that?" Randy said, clearing his throat. Officer Butler could just imagine Randy sitting at his desk, his feet propped up, and holding the phone receiver under his chin with his shoulder.

"I've been reading the journal for the last hour, and I just read an entry from February, 1993, the day Bea Miller kidnapped a baby from a park in New Orleans."

Officer Butler heard clanking, like the sound of the telephone hitting a metal desk, and then a loud *crash.* "Sorry about that, I just fell backwards in my chair. Come again?" Detective Baker said.

"Bea kidnapped a *baby boy* from a park in New Orleans in 1993. His name was Timothy Johnson. It says here both of his parents were attorneys. He is the boy they now call Joshua."

"*Oh my God*, you have to be kidding me! I'll make contact with the police in New Orleans right away."

"And that's not all. David is her *only* biological child. When he was born, there were some complications; the doctor told her that she wouldn't be able to have any more children. That means she not only kidnapped Joshua, but John, as well. I haven't reached that part yet; but if she did it, then I'm sure she would have written about it."

"*Then get back to reading!*"

Officer Butler hung up the phone and called Chief Felder. He hadn't talked to him in a week or two, and needed to fill him in on the case. Chief Felder wasn't in, so he didn't bother leaving a message. Even though Officer Butler was enjoying his temporary assignment, he missed his friends and co-workers from the police department. He had worked side-by-side with some of them for many years and had seen them through marriages, babies, divorces, and deaths. They were like family—the kind of family you could always count on.

Be Careful What You Wish For

Growing restless from sitting and reading, Officer Butler decided to go to the gym for a little while and burn off some of his excess energy. He was starting to grow frustrated with all of the wrongs Bea had committed. For a while, he had felt sorry for her; but at any point in time, she could have put an end to the cycle and decided she didn't want to follow that path any longer. It didn't matter how badly she was broken. It was Bea's decision to continue the downward spiral and not seek professional help.

While at the gym, he caught a snippet of the early news. He was surprised when Bea Miller was the lead story. It had already leaked to the press that she had kidnapped a child from New Orleans. It also showed a happy, tearful reunion of Charlie (also known as Mikey) and his parents. The parents seemed happier to see Charlie than he seemed to see them; most likely because they were virtual strangers to him. How horrible it was to think Charlie was apprehensive of the two people who obviously loved him, and was more comfortable living with a serial kidnapper. *No wonder the kid had nightmares.*

On his way home, Officer Butler stopped in to see his mom and dad. Reading about Bea and her horrible life made him appreciate what he had all the more. He kept hugging his mom, and she asked him—more than once—if something were wrong. He could only shake his head and thank God for his incredible family. When he got out to his car, he noticed he'd missed a call from Detective Baker. Quickly, he hit redial wondering what was going on.

"Rich, I just wanted to let you know—David Miller has been released. Once word had gotten out that Bea had kidnapped that boy from New Orleans when David had been only two years old, it became apparent that David hadn't done anything wrong. Sure, he was along for the ride—but what choice did he have?"

"So, where is he now?"

"I believe he went back to the trailer."

Officer Butler put on his turn signal and headed to Crimson Lane. When he knocked on the door, David answered and invited him in.

The first words out of his mouth surprised Officer Butler. "When do I get John back? I was told she kidnapped Joshua, but I want John. We are brothers and we need each other to get through this."

Be Careful What You Wish For

Officer Butler hated to be the one to break the news to him, but he did.

"I feel as if a part of my heart has been ripped out," David said in disbelief. "I just can't believe she kidnapped *four* kids. I *remember* when John was born, how in the world did she pull that off? He was a newborn for Christ's sake. Where did she get him?" David watched Officer Butler, disillusionment in his eyes.

"We don't know that part yet, but I'm sure we'll find out. It's only a matter of time."

"How did you find out about Joshua?"

"She wrote about it; every detail of how she went to New Orleans, found Timothy, and then stole him from a Nanny who'd come to trust her, when she wasn't looking. It's all there in the journal."

"You're kidding me . . . where was *I?*"

"You were with her."

David just shook his head. "Now I know why she clung to me so much. After Dad had died, I was her *only* family."

After telling David to stick around and stay out of trouble, Officer Butler headed home to read some more, hoping to discover the details of the day John became a Miller.

July 27, 1993

With two babies, I hardly find the time to take a shower, much less write in my journal. But the boys change so much every day, I feel the need to document all of it. Henry is so happy now that he has two sons; and I'm happy because Henry is happy. I love him so much and don't know what I would do if anything ever happened to him. He hasn't been driving as many over-the-road jobs. He said he wanted to spend as much time as possible with me, David, and Joshua. I honestly lucked out. Joshua looks so much like David, it's uncanny.

August 14, 1994

It happened again today. I was at the park pushing Joshua in a stroller. David was walking beside us, stopping every so often to pick up a rock or a twig. What is it with little boys and rocks? Actually, what is it with little boys and anything that involves dirt? So, anyway, we were

*walking along, and I heard rustling, as if someone were following us.
Every time I turned around, there was no one there. But then, the
direction of the wind changed, and I smelled it—a Camel, unfiltered
cigarette. Oh no, Papa found me again, I just know it. What am I going
to do now? Henry doesn't even know about Papa! God help me.*

October 21, 1995

*David is four and Joshua is two. I almost fainted when Henry
mentioned he missed having a baby in the house. "Wouldn't it be great if
we could have another baby?" he said out of the blue one evening. At
first, I wasn't even sure I heard him correctly. But then he repeated it. I
told him I like that the boys are more self-sufficient. He agreed it was
nice, but he also said he would certainly enjoy having another boy, so he
could call them "My Three Sons". Henry is an only child and always
dreamt of having a large family. He made me promise to think about it.
What's there to think about? If another baby will make Henry happy, I
just have to figure out a way to get one.*

November 30, 1995

*Having thought about the baby idea, I decided to see if I could
get a job at Mercy West Hospital in Spanaway, a great hospital about
forty-five miles from where we live. It's not a large hospital, but it is well
known for their Maternity ward. Their Labor & Delivery unit is top
notch, as well. I once heard that some hospitals allow volunteers to come
in and help with the babies, especially the newborns with special needs.
I'm not sure that's the case still, but it's worth finding out.*

December 13, 1995

*I went to Mercy West today. I spoke with three different people,
and after a series of conversations, which combined lasted a total of
forty minutes, they offered me a job. I told them I didn't want a paying
job, I wanted a volunteer position. I knew if they actually paid me, they
would find out my true identity. I told them my name was Laverne, and I
live in Spanaway.*

*I wasn't sure how Henry would react about my volunteer
position; but when I told him, he was genuinely excited for me. Since
Joshua came home, Henry has been doing more local deliveries so he
could stay closer to home. But now that I'm going to be working, he said
he'd like the change of pace so he decided to take more over-the-road
jobs.*

Be Careful What You Wish For

January 22, 1996

I totally LOVE my job. Seeing all the babies, especially the ones that need more attention, makes me realize how lucky I am. This past week there was a baby girl born weighing only a pound and a half. She is such a survivor. The doctors think that she will gain enough weight to be able to go home in about six weeks. Her mom was already discharged, so I get to hold her a lot when I'm there. She is utterly adorable, so tiny and delicate. Human contact seems to do her a world of good. I hope I have a little girl someday. I don't know what it is, but girls are so different from boys. Everything about them, from the way they smell to the way they stretch and yawn.

March 7, 1996

A twelve-year-old girl had a baby today. She was raped. She decided to give her baby up for adoption. Poor thing, he's addicted to crack, and he cries all the time. Just think, if Papa hadn't made me get an abortion, my baby would be almost twenty years old now.

Once the adoptive parents found out that the twelve-year-old mother was doing drugs all throughout her pregnancy, they decided they didn't want the baby. It's the saddest thing. He will stay about another month and then go to a foster home. No one will want him. He's only two days old, and he's already damaged. I just don't understand how someone can do that to an innocent baby. It took Papa fifteen years to damage me. Oh wait, I forgot, I was damaged from the beginning because I killed my mother . . . or so Papa says.

April 1, 1997

Hard to believe I've been working at Mercy West for over a year. I truly enjoy my job there. I get along well with my co-workers, and they all seem to love me. They tell me all the time how terrific I am with the babies, and that makes me happy. But, I can't lose focus and forget the reason I decided to volunteer there to begin with. I've been there long enough to establish their trust, now I need to set my plan in motion.

May 10, 1997

I decided to survey the area and locate all the security cameras. When Kelly went on break, I spotted three cameras in the nursery itself. Two were rotating back and forth over the cribs. The third one, which was stationary, was positioned on the only door to the nursery. I wondered what would happen if I picked up and baby and walked out with it. I figured I wouldn't go far, just down the hall and back to see what might happen. I didn't know if an alarm would sound, or what, so it was an experiment that was way overdue.

I met Kelly in the hall as she was coming back from break. When she saw me, she wanted to know what I was doing. I told her the baby was a little fussy, and I thought if I took her for a walk down the hall she might settle down. I told Kelly it seemed to work because she had stopped crying.

Kelly gave me a disgusted look, pushed her half glasses up on her nose and said, "Typically the only person allowed to remove a baby from the nursery is the nurse assigned to the patient or the pediatrician."

I apologized profusely. Now that I know the rules, I'll just have to figure out a way around them.

May 11, 1997

Today when I was walking down the hallway, just starting my shift, a new mother called out to me from her room. She told me she wanted to see her baby and had pushed the call button several times, but no one answered. I was told at my new hire orientation that the patient's care and satisfaction should always be my number one priority. I explained to the new mother I didn't think I was authorized to bring her baby to her, but I would check.

I went into the nursery and told Kelly what had happened. Kelly seemed disgusted and said, "Oh that lady. She's a real piece of work. If you want to take her baby in there, be my guest. It's the little boy in the first row on the left. Just push him there in the crib."

I could not believe my ears. I had just found a way to take a baby out of the nursery. I pushed him down the hall, in his crib to his mother, just like Kelly told me to. When I returned to the nursery, I wanted to double check with Kelly because I was certain she told me yesterday I couldn't take a baby out of the nursery. She explained I could not just pick one up and walk out, but if a doctor or nurse gave me permission, that was entirely different.

Be Careful What You Wish For

June 14, 1997

I took advantage of my newfound knowledge and used every opportunity to visit with patients and bring their babies to them. It seems the nurses are grateful for the extra help, and I am grateful to have the freedom to do so. I think they are getting sick of me asking.

June 16, 1997

I was right. They were sick of me asking. Today I was given clearance to take the babies out of the nursery without asking permission. Can you believe that? Now I know how a starving person must feel at a smorgasbord.

November 15, 1997

Tonight over dinner, I told Henry that I was pregnant. I have been at Mercy West for almost two years now, and they trust me a great deal. The only thing is, once I set the plan in motion I will have to quit working there, and I genuinely love my volunteer position. Oh well, I love Henry even more.

Needless to say, Henry was surprised when I told him. It had been such a long time since he'd mentioned having a third baby that he must have thought I'd dismissed the idea completely. He told me we needed a bigger house. I told him I didn't need a bigger house, but a larger vehicle would be helpful; perhaps one of those conversion vans. I've seen some that are pretty elaborate, almost like a hotel room on wheels. I told Henry I didn't need anything that nice, just something roomy. Henry leaned over and told me I was the best thing that ever happened to him. I feel the same way. I don't know what I would do without him.

November 16, 1997

On my way home from work today I stopped at a Chevy dealership. I traded in my old Impala, for a slightly used, 2 year old, navy blue, Chevrolet conversion van; it looks brand new and only has 18,000 miles on it. It has a raised roof and a light blue stripe down the side under the big, slightly tinted windows. I can't wait to make curtains to hang in each one. The salesman said it could seat six, as it has a bench seat along the far back, as well as a captain's chair in the center. It is the van I pictured in my head when I mentioned it to Henry. It is totally perfect, and all my plans are falling into place.

Be Careful What You Wish For

Oh no, Officer Butler thought. *This isn't looking too good. I remember that ID bracelet we found in the safe; it said Baby Boy Logan, and it was from Mercy West Hospital. I bet that's John.* To confirm the date, Officer Butler glanced through his notes. The ID bracelet said DOB 06-12-98. *Yep, that's it. Maybe we can get a hold of Kelly as another witness. If she's still around, I'm sure she remembers the day Baby Boy Logan disappeared. I am just flabbergasted how Bea was able to pull these abductions off. She had a husband who adored her. Didn't he get suspicious when she wasn't looking pregnant?*

The next morning, Officer Butler got up early and went to the Federal Building to see Detective Baker. It had been over a week since he last talked to him. He wanted to know how things were progressing, and when the he thought it might go to trial. Detective Baker told him the idea had been tossed around that they may need a change of venue since it seemed everyone within a two hundred mile radius knew about Bea Miller and what she had done. However, since the news of the child that had been kidnapped in New Orleans hit the airwaves, it was now an international story; and no matter where the trial may be moved, it was not likely the jurors would feel any differently. The bottom line was . . . everyone knew she was guilty. There would be none of this "innocent until proven guilty" crap. It was unfortunate for Bea Miller, but this was a case of "guilty until proven innocent." Mr. Monroe certainly had his job cut out for him. If the jury didn't find her guilty, it *would* be a miracle.

They talked more about the journal, and what he'd just discovered about two possible witnesses; Tammy and Kelly.

"I think I've found another possible witness or two, but I'll need some time to read further. I need to see if my gut feeling pans out. The one was a co-worker of Bea's at the truck stop where she met her husband, Henry."

"Naw, doesn't sound like she could add anything worthwhile. If you'd like to track her down and talk to her on the phone, then that would tell us more. Just working with Bea, unless she was her partner in crime, won't sway the jury one way or the other. You said there were two. Who is the other one?"

"Her name is Kelly. She was a nurse at the hospital where Bea volunteered in the maternity ward."

186

"A nurse, you say? Might be worth looking into. The jury always seems to like someone who's educated. For some reason they take their testimony more serious. But you're not going to have a lot of time, the state is currently canvassing jurors and the trial's supposed to start in about two weeks."

"Two weeks? Are you sure? That's really fast. I'd better get busy reading."

Detective Baker laughed as Officer Butler turned and left the station.

ᯤ *Chapter Twenty-One* ᯤ

James Monroe had been poring over his notes, trying to figure out how they were going to get Bea Miller out of this mess. Even if she told the jury she had done it for the children, it still didn't give her the right to kidnap those kids. He felt their best plea would be insanity, but Bea wouldn't hear of it. Anxious to find out how she got John, he went back over to see her. She was sleeping when he arrived.

"Up and at 'em, Bea," he said tapping her lightly on the bottom of the foot. "I need for you to tell me how you kidnapped John, so I can determine how much more of a hole you've dug yourself into—and if we are ever going to get out of it."

Bea sat up and rubbed her eyes. She was quiet for a moment before she began. "Well, I told you I got a job at Mercy West in the Labor & Delivery Department. My plan was to work there long enough to establish trust, and then remove a healthy baby boy from the nursery. It was in the winter of 1998. Henry was still gone four to five days a week driving around the country, making deliveries, and David and Joshua were in school. David was in the first grade, and his teachers told me he was one of the smartest kids in his class. Joshua, just into preschool, was learning skills that would help him when he started kindergarten in the fall. I still volunteered at Mercy West five days a week, but gradually began to cut back on my hours. Around the house, I always wore a pregnancy suit. They came in different sizes so I had one for three months, four months, five months and on up. I was surprised how they actually looked and felt like the real thing. I also bought several maternity outfits to wear when Henry was at home. I couldn't believe how easy it was to fool him. I made sure the lights were turned off before we went to bed, and he never saw me without my maternity clothes on."

"Didn't you feel guilty lying to Henry?"

"No . . . not at all, Henry was the one who wanted another son. I did it for him. In late May, I turned in my two-week notice. I told them we had received a phone call the night before, and that Henry's mother was terribly ill and we needed to go back to South Carolina to look after her. They told me they were sorry to see me go. They wanted to give me a going away party, and they said it would mean a lot if I invited Henry.

Be Careful What You Wish For

Can you imagine that? How would I explain *that* to Henry? Around the house I got bigger and bigger, and Henry got more and more excited. At some point, Henry told me he was certain this would be our last baby, and he wanted to savor every moment. I told him I had a feeling this baby was another boy, and he was overjoyed."

"Okay, Bea. Stop stretching it out. Just get to the part where you kidnapped John."

"It wasn't kidnapping! It was the 14th of June, 1998. Henry was on his way to Dallas. He had a load of lumber to deliver. I figured that would give me about six days to make sure my story was plausible. Four hours after Henry left, I contacted him on the CB radio to tell him my water broke. Of course, he was disappointed that he was going to miss the birth *again*, but I assured him he wasn't missing much—and when he got back home, I would be waiting with our new baby. Henry and I had become really good friends with one of our neighbors, Mrs. Wilson. She was a retired pediatrician's assistant, and volunteered to take care of David and Joshua in the event I went into labor when Henry was out of town. I told Henry I dropped the boys off at Mrs. Wilson's house and that I was getting ready to head to the hospital."

"Did he believe you?"

"Sure he did. Why wouldn't he? I pulled into my parking spot in the underground parking garage at Mercy West. I made certain to bring the car seat with me. I took the elevator to the seventh floor, just as I had every other day. Two hours later, I was sitting in the nursery rocking a fussy baby girl when Madge, the nurse on duty, had to run an errand down to the records department. Once Madge had left, I heard the words Papa said to me; *if you see something you want, take it.* This was the first time in years I could hear Papa speak to me, almost as if he were in the room with me. I pushed Baby Boy Logan out of the nursery and down the hall to an empty patient room. I put on a pair of rubber gloves, cut the security ID bracelet from his ankle, and placed it in my pocket. I picked him up gently and took the stairs—it was the first time I had ever done that, and went down to my van. I placed him in the car seat and went back up to the seventh floor. I took the empty crib and wheeled it back to the nursery, putting it in the back room with all the other empty cribs. When Madge returned, I was sitting in the same rocker gently rocking the same baby girl. Thirty minutes later, I finished my volunteer shift and hugged my coworkers. 'Laverne' turned in her hospital ID badge and left the hospital, and I never looked back. I didn't think anyone would suspect me . . . after all, I left the hospital the same way I came in—empty handed."

"So, it was that easy?"

"Yep . . . my plan worked like a charm." Bea smiled, feeling very proud of herself.

"And tell me, Bea, why did you feel Baby Boy Logan needed to be rescued?"

"Funny you should ask. His parents were young and didn't have any medical insurance. They weren't even married for God sakes. I wondered how they were going to take care of him, so I decided he would be better off with me that with people who couldn't afford to raise him. I did them a favor that day. Babies are expensive."

Shaking his head in disbelief was all James Monroe could do.

"But, along with the good news came some bad news. When I returned home from the hospital with Baby Boy Logan, whom I'd named John Henry, two patrol cars were waiting in my driveway. At first I thought they knew I took the baby. I pulled into the garage and got out of the van. They took me inside and then told me my Henry had been killed in a motorcycle accident. I was very confused and thought they had the wrong person because Henry didn't even own a motorcycle. But, then the troopers explained the details to me. It seems Henry was driving his semi-truck when a motorcycle switched lanes. Henry's truck jackknifed and slid over the embankment. The motorcycle driver, who had been left unharmed, ran to his aid, but when Henry's truck caught fire there was nothing he could do."

"Oh my gosh, Bea, I am so sorry."

"I was numb. They left me to mourn the death of my beloved Henry. An hour later, I remembered John was still in the van. Thank goodness our house sat in the shade, and the van was parked in the garage where it was cooler. By the time I got out there, John Henry was screaming his little fool head off. I shut the garage door and took him inside. Since Henry was badly burned, there was no open casket or funeral. I decided to have him cremated and a private memorial service was held. The only people in attendance were a couple of his employees and me. Henry's ashes were handed to me and I took them home and

190

spread them over the backyard, a place where we had many happy memories. I went to Mrs. Wilson's and picked up the boys. Now I had three boys and no Henry. I wondered what in the world I was going to do."

"I'm sure Henry had life insurance, didn't he?"

"I thought the same thing, but I quickly found out Henry had no life insurance. Since I didn't know anything about the trucking business, I decided to sell Miller Trucking to one of Henry's employees for a song. I made up my mind that the boys and I needed to move to another city; a change of scenery would do all of us some good. Since we were only renting in Seattle, I didn't need to worry about selling the house. I decided to leave the furniture and take just a few necessities. While I was rummaging through a drawer that contained all of our important papers, I ran across a small box from a jewelry store. I opened it and inside I found a charm bracelet. It had three charms; one that was shaped like a football and was inscribed with the name DAVID, one in the shape of a baseball said JOSHUA, and the third one, which was shaped like a bowling ball, had been left blank. I remember holding that bracelet up to my chest and crying and crying. Henry was so good to me. At that time, I had no idea how I was going to live without him."

"So that's how you acquired the charm bracelet, which is now being held as evidence."

"Yes. Henry had purchased it for me as a surprise. Once John was born, I had his name put on the bowling ball, and then I added the soccer ball when Mikey came. At some point, I bought the princess crown because I knew eventually I would have a little girl. Do you think they will give it back after the trial?"

"Bea, I don't think you will be wearing jewelry where you are going."

"I'm not going to jail, remember? I told you they would understand when I explained everything."

"Yes, I remember what you told me, but I don't think you have a snowball's chance in hell of worming your way out of this one. I know I asked before, but just to be sure, did you write about taking John in the journal?"

191

Be Careful What You Wish For

"Absolutely . . . I documented all the things that made me who I am today."

"Is there anything else you wrote that I should know about? You didn't hijack a school bus full of kindergarten kids at gunpoint and kill them all did you?"

"Are you trying to be funny?"

"Yes . . . I thought a little humor might make the situation appear less grim than it is. So what did you do after you found the bracelet?"

"I knew we needed to leave Seattle, but I didn't know where we should go. David kept asking me where Daddy was . . . I told him he was in heaven. When I told the boys we were moving, David asked if we were moving to heaven. I remember thinking, 'I wish we could, David, I wish we could.' Finally, I just packed the kids in the van and we left. We stopped to eat at some greasy spoon along the way and I overheard someone talking about North Dakota. It was one of the few western states that Papa and I had never visited, so, I figured it wouldn't hold any unpleasant memories. I had driven for seven hours before we stopped for the night, guessing we would arrive in North Dakota sometime the next day. As soon as we got across the state line, I stopped at a real estate office and explained my situation. One of the realtors recommended Bunting Valley, not far from Fargo. She said it was a very family-friendly community and had a lot to offer. She put me in touch with another realtor, closer to Bunting Valley, and that realtor found us a place to rent; the furnished house trailer on Crimson Lane where I was arrested. I paid the first and last month's rent, and we moved in the next day. We didn't have many things, so it didn't take too long. I registered David and Joshua for school in our new neighborhood and found a daycare for John. I knew I had to find a job—the sooner the better. School would start in just two weeks, so once they were in school, I planned on pounding the pavement until someone hired me."

"Did you have a skill set—besides shoplifting?"

"Not actually, but that didn't discourage me. On the first day of school, I dressed the boys in matching outfits; jeans and green John Deere t-shirts. I walked them to the end of Crimson Lane to catch the bus. I packed them a lunch and took pictures, just as I thought a loving mother would do. I don't remember ever getting them developed. Anyway, as soon as the bus pulled away, I noticed a factory across the

192

main road. I couldn't believe I never saw it before. After I had dropped John off at daycare, I went to the factory to apply for a job. As it turned out, it was Al Dente' Macaroni and they had several positions that I qualified for. After I had looked at the list of open positions, I decided I would like to work quality control near the conveyor belt, inspecting the boxes filled with macaroni before they were sent down the line to be sealed. I completed the new hire paperwork on the spot, and they gave me three olive green one-piece uniforms and a box of hairnets. My first day was the following Monday."

"Isn't that the macaroni warehouse that went out of business?"

"Yes, it did some years later, but that was after I worked there. Anyway, I worked alongside Blanche, this petite woman who seemed to have the perfect life; perfect hair, perfect house, perfect husband, and of course, the perfect little girl. Her name was Morgan. I was extremely jealous that Blanche had a little girl, when all I had were three boys; three truck-loving, pants-wearing, *boring* boys. No, frilly dresses, dance lessons, pink and purple rooms; it was just blue, blue, and more blue! *Ugh!* I wanted a girl so badly, and I remember wondering why God was punishing me."

"Did you ever think it may have been because you deserved it?"

"Bite your tongue, Mr. Monroe," she scolded. "No one deserved to work with Blanche and hear her stories and see her pictures. Every single day it was something else Morgan did, or something else Morgan said. I grew utterly sick of it, I was this close," Bea held out her thumb and index finger with about an inch between them, "to strangling her with my own bare hands!"

"What happened then, Bea?"

"I worked there for a while, but one day I was going up a set of steel grated steps to where the lunchroom was located on the second floor. I don't remember what happened, but somehow I slipped and fell. I was told that there was blood was everywhere, and they ended up having to call an ambulance. Four hours later, I had forty-two stitches down the back of my head. I was told my head would heal, but I managed to twist my back in such a way that I will be in constant pain. That's why I hate this stupid mattress." Bea paused to pound it with her fist. "My back was already bad, but now it's even worse. I decided to sue Al Dente' and I won a small settlement. But, the best part was that I was disabled in the

193

fall, so I wouldn't have to work another day of my life. I used the settlement money to buy the trailer. Since it was so old, my landlord only wanted fifteen thousand dollars for it. I thought not having to work was going to be great, but just sitting around the house was very depressing. I wished I could afford to buy new furniture, but there was no way. My disability pay was only seventy percent of what I was making, which wasn't much. Don't get me wrong, it was enough to live on, and sometimes I had a little extra, but I wondered why I couldn't get lucky, as Henry had, and win the lottery?"

"Okay Bea, I think that's enough for today. They should be setting the trial date soon. Have you given any more thought to a witness?"

"Yes. How about Mrs. Brown? She's my next door neighbor over on Crimson Lane. I have always been nice to her. I'm sure she would have many kind things to say about me." James Monroe just stared at Bea incredulously. "Don't tell me . . . the prosecution has already asked her?"

James Monroe, with nothing to say, nodded his head, "yes."

ᥰ *Chapter Twenty-Two* ᥱ

Officer Butler had been reading the journal for a few hours. It was like one of those "Movie of the Week" films on Lifetime TV. Some of the things were so far-fetched, he had to keep reminding himself that this was a true story. Reading how Bea had kidnapped Baby Boy Logan made him sick to his stomach. Never mind the fact that she hadn't given them her real name, or address, and had gotten away with it *again*. At least now he knew how Henry had died and how Bea had acquired the bracelet. *Henry must have gotten it for her as a surprise. How horrible it must have been when she found it after his death.* He used his thumb to flip through the remaining pages of the journal. He had read well over half and Bea had already kidnapped two kids—two more to go.

He put down the journal and dialed the number for Detective Baker who answered on the second ring.

"I know the details of John's abduction. The entire story is here in the journal."

Detective Baker chuckled. "How dense *is* this woman? It's one thing to write it down, but for her to have written it down and then leave it behind, it's almost as if she were begging to get caught. The only problem is, Rich, she was indicted on two counts of kidnapping; Maggie and Mikey. The kidnapping of Joshua and John may not be admissible."

"You've got to be kidding me . . ."

"No, I'm afraid our justice system is very explicit. However, that's not to say we can't mention it in court. I'm sure Monroe will object, but at least we'll get it out there. I'll make sure Hildebrand knows about it."

"Well then, I guess I don't need to read anymore, if we can't use it, and I guess contacting Kelly as a witness is a moot point."

"It's up to you. But remember, that journal is evidence, so you'll need to bring it back before the trial."

"I must say, I'm enjoying it. It's so bizarre, sometimes I feel as if I'm reading a novel. Bunting Valley is such a small town—and, pardon the cliché, but it's 'a place where everyone knows your name.' To think that someone like this could be living among us . . . it just baffles my mind. I was always skeptical when I saw those interviews on the news."

"What interviews?"

"You know . . . like when someone kills fifteen people and the media talks to a neighbor who says 'He was always such an amiable man.' I always wondered how it was possible that they didn't know they were living next to a serial killer, or kidnapper in Bea's case. I guess I got my answer."

"Yep . . . what happens behind closed doors is a mystery. If you're enjoying the journal, keep reading. Even if we can't use it, it wouldn't hurt the case any, that's for sure. The more we know about her, the better off we'll be. Oops, my other line is ringing; can you hang on just a minute?"

While he was on hold, Officer Butler jotted a notation in his notepad. *"November 23, 2000 . . . first time Bea mentions wanting a girl."* A moment later, Detective Baker was back on the phone.

"Rich, if you can tear yourself away from the *novel*," Detective Baker snickered, "can you come to the Federal Building for a meeting with Mr. Hildebrand? He has some questions, and I'd like you to be there."

"Absolutely, I'll be right there."

The Federal Building was an old structure sitting in the heart of the city. It took up two city blocks and employed well over five hundred people. It was a court of general jurisdiction, handling both civil and criminal cases. There were ten judges that presided over both types of cases which numbered more than sixteen hundred each year. Directly behind the main courtroom, there were six jail cells. This is where Bea was being held, awaiting trial. When the trial ends, if she's found guilty and depending on the sentence, she would be moved to another women's prison some thirty miles away. When Officer Butler pulled into his parking spot, he noticed TV crews from CNN and the local affiliates camped out in front of the building.

Detective Baker and Prosecutor Hildebrand were waiting for him when he arrived, and when it was all said and done, they decided their list of witnesses would consist of: Detective McClure, David Miller, Edna Brown, Tim Taylor, Nancy Novak (Mikey's—aka *Charlie's*—

biological mom), and possibly Benita Adams. Officer Butler would be called *only* if they felt things were going badly and they thought his testimony might make a difference. Prosecutor Hildebrand said he needed to meet with each of the witnesses prior to the trial, so he could determine what they knew that would be the most damaging. He indicated Benita Adams might be a stab in the dark, since she only knew Beatrice for the first six years of her life—and that didn't have anything to do with the kidnappings. Her testimony might do more harm than good. Prosecutor Hildebrand was still hoping Bea would take the witness stand in her own defense. He had requested it, but hadn't heard yet if she had agreed to oblige the court. They didn't have many exhibits; but, they did have the charm bracelet, the journal, the safe, and the few items assumed to have been purchased for Maggie confiscated from the Miller trailer.

The trial date was finalized and added to the court docket for Wednesday, October 31, 2010. Officer Butler was told to reach Benita Adams and get her into town, just in case. The other witnesses would be contacted through Mr. Hildebrand's office.

On the way home, Officer Butler stopped by to check on David. He seemed to be doing okay on his own. He had cleaned the trailer, and it looked a lot better than the last time Officer Butler had seen it. David, still in shock and denial, couldn't believe Bea was capable of committing such horrendous crimes. Officer Butler told David he would be needed on October 31st as a witness. He also told him his great-aunt, Benita Adams, would be coming into town. David wasn't aware he had an aunt.

"Will Bea be there?" David asked.

"Yes, I'm afraid so. You can't avoid it any longer. You'll have to see your mother."

"She's not my mother. A mother is someone who is loving, kind, and nurturing. She was never any of those things. She's not my mother. She is Bea Miller, a serial kidnapper and a virtual stranger to me."

Officer Butler, thinking of David's comment, went home and phoned Benita Adams. She said she was excited to see Bea after all these years. He explained to her that she wouldn't really "see" Bea, she would just see her in the courtroom, and Benita sounded disappointed. He told her about David, and Benita said she might want to meet him; she'd have to let him know. He then picked up the journal and commenced reading.

Be Careful What You Wish For

May 15, 2003

The older David gets, the more he becomes my best friend. I can't wait for him to get off the school bus every day, so I can ask him about his day. I don't have anyone else to talk to. Our neighbor, Mrs. Brown, is nice, but she's so nosey. I hate to tell her anything because I can only imagine how she likes to gossip. My life is hard enough without the neighbors shunning me.

September 30, 2003

I'm terribly depressed. The boys are back in school, and I want a girl more than anything. I know if I had a girl, life would be so much better. We could do things together, just like me and Aunt Nita used to do. I think I'll mention it to David and see what he thinks.

October 5, 2003

Well, I told David I want a girl, he looked at me as if I expected him to impregnate me. He is very funny. When I told him my plan of taking one from the grocery store, he thought I was crazy. I know I could do it. It's been a while, but stealing is a skill you never lose. He told me kidnapping is against the law and blah, blah, blah. I stopped listening.

October 17, 2003

I've made up my mind. Tomorrow I am going to find my little girl. It's mighty cold out, unseasonably so. The weather man predicted snow. It's not even Halloween yet and it might snow. I hate winter. I hate being shut up indoors months on end. I hate having to bundle up like a caterpillar in a cocoon just to walk out and get the mail. But, this coming winter, I will be bonding with my little girl. I can't wait!

October 18, 2003

Something horrible happened. I got up early and went to Greenfield, to the Stop-N-Save supermarket. I was going to look for my new daughter. The Stop-N-Save is about 40 miles from where I live. I parked in a handicapped spot and went in. I chit-chatted with a couple of workers, mostly about the cold weather, and even though, I wasn't actually going grocery shopping; Papa taught me to put a few things in my cart so that it looked like I was. It was less obvious that way, so I did. I rounded the corner at the end of the cookie aisle, and there she was. A beautiful baby girl all bundled up in a yellow snowsuit, lying in the seat attached to the cart. I heard Papa, loud and clear; if you see something

Be Careful What You Wish For

you want, take it. I followed the baby and the lady with her for a few aisles, making sure I didn't draw attention to myself.

The lady pushed the cart to the end of an aisle, and then backtracked to get a box of something, cereal I think, and I saw my chance. I swooped in, grabbed the baby, and was out the door. I threw her in the car seat and sped away, stopping a few blocks later to buckle her in. I was ecstatic. She looked as if she were seven to eight weeks old. Since I had worked at Mercy West so long, I became a fairly decent judge of things like that. I kept looking at her in the rearview mirror. She was beautiful. At one point, I told her that her name was Michelle.

Michelle and I rode all the way home, and she cooed and giggled. I thought, "Wow, I lucked out and found the perfect baby with the perfect temperament." We got home and then it all went downhill. When I unzipped the snowsuit, I couldn't believe my eyes. Michelle was dressed in a pair of navy blue pants with a light blue t-shirt. The t-shirt had baseballs all over it.

I ripped off "her" pants and looked in the diaper. Michelle wasn't a girl at all! "She" was a boy! Another stupid boy! I don't want another boy! I don't want the three I have, and now I have another one.

Michelle grew hungry and started to cry. I told her to shut up, and as soon as I heard the screech of the school bus brakes, I rushed to the door and yelled for David. He ran home, and I told him what I had done. I asked him to get rid of it. I don't know if I actually meant it, but I couldn't stand the thought of having another boy. David refused, so we decided to keep it. Its name is now Michael, and I am a single mom with four boys. God help me.

December 15, 2003

I couldn't wait for the boys to get on the bus today. I dropped Mikey off at day care and drove 45 minutes to a casino. I had been saving a few dollars here and there, hoping to turn it into a million. As soon as I walked in, the flashing lights were all around, inviting me in. I began stuffing quarters into a slot machine decorated red, white, and blue. Pull after pull turned up nothing substantial, but I won a few dollars and lost a few dollars. A few hours later, just as I was about to call it a day, I smelled it; Camel, unfiltered cigarettes. "Hello, Bea," a voice behind me said. I froze. I'd recognize that voice anywhere. I couldn't decide if I should turn around, ignore him entirely, or scream. I

199

wanted to scream, but somehow, that seemed a bit much. After a minute of silence, he spoke again. "Come on, Bea, don't be like this."

I finally turned around and looked at him. "What do you want, Edward?" I said. He asked me for a hug and feeling like a little girl again, I stood up and gave him one.

Edward wanted to go somewhere and talk. He wanted to reminisce about all the good times we had. "Exactly what good times are you referring to?" I said. "The time you made me sit in jail for five days? Or how about the first time you took me to the store, when I was just a child, and made me put that steak in my shirt? Then there was the time you threw Aunt Benita out just because she loved me. Oh, I know, how about the good time we had the night I left, when you raped and almost killed me? Yeah, those were some good times, alright." I couldn't believe I had the nerve to stand up to him.

He started in with how much he has changed, and how he wants to become part of my life and prove it. He actually had the nerve to say he had missed me. I told him I want no part of him and left. He followed me out to the parking lot. My car threw stones and dirt all over him as I sped away. What am I going to do?

April 21, 2004

I stayed indoors the rest of the winter, fearful that I might run into Papa. Today Mikey and I were outside, and Mrs. Brown poked her nose out. She saw Mikey and invited us over, to talk and catch up.

I told her about Mikey, and I concocted some crazy story about my sister dying of breast cancer, leaving me custody of Mikey. Mrs. Brown fell for it, hook, line, and sinker. She is so stupid.

Then she told me she had been going over to the new senior center and had met a nice man by the name of Edward. Oh my God. It's Papa! He's trying to use Mrs. Brown to get close to me. She told me the seniors have a luncheon every Wednesday. I am going to go and confront Papa. I want to know what he's up to.

April 26, 2004

I went over to the Senior Center, and Papa was there. He admitted he had been following me since I left for Seattle. I knew it! He knew I had four boys, and he wanted to be the grandfather he knew he could be.

200

I told him to leave Mrs. Brown alone. He said he would leave her alone if I agreed to let him see the boys. I told him I would think about it and let him know. We agreed to meet in two weeks.

May 1, 2004

I am torn. I don't want Papa around my kids, yet at the same time, it would be nice to have the extra help. I just don't know what to do. If he has changed, like he claims, I wouldn't mind letting him back in my life, but at the same time, if I heard it once, I heard it a million times; there is no cure for evil.

May 8, 2004

I met Papa and told him I was real apprehensive. He said he understood and then he told me he was dying. He had black lung and wouldn't be around much longer. His only wish was to get to know his grandsons. Now what am I going to do? I had almost decided against it, but now that I know he's dying, I don't know if I can let myself be that cold and cruel. I told him I would let him know next week, and we agreed to meet same time and same place.

May 15, 2004

Today I took Mikey with me when I met Papa. I'm sure I'll live to regret it, but they got along quite well. Perhaps I can give him Mikey and he'll leave me alone. It was the oddest thing, but Papa was running and chasing Mikey, and he didn't show any signs of having black lung. I hope he's not at it again. I'm a little smarter this time around. We agreed to meet next week for another play date.

May 22, 2004

Okay, it's getting pretty obvious; Papa doesn't have black lung any more than I do. No coughing . . . no wheezing . . . I finally asked him about it, and he said, "Some days are good, and some days are bad— I've learned not to question it, but accept it as a gift." That's a load of shit if I ever heard one! He keeps asking me when he gets the meet the other three boys. School is out soon. I don't know how much longer I can stall him about seeing the kids. I don't ever remember Papa liking any kids. I wonder why he is so hell bent on getting close to mine.

Be Careful What You Wish For

May 25, 2004

I've been thinking about it, and I am going to ask him, outright, if he has black lung. I'll tell him if he doesn't tell me the truth, he will never get to see the boys.

May 29, 2004

You are not going to believe what happened today . . . Mikey and I went to meet Papa, just like we have been for the past month. We decided to take Mikey to a playground. Papa pushed him on the swing set and ran around chasing him. Again, there was no coughing or difficulty breathing.

During the ride back to where Papa had left his car, I asked him— point blank, if he were dying. He fed me some load of shit that all of us are dying, but I finally got it out of him that he hadn't been truthful and that he wasn't dying any sooner than anyone else.

Then, he got mad and started ranting about how he has followed me for years, and he stuck by me when I married Henry and had the boys, waiting for the perfect opportunity to come back into my life. As long as Henry was alive, he knew I would never need him. I asked him what he was talking about. Papa looked at me and said, "Who do you think was driving the motorcycle?" and then he laughed. Papa had deliberately run Henry off the road, so that he could worm his way back into my life, and he thought it was funny? "You should have been there Bea. I ran over to him and pretended to help him, and that was when the whole truck went up in flames. I couldn't have choreographed it any better."

I started hitting him. I hit him on the face, arms, legs, head, wherever I could. I could not believe he killed my Henry. The love of my life was dead, and Papa was to blame. I lost it. I started screaming. Finally, I looked at him and said, "I can't believe you killed my husband."

Papa never missed a beat. "So . . . ? You killed my wife. Now we're even."

I didn't have the strength to hit him anymore. I put my head down and muttered, "Just when I thought I couldn't hate you any more than I do . . . you son-of-a-bitch. You killed my Henry." What happened after that is a blur, but before long, I was in my driveway and Papa was

202

behind me. I walked back. He rolled down the window and had the nerve to say, "Do I still get to see my grandsons?" I balled my fist up and punched him, square in the nose. Blood started gushing. He accused me of breaking his nose, and called me a bitch. I grabbed Mikey up and took him with me into the house. I heard Papa yell that he wasn't done with me yet.

Officer Butler stopped reading and shook his head. *Oh my God. I can't believe it. Edward deliberately ran Henry off the road so he could get close to Bea and his grandsons.* He picked up the phone and called Detective Baker.

"I'm still reading the journal. I just finished reading where Bea's father, Edward, killed Henry Miller, Bea's husband."

"What? How did he do that?"

"He ran Henry off the road, and Henry's truck caught on fire. He burned to death in the crash. Can you imagine that?"

"It just keeps getting better and better . . . how much more do you have to read?"

"Not much . . . maybe ten or so entries. As time went on, she didn't seem to write as much. I have passed the section where she kidnapped Mikey, though."

"Really . . . ? Did you learn anything new?"

"Not really . . . it's pretty much the same story David told. Is there anything new going on there?"

"The jury selection has been finalized. The state has picked over forty people, and they have already sent out the letters letting the jurors know. They will all report on Monday and after the examination phase, it will probably be narrowed down to fifteen or twenty. I think the state is planning on having twelve jurors and several alternates."

With only four days until the trial, Officer Butler wanted to complete reading the journal. Once he signed it back in as evidence, he would, quite possibly, never be able to get it back again to finish reading it; and the funny thing was, he just had to know how the story ended, even though he was well aware of the outcome.

Be Careful What You Wish For

September 17, 2005

It's been over a year, and I still live in fear Papa is going to come back. From time-to-time, I think I smell his cigarettes, but I try to convince myself my mind is playing tricks on me. Just to be on the safe side, I now drive the boys to and from the bus stop, for fear he might kidnap them. I did something today I never thought I'd do. I went out and registered for a hand gun. I don't know if I could ever use it, but I feel better knowing that I'll have one if I need it. Papa probably thinks he has me right where he wants me; scared and alone.

August 1, 2006

Today I was doing some fall cleaning. I don't know what got into me; I hate housework, but today I felt domestic. I washed down all the walls in the living room and beat all the dust, and dirt from the rugs. I started on the dishes then, and had been at it for a little while when, with my elbows deep in a sink of soapy water, I jumped when someone knocked on the front door.

I assumed it was Mrs. Brown, but when I opened it, there stood Papa. I tried to slam the door, but he put his foot in the way, so I couldn't. I pushed with all my might, but he managed to get inside the trailer. He grabbed me by the hair and slammed me up against the wall. I could only imagine I must have looked like a rag doll in his strong grasp. The smell of alcohol was so intense—it was as if it were oozing out of his pores. He slurred his words as he demanded that I let him see his grandsons. I told him they were at school, so he decided to sit and wait for them. In the meantime, he told me to cook him a steak.

I went into the kitchen and banged around on pots and pans pretending to be cooking. All I could think about was the hand gun, which was on the opposite end of the trailer, in my nightstand. Papa yelled, "Don't try anything stupid, or I'll kill you and take those boys when they get home."

I told him I was just in the other room making him a steak. I banged a little louder as I peered around the corner from the kitchen and saw him with his head leaning back against the sofa with his eyes closed. Suddenly, he jerked upright and yelled, "I don't smell anything cooking in there!"

I went back into the kitchen and hit some pans together. I told him I was working on it. Papa started snoring so I tiptoed past him, *down the hall to my bedroom. I grabbed the gun and crept slowly down the hallway. I stood there wondering what I was supposed to do. If I shot him while he was sleeping on the couch, it would look as if I'd killed him in cold blood. I needed to get him to come towards me. I knew, once I did this, there would be no turning back. Either I had to go through with it and kill him, or he would kill me. "Edward", I yelled.*

He stood, albeit wobbly, and came towards me. I shut my eyes and squeezed the trigger. The bullet shot across the room and hit him just below his chin, in the neck. Papa fell backwards, but he didn't stop. He tried to get back up, and I shot him again. This time he went down and never moved. While Papa lay on the floor, in a pool of his own blood, I dialed 911. I told them I had killed an intruder in my home.

They came out quickly. Papa was pronounced dead at the scene. Mrs. Brown was standing on her deck as they wheeled him out on a stretcher in a black body bag. I had to go to the police station to fill out a report. They took pictures of my bruised and battered body, and I was free to go.

August 3, 2006

I received a call today from the police station. The court had ruled that I had shot the intruder in self-defense, and I was cleared of any wrongdoing. Can you believe that? I shot, and killed Papa, and I got away with it. I hope you rot in hell for everything you did to me!

She had killed her own father and gotten away with it. It was true what David had said, she was the luckiest person alive, and she could worm her way out of anything.

ᶜᴼ *Chapter Twenty-Three* ᵒᵂ

I t was two days before the trial and Benita Adams had arrived in town. Officer Butler told her that he would pick her up from the airport and take her to her hotel. He was, however, not expecting the person who walked down the ramp. Benita was quite striking, despite her age, and was truly elegant. She looked like a movie star, wearing a long ivory coat with matching hat and gloves. She had brought *four suitcases* and Officer Butler was having a tough time trying to figure out *what* in the world she could have brought with her that would have required so many of them. She was a *witness* . . . at a *trial*, for Pete's sake. It wasn't as if she were going on vacation. When she saw him eyeing the baggage, she lifted her hand and lightly touched her chest, "I never know what to pack. It always drove my late husband nuts."

Benita had made reservations at a five star hotel downtown close to the Federal Building. "I know you told me all my expenses would be reimbursed, but don't worry about it. I have more money than I know what to do with. Mr. Adams was an oil man and left me millions."

They rode in silence most of the way. When they turned off the highway and headed towards downtown, Benita reached over and touched Officer Butler's arm. "Please take me to see David. I've been thinking about it, and I'd like to meet him."

"Are you sure?"

"Yes, I'm sure. I'm an old broad, and there's no telling how much longer I'll be around. If I want to meet him, this may be my only chance."

Officer Butler turned around and got back on the highway, headed in the direction of Bunting Valley. He pulled off the main road into the trailer park and Benita got a sour look on her face, almost as if she had tasted a lemon. "*This* is where he is?"

"Yes. This is where they all lived up until the arrest. David's here now all by himself." Officer Butler turned into the driveway and Benita looked as if she were going to pass out. "Are you alright, ma'am?"

"Yes, yes, I'm sure I'll be fine. I just can't believe Beatrice lived here."

Officer Butler climbed out of his car and walked around to open the door for her. He could tell she was used to being taken care of. He asked her to wait while he knocked on the door and spoke to David. Minutes later, David opened the door and invited them in.

Benita acted as if she didn't want to sit on the furniture, but she must have gotten tired of standing because she finally sat down on the very edge of the sofa. David offered her a cup of tea, which she declined. Officer Butler noticed something different about David. He no longer looked like the teenage boy who had climbed out of the back of the van in the black t-shirt only a few weeks ago. He had on a navy blue polo shirt and a pair of jeans. His "jet black" look was gone and his hair appeared to have been highlighted or colored, and was cut and styled. He had been transformed in these few short weeks and looked quite presentable.

"You look quite nice, David. How are things going?" Officer Butler was pleased at the changes and had to say something; the Lord only knew when the last time was that David had received a sincere compliment.

"Good. I just got a job. This is my uniform," he said holding his arms out.

"That's wonderful news . . . where at?"

"At the Music Mart . . . you know, I told them about the CD I stole years ago and how sorry I was. I think the manager felt sorry for me and offered me a job."

"I'm sure that's not why they hired you, but that was nice of you to tell him. Shows true character when a man can own up to his mistakes."

"I am going to register for some college courses in the spring. If all goes well, I hope I can graduate in four years and get a good job."

"Do you have any idea where you might go?"

"I thought I'd start out at the community college and then transfer. I don't have any transportation, so I have to walk, or take the bus everywhere I go. I am barely paying the bills here with the money I make at Music Mart."

Benita just sat and listened, seeming to enjoy the banter between Officer Butler and David. Finally, feeling as if he were monopolizing the conversation, Officer Butler turned to Benita. "David, you know Benita took care of your mom for the first six years of her life?"

"She did?" David's eyes lit up.

"Yes. Your grandma, Marcy, died a few days after your mom was born; and your grandpa, Edward, called Benita and asked her to move in and help out. Isn't that right, Benita?"

"Yes, that's correct. Your mom was such a wonderful little girl. I loved her so much, David. She and I were best friends. We did everything together."

"So what happened? Why did you leave?"

"I had no choice. Your grandpa, Edward, who was my brother, was not a very nice man. He had a temper he could turn on and off like a light switch. I did something that made him angry, and he kicked me out."

"What could you *possibly* do that would make him so mad?"

"It's kind of foolish, now that I look back on it. Edward found out that your mother and I celebrated her birthday every year and he got mad."

"What?"

"Your grandpa blamed your mom when your grandma died, so he punished her by not letting her celebrate her birthday. I thought that was a horrible thing to do to a little girl. Beatrice didn't kill Marcy. What killed her was the pneumonia, and *that* was Edward's fault."

"He wouldn't let her celebrate her birthday . . . *ever?*"

"No. He told her that she had killed her mother, and she wasn't going to get to celebrate living when others have died because of her."

"Oh my God . . . *that's horrible.*" David hung his head.

"That's all in the journal, David. I told you, you might feel different after you read it."

"What else can you tell me?"

"Well, for starters, you look just like her."

"I do?"

"Yes, you do. She was always the picture of health. I said, more than once, she should have been a poster child for what a healthy child *should* look like; rosy, pink cheeks, snow white skin . . . she was lovely. I loved dressing her up. She was like a baby doll to me."

Officer Butler could tell David was genuinely enjoying his visit with Aunt Benita. "Where are you staying?" David asked her.

"Downtown at the Princess Regency."

"You are welcome to stay here. There are three bedrooms and only one of me."

"That's quite alright, but thanks for the offer. I'd rather be downtown, closer to the Federal Building. How much is the rent here, in this . . . ?" Benita threw up her hand, indicating the trailer, but not sure what to call it.

"I don't have to pay rent. Mom bought this trailer when she won a settlement from her former employer. But I do pay utilities and taxes, which are about three hundred fifty dollars a month."

"You have to pay three hundred fifty dollars a month to live ere?" Benita frowned.

"Yes, ma'am . . . that's a really good price, actually."

"I'll tell you what, David. I have my checkbook right here." She reached in her Gucci bag and pulled it out. "I'll write you a check, for let's say, twenty thousand dollars. That should pay your bills for the next four years, so you can concentrate on your studies."

David gulped so loudly that Officer Butler could hear him from across the room. "That's okay, ma'am. I'm doing fine on my own. I do appreciate the offer . . . really, I do; but I can't take your money."

"Have I offended you? If so, David, I didn't mean to."

"No, no, it's not that. It's just, this is the first time in my entire life I have been on my own, responsible for everything. I know if I don't pay the water bill, I don't have any water. If I don't buy groceries, I have

209

nothing to eat. If I don't pay the electric bill, I have no lights. As stupid as it may sound, I like that feeling." David smiled.

Benita and Officer Butler stayed a little while longer and then he drove her back to her hotel. "David is a nice boy, isn't he?" she said as he stepped out of the car and walked around to open her car door.

"Yes, he is. He seems to have a good head on his shoulders, and somehow, he grew up knowing right from wrong. Now that he's out from under Bea's influence, I expect that young man to do great things."

"I hope you're right," Benita said, adding, "You don't have to walk me all the way in. I'll be fine."

"Are you sure?"

"Absolutely! I'll see you in court."

The trial date was rapidly approaching, and Officer Butler had about ten more entries to read. He wanted to finish the journal before the opening arguments. After dinner, he settled down in his favorite easy chair and started reading. He had to look back to see what had happened last. *Oh yeah, she killed her father, how could I forget that?*

August 22, 2006

For the first time in a long time, I feel as if a tremendous burden has been lifted; I am free. I no longer have to look over my shoulder every time I go out. I no longer have to hide my children. I no longer panic when I smell cigarette smoke. Papa is dead, and I killed him. He won't be bothering me ever again.

February 7, 2008

The older the boys become, the less they need me. This gives me more and more time to sit and think what life would be like if I had a little girl. I was so happy when David was born, but after that, the other boys were just for Henry. If only Mikey had been a girl; a cute and dainty little girl. I would take her shopping, and we could get our nails done. My life would be much better if I had a girl.

April 4, 2008

Today I was doing some laundry, and I decided to strip the beds. When I entered the room shared by John and Mikey, the smell of urine was so strong, my eyes actually watered. Upon closer investigation, I could see where it was still wet from the night before, and there were several other dried stains. John is eight years old and Mikey is five. No one should be wetting the bed. As soon as the boys got home from school, I took John into another room to talk to him. He finally confessed it was Mikey. I knew it. That kid has been a pain in the ass since day one.

So, I took Mikey aside and explained to him, "We are not animals and we do not wet our beds. If you are going to act like an animal, then I will treat you like an animal." I told him for the next week he had to sleep in a cage. He looked up at me through those thick bottle cap lenses. "What?" he said, tears welling up in his eyes.

I did not relent. I made him sleep in the cage, and I told him, if he wet the cage, I would add another week to the punishment.

April 12, 2008

The punishment is over, and it worked like a charm. Mikey kept the cage dry, so he's back in his bed. I placed the rabbit cage out behind the house, just in case I might need it again sometime. Any day now, they are going to knock on my door, and present me with the Mother of the Year award, I just know it.

September 4, 2009

I was standing in the kitchen, today, washing up the lunch dishes and I heard music. It wasn't terribly loud, but it was there, nonetheless. I walked out into the living room, and the music got a little louder. I asked Josh if he heard it, but he didn't. I started down the hallway to the bedrooms. The further away from the front of the house I got, the quieter the music seemed to get. By the time I reached my bedroom, it had stopped altogether. I went back to the living room and opened the front door and found the source of the music. The van, sitting in the driveway, was vibrating from the base on some rock 'n roll song. I slipped my flip-flops on to go out and investigate.

The closer I got to the van, the louder the noise got; in addition to the music, I could hear talking, laughing, and coughing. I stood outside and listened for a moment and couldn't make out any of the voices except David's. I flung open the side door, and cigarette smoke hit me in the face. Two of the five boys that had been seated on the floor stood and made a beeline towards the open door. I managed to grab one by the arm and pushed him back to the floor. I looked at David and said, "What in the hell is going on?"

David acted like an alien had taken over his body and he started talking in this weird language. He said something about him and his peeps enjoying the vibes. I could tell he was trying to impress his "peeps". The way he was acting, I thought he had been drinking, but he said, "Chill, Mom. All we have are cigarettes. It's all good." I told him it was not "all good." I asked him to hand me the pack of cigarettes. I told them I would not tell their parents if they made a deal with me. Hesitantly, they all agreed. I handed each of them a cigarette and told them they had to eat it, right in front of me, from the filter down to the last crumb of tobacco. They looked at me as if I had lost my mind. "Eat up, boys, or I'll call your parents. Due to the coughing I heard out here, my guess is this is the first time you've done this, and I'm determined to make it your last."

One by one they stuck them in their mouths. One by one they chewed and swallowed and chewed and swallowed. A couple of them gagged and turned a little green, but none of them puked. David finished his first. "Gee, David, would you like another?" I jokingly said as I held the pack towards him. David put up his hand, "No. No. I don't want anymore. I don't ever want to see another cigarette as long as I live." Lesson learned.

April 23, 2010

It's spring time again. This is the time of year when I get the itch for a little girl. When I got out shopping, I see the Easter dresses and bonnets, and all of the little girls are dressed in their bright new clothes and flip-flops, I want one so badly. I mentioned it to David, and he tuned me out. Doesn't he know how vital this is to me? Doesn't he care?

June 14, 2010

School's out for the summer and David graduated this year. Pretty soon he will be going off on his own, and I will be stuck here with those other three boys who don't even belong to me. I want a girl—and this summer I am going to get one! I don't care what David says, he can't talk me out of it.

There is only one more entry, the day Maggie Taylor went missing.

Be Careful What You Wish For

July 17, 2010

Today is the day I get to meet my daughter. I wish the boys would get up already. The sooner we get to the lake, the sooner I will find her, and the sooner we can all get home.

I know I will find the perfect little girl there. There will be no mistake this time. I already filled the boys in and told them if they so much as uttered a word to anyone, as to what goes on at the lake; I will personally cut their tongues out. And I mean it. I've waited for this day far too long; no one is going to mess it up. I feel like I could literally kill anyone who gets in my way.

I hope she's little, but not too little. I know I don't have the patience to go through the terrible two's all over again. I wonder what her name is. I hope it's a pretty name, so I don't have to change it.

It sure put things into perspective and helped Officer Butler realize a lot of things, mostly how Bea Miller turned out the way she was. He wished, just once, she would have written how horrible she felt about doing something wrong; that she had revealed *some feelings* of guilt or remorse, *something*, but there was nothing. He picked up the phone and called Detective Baker.

"Hi Randy . . . I just finished the journal. What a story it has to tell."

"Did you learn anything new?"

"Yeah . . . Bea Miller shot and killed her father. He pushed his way into her home, and she got a handgun and shot him. I'm not saying he didn't deserve it, but the fact that she got away with it just blows my mind."

"Maybe that's something we can bring up at trial."

ᐭᔮ Chapter Twenty-Four ᔭᐭ

The day of the trial was finally here. In some ways, it seemed like it took forever to get here; but in other ways, it seemed just yesterday little Maggie Taylor went missing from the beach. Officer Butler managed to get to the Federal Building early to turn the journal back over to Detective Adams since it would be needed as evidence.

Bea was dressed in a two-piece white suit with a cobalt-blue, silk blouse. She had her hair pulled back in a tight pony tail and was wearing bright red lipstick. She sat at a table next to her attorney, James Monroe. The courtroom was crowded. Friends, neighbors and other who were just curious came out to see the serial kidnapper. Officer Butler saw Abby Taylor in the audience and managed a wave.

Bang, bang, the gavel rapped sharply on the Judge's bench gaining everyone's attention. "All Rise. The Superior Court of Fargo is now in session, with the Honorable Judge Nelson presiding," the bailiff said loud and clear. Everyone in the courtroom remained standing until the judge came in and took the bench. The judge then asked the bailiff to call the day's calendar. The bailiff looked at the court paper in front of him and read aloud, "Your Honor, today's case #106078 is the State of North Dakota vs. Beatrice Miller."

The judge, a middle aged man with dark hair and bifocal glasses turned to face the attorneys for each side. "Are you ready to begin the trial?"

"Yes, Your Honor." Gregory Hildebrand was the first to open the trial. He stood with confidence, looking as if he had been doing this his entire life. With all eyes on him, he walked over to the jury box and prepared to deliver his opening remarks. Wearing a two-piece, navy blue suit and matching tie, he paced in front of them, taking his time. He waited several moments before he looked directly at the jury and spoke. When he did, he presented the charges against Beatrice G. Miller and the details of two counts of kidnapping.

He concluded with, "We are going to prove beyond a reasonable doubt, that Beatrice Miller kidnapped these two children. She did so willingly and with the full knowledge of what she was doing. The state will prove beyond a reasonable doubt, that Beatrice G. Miller, with aforethought and malice, did act of her own volition to kidnap Charles Novak and Margaret Taylor; and to date, shows no remorse for her deeds. No one forced her to commit these crimes. When this trial has concluded, the prosecution will have proven that she did commit these crimes willingly. At that time you will see she has lived a life of crime and she deserves to be punished to the fullest extent of the law. You, the jury, will be called upon to return a verdict of guilty on two counts of kidnapping. It is time for her crimes to come to an end." Gregory Hildebrand returned to his seat.

James Monroe stood up wearing a tan suit with brown cowboy boots and surprised Officer Butler, who was sitting in the audience, by agreeing with Mr. Hildebrand. He agreed that Bea had taken two children, but she was not in her right mind. She grew up in a household where she was abused and neglected. Her father taught her how to lie, cheat, and steal, and she did not know any other way to survive. It was learned behavior . . . learned behavior that she could not stop.

Gregory Hildebrand called his first witness—Benita Adams. Bea seemed happy when her Aunt Nita walked down the aisle and took a seat in the witness box. She looked just like Bea had remembered her, only older. Now that Bea got to see her in person, she was certain that it *had* been her on the street corner in Dallas. Benita Adams was dressed to kill. If Officer Butler didn't know any better, he would have thought she had hired a designer to create a wardrobe for her appearance in court. She stated her name and the bailiff swore her in, and the testimony began.

Mr. Hildebrand walked up and leaned on the witness box. "Mrs. Adams, please state your relationship to the defendant."

"I am her aunt. Her father is my only brother."

"What can you tell me about your niece?"

"Well, I haven't seen her in many years. I lived with her and Edward until Beatrice turned six."

"And you haven't seen her since?"

"I didn't say that."

"So what are you saying?"

"I saw her once in Dallas. She was sitting on a street corner in a wheelchair with a sign begging for money."

"How do you know it was her?"

"Beatrice was my pride and joy. I could never forget those eyes, the same eyes that looked at me as I turned my back and walked out on her."

Officer Butler was shocked. Obviously, Benita had met with the prosecutor because how else would Gregory Hildebrand have known this? Officer Butler read it in the journal but didn't tell anyone about it.

"Is your niece handicapped, Mrs. Adams?"

"No, not that I'm aware of . . . I read in the paper shortly after I saw her about swindlers who were doing that very thing to take money from innocent people."

"Doing what thing?"

"Pretending to be homeless or penniless, begging others to hand over their money, when all they had to do was go out and find a job."

"No further questions, your honor." Mr. Hildebrand took a seat.

"Mrs. Adams," James Monroe began, "Tell me about when you lived with Bea and her father."

"I moved in with them when Beatrice was a couple of days old. Beatrice's mother died shortly after childbirth and Edward contacted me and asked if I would move in and help out."

"Did you?"

"Of course, I did. Beatrice needed me."

"What was her father like? I believe you said his name was Edward."

"Edward is my brother, and I will always love him, no matter what."

"That's not what I asked, Mrs. Adams."

The judge spoke up, "You have to answer the question, Mrs. Adams."

"Edward had a very short temper and, at times, could be considered abusive."

"Please tell the jury about the birthday celebrations."

216

"Edward forbade us to celebrate Beatrice's birthday. He told her many times she had killed her mother, so she was not allowed to celebrate living when others have died because of her."

"What did you think of this?"

"I thought it was awful. Beatrice no more killed Marcy than I did. For that man, my brother, to shoulder her with that guilt for her entire life . . . it's just not right."

Mr. Monroe picked up the journal and began reading one of the first entries. Officer Butler remembered it immediately.

"July 9, 1966: Aunt Nita told me a month before my first birthday that she asked Papa what we were going to do to celebrate. According to Aunt Nita, Papa still blamed me for Mama's death and he got angry each time Aunt Nita brought up my birthday. Papa told her I didn't deserve to celebrate living, when others had died because of me. Of course, Aunt Nita said she always came to my defense, telling Papa he was being ridiculous. But, that didn't matter. Papa hated me and wouldn't change his mind. He told her many times he didn't want me to forget the misery I had caused the day I was born. As I got older, I remember him telling me too."

Mr. Monroe closed the journal and looked at the jurors. "I just read an entry from a journal belonging to Beatrice Miller, found when a search was conducted at the Miller residence. Please list it into evidence as Exhibit A. Mrs. Adams, does that sound like something that happened when Beatrice was a small girl?"

"Yes." Benita leaned in to the microphone and spoke louder than necessary.

"You say you left when Beatrice was six years old, is that correct?"

"Yes, that is correct."

"And you say you saw her on a street corner in Dallas some years later, is that correct?" Monroe was pacing back and forth as if Benita Adams was a mouse and he was going in for the kill.

"Yes."

Be Careful What You Wish For

"How can you honestly say you know for sure that girl on the street corner was the defendant, Beatrice Miller? Surely her looks changed after all those years?"

"Honestly, they hadn't changed that much. Sure, her baby teeth were replaced by adult teeth and she was a little bigger but she still looked the same. She still had the same nose and the same color hair. Her eyes, I could never forget her eyes. I knew, without a shadow of a doubt, that was Beatrice."

"Why didn't you speak to her?"

"I was with my husband and, I'm sorry to say, I didn't want him to know I knew someone who was homeless and begging on the street corner."

"No further questions." Benita Adams stood up and stepped down from the witness box. The bailiff took her arm and started to lead her out of the courtroom. She turned and looked at Bea. Officer Butler could read her lips. "I'm so sorry," she mouthed to her. Bea smiled in response.

Not wasting any time, Mr. Hildebrand stood and stated, "Next, the State of North Dakota would like to call David Miller to the stand."

David entered wearing a suit and tie; and after stating his name, was sworn in. Officer Butler could tell he was trying to avoid looking at his mother. Officer Butler figured even if he wouldn't accept her money, Aunt Benita had found a way to buy him some new clothes.

"David, please tell the jury what happened in the fall of 2003."

"Bea went to the Stop-N-Save—the one in Greenfield—and took a baby boy from a shopping cart there. She thought it was a girl, but when she got it home and found out it was a boy, she panicked and asked me to get rid of it. When I told her I wouldn't, she threatened to cut off his penis and dress him like a girl."

"And who is this child she took in the fall of 2003?"

"I've been told his real name was Charlie Novak. We call him Mikey."

The gasps from the jury were deafening. "No further questions."

218

Be Careful What You Wish For

Mr. Monroe stood and walked over to where David sat. He kept walking back and forth in front of the bench saying, "David, David, David, David," lightly tapping his lips with his index finger. "You stated your mom took a child from the Stop-N-Save in the fall of 2003, is that correct?"

"No, I stated Bea took a *baby boy* from the Stop-N-Save in the fall of 2003."

Mr. Monroe chuckled. "How old were you when this happened?"

"I was twelve."

"And, as a twelve year old boy, did you not think about calling the police?"

"I threatened to call them if she hurt Mikey."

"But not because she kidnapped a baby?"

"No. She told me his mom had left him unattended in the cart. She thought Mikey was better off with us."

"And was he?"

"That's hard to say."

"No further questions, Your Honor."

After a short fifteen minute recess, Detective McClure was called to the stand. He told about the day Charlie went missing, and the frantic call that had come into the station. He concluded with the DNA results which proved Charlie and Mikey were one and the same. Mr. Monroe passed on the cross-examination, and Nancy Novak was called to the stand.

"Mrs. Novak," Prosecutor Hildebrand said, "Do you remember the day Charlie disappeared at the Stop-N-Save?"

"Yes. I remember it well."

"Can you tell us about it?"

Mrs. Novak took a deep breath. "I got to the grocery store around nine-thirty to do some grocery shopping. I had dressed Charlie in his new snowsuit since it was so cold out. That was the fall it snowed before Halloween. I went in and grabbed a cart. I took one with an attached infant seat, so Charlie would be comfortable. We were going up and down each aisle, and I kept talking to Charlie the way I always did. When I spoke to him back then, he always smiled at me with one of those toothless, baby grins. The whole time we were shopping, I was playing peek-a-boo and other games with him to keep him happy. Charlie and I went down the cereal aisle and I was so busy talking to him, I forgot to grab a box of cereal I knew we needed. Once I rounded the end of the aisle, I remembered the cereal; so, I stopped the cart, turned around, and went back to grab it. When I came back, Charlie was gone."

"Gone, you say?"

"Yes, gone."

"What happened after that?"

"I called the police and Detective McClure was there in a short while. He questioned several of the workers and shoppers, but no one saw anything. It was as if Charlie had vanished into thin air."

Gregory Hildebrand took his seat and said, "I have no further questions for Mrs. Novak."

James Monroe stood and tucked his thumbs under his suspenders, sliding them up and down. "Mrs. Novak. Are you telling the jury that you left your infant son *unattended* in a shopping cart—in the grocery store?"

"Yes, but he was no more than twenty feet away from me. I was just around the corner!" Mrs. Novak seemed agitated.

"Could you see him the entire time you were getting the box of cereal?"

"No, I couldn't see him, but I knew he was there. I was only gone a few seconds."

"Apparently long enough for someone to take him."

Mrs. Novak spoke up, "Yes, I went around the corner, and I have played that scene over and over again in my mind. If I had it to do again, I wouldn't have done it, but I did—and I can't take it back. However, that doesn't give that woman," she pointed at Bea, "the right to come in and take my baby." Nancy started to cry. "When I think back on all the things I missed; his first tooth . . . his first step . . . his first word . . . his first day of school, and the first time he said Mama, *which he said to her*," she pointed at Bea again, "and not *me*, the pain is unbearable."

"Where is Charlie now?"

"He's at home."

"And where is home, Mrs. Novak?"

"New Mexico. We moved there after Charlie disappeared."

"How is he?"

"He has not adjusted well. He is scared of his own shadow. It's obvious his health has been neglected, and he can't remember the last time he saw a doctor. The little boy I got back is not Charlie. It's Mikey, the little boy she made him into." Nancy Novak looked at Bea with such hatred.

"I have no further questions, Your Honor."

Court was recessed for one hour; and after lunch, Edna Brown was on the stand.

The prosecutor asked her to tell about the day she first met Mikey.

Mrs. Brown smiled. "This is a good story . . . a sad one, but a good one." Officer Butler remembered that was exactly the way she had started the story when she told him. It was almost as if she had repeated it so many times, she had stored it in her memory bank. "Elizabeth, Bea's sister, and Bea were about five years apart in age. Elizabeth was always mature, and she seemed mostly grown when Bea came along, so Bea felt as if she were an only child. Elizabeth was very intelligent and graduated from high school early when she was just sixteen years old. She went off to Europe and never came back. Then one day, out of the blue, she contacted Bea and told her she had started the adoption process to adopt a lovely little boy. And since both of *their* parents were dead, Elizabeth wanted for her adopted son to know his only living relative as well as his cousins. It took four long years, but when Mikey came into her life, she decided that it had all been worth it. Elizabeth spoiled him rotten. Shortly after Elizabeth adopted him, she tragically found out that she had Stage IV terminal breast cancer. She went downhill extremely fast, and when she died, her Last Will and Testament stated that Bea was to get sole custody of Mikey."

Be Careful What You Wish For

"Mrs. Brown, where did you hear that story?"

"Bea Miller told it to me. She was sitting in my living room and told me every word."

"Mrs. Brown, are you aware that Mikey was kidnapped?" Gregory Hildebrand asked.

"Well yes, I know that now, but back then, I thought Bea told me the truth. She seemed so sincere when she said it. I had no reason to doubt her."

"Are you familiar with a man by the name of Edward Noslen?"

"Yes. I met Edward at the local senior center." Mrs. Brown looked confused.

"What happened to Edward Noslen, the man you met at the senior center?"

"He had to go back to San Francisco to supervise the reconstruction of his home after a fire destroyed it."

"Where is Edward Noslen now?"

"I have no idea."

"Are you aware that Edward Noslen was Bea's father?"

"No, I didn't know that." Mrs. Brown looked over at Bea and furrowed her eyebrows.

"Furthermore, are you aware Bea Miller shot and killed Edward Noslen in her home?"

James Monroe shot up out of his seat like someone had stuck him with a tack. "*Objection,* Your Honor. The prosecution is stating facts, which are not in evidence. We are not here to discuss the death of Edward Noslen. We are here to determine whether or not Beatrice Miller kidnapped two children while being of a sound mind."

"Sustained," the judge spoke clearly. "Stick to the charges at hand, Mr. Hildebrand," the judge warned.

"Yes, Your Honor . . . I have no further questions for Mrs. Brown."

"I don't have anything either." Mr. Monroe shuffled his cowboy boots against the wooden floor and took a seat.

222

Be Careful What You Wish For

Next to take the stand was Tim Taylor. He told the jury the pertinent details of the day Maggie had gone missing, and he shared the pain and anguish Bea Miller had caused him and his wife, as well as their extended family.

Mr. Monroe stood up and began his cross-examination of Tim. "Mr. Taylor, isn't it true that you and your wife were not watching Maggie at Lake Gerber?"

"No. That's not true at all. We had been watching her the entire day."

"Then how did she vanish if you were watching her? Did a magician make her disappear in mid-air?" Mr. Monroe chuckled.

"We took our eyes off her for *one minute,* and then she was gone."

"Mr. Taylor, wasn't Maggie in the sand down by the water?"

"Yes, that is correct."

"Does she know how to swim?"

"No, she can't swim."

"So you left your three-year-old daughter who can't swim, inches from a lake, while you took your eyes off her for one minute . . . is that correct?"

"You are making it sound worse than it was."

"Answer the question, Mr. Taylor," Mr. Monroe said sternly, leaning on the witness box.

Tim sighed, feeling like he was the one on trial. "Yes, that is correct."

"No further questions." Mr. Monroe smiled as he took his seat.

The last person to be called to the stand was Beatrice Miller. Bea was white as a ghost and walked slowly to the witness box. After she was sworn in, Gregory Hildebrand nearly leaped from his seat. He had been waiting for this moment ever since he heard he had been assigned to the case.

"Good afternoon, Ms. Miller. How are you today?" he smiled.

"I'm fine."

"Do you know why we're here today?"

"Yes. I was told I kidnapped a couple of children."

"Did you?"

"Not so much kidnapped as removed them from an unpleasant situation. Kidnapped is such an ugly word."

"What type of ugly situation?"

"Mikey was left alone in a grocery store. Maggie was left alone on a beach at the lake. It doesn't take a rocket scientist to figure it out. What kind of parents would do that?"

"What about the other two . . . ?"

"Which two . . . ?"

"Let me read an excerpt from your journal." Gregory Hildebrand opened it and began, *"June 13, 1998: Today is the day my baby is going to be born."*

"Side bar, Your Honor," Mr. Monroe stood at the judge's nod, and practically ran up to the judge's bench. The judge called Gregory Hildebrand up, placed his hand over the microphone at his seat, and then had a brief conversation with counsel. Officer Butler couldn't hear what they were saying, but when the trial resumed, they were no longer talking about the entry in the journal.

Gregory Hildebrand started again. "Can you tell me about your upbringing?"

"I had a horrible childhood. Mama passed away when I was a couple of days old, and Papa hated me for the rest of my life because of it. He beat me, starved me, broke my bones, gave me black eyes, sold me for sex, raped me, and treated me worse than most people treat their pets. It was much *worse* when I didn't do what he told me to do."

"Why didn't you leave?"

"I did. I ran away from him when I was fifteen years old."

"Where did you go?"

"I went to Seattle, Washington."

"After you ran away, what was your life like?"

224

"It was better. I worked and paid my own way."

"Did you continue to steal?"

"Every so often . . . I did."

"Did you not say your Papa was worse when you didn't do what he told you to?"

"Yes I did."

"Well, if he told you to steal and he was no longer there, why did you continue to do so? He could no longer beat you, so you knew exactly what you were doing, isn't this correct?"

"Stealing was the way for me to make ends meet. Without it, I wouldn't have survived."

"So, stealing is okay in your book?"

"No, I wouldn't say it's okay, but sometimes you have to do what you have to do."

"Tell me, do you feel bad taking those children from their families?"

"No, I don't feel bad."

"No further questions, Your Honor, but before I rest my case, let me show the jury a charm bracelet belonging to Bea Miller. It was found in the sand at Lake Gerber where she—how did she put it—removed Maggie Taylor from an unpleasant situation." The jury laughed. "Let it be listed as Exhibit B, and if it pleases the court, the prosecution rests."

"Mr. Monroe, do you have any further questions?" The judge looked directly at the defense table.

Mr. Monroe approached Bea, and then leaned in front of her. "When you continued to steal after you ran away, besides using it to make ends meet, were there any other reasons?"

". . . because Papa told me to do it."

"How could 'Papa' have told you to 'do it' when he wasn't there?"

"I could hear him talk. He spoke to me and told me to take things."

225

Be Careful What You Wish For

"Did this happen often . . . ?"

"No, he didn't, not often, but when he did, I listened."

"What would he say?"

"Same thing he always did. He told me 'if you see something you want, take it. Don't wait for someone to buy it for you. Don't wait to save enough money. Just take it.'"

James Monroe sat back down and announced, "No further questions and the defense rests." Bea was ushered back to her seat, next to James Monroe.

Gregory Hildebrand rose to give his closing arguments. "Ladies and gentlemen of the jury . . . Bea Miller has admitted to taking two children who didn't belong to her. She has admitted that she feels no remorse in doing so. If you don't punish her for what she's done, your children, your grandchildren, your nieces, and your nephews may be her next victims." Mr. Hildebrand took a seat to allow James Monroe to state his closing arguments.

Mr. Monroe rose and walked over to the jury. "Ladies and gentlemen; while Bea Miller has admitted to taking two children, she has also admitted that her father communicated with her, while not in her presence. This does not sound like the testimony of a person who is entirely sane. She thought she was doing a good thing by rescuing these children from a family where she thought they were not wanted. She does not deserve to be placed in prison. She needs medical attention and therapy to help her deal with a past that still haunts her, so she can move on and become an upright, law-abiding citizen. Please check your conscience before you make your decision. Make no mistake about it— putting her in prison would only make matters worse." James Monroe took his seat and draped his arm around Bea's shoulders.

The judge gave the jury instructions, and then they were led into another room for deliberation. Within a half hour, the jury returned to the courtroom, having reached a verdict.

After they were seated, the judge spoke. "Has the jury reached a verdict?"

"Yes, Your Honor, we have." The jury foreman then handed a piece of paper to the bailiff who, in turn, took it over to the judge. After

226

the judge had read it and refolded it, he returned it to the bailiff who took it back to the foreman.

"How do you find, the defendant, Beatrice G. Miller?"

The foreman cleared his throat, and began to read. "We the jury, find Beatrice G. Miller guilty of two counts of kidnapping; one, a male infant by the name of Charles Novak at the Stop-N-Save in the fall of 2003; and the second victim, Margaret Taylor from Lake Gerber on July 17, 2010."

The whoops and hollers were thunderous. Officer Butler ran and grabbed Detective Baker's hand. "We did it, man, we did it."

Gregory Hildebrand had won his first, high-profile felony case on his own—and he was overjoyed. Television crews were already surrounding him, leaving him little—if any—room to walk.

Bea Miller was led away to be placed in the women's prison until sentencing. Detective Baker guessed she would get the maximum sentence; a fine of ten thousand dollars and twenty years imprisonment for each kidnapping. Either way, Bea Miller wasn't going anywhere anytime soon.

Two weeks later, Officer Butler was back at the police precinct in Bunting Valley, manning the K9 unit. Even though he had enjoyed working on the Miller case, he was happy to be home. Chief Felder told him how proud he was for all the work he'd done and reminded him again that he planned to recommend him for the Lead Detective position when Detective Stephens retired.

On his way home from work that night, Officer Butler decided to stop by and see David. Surprisingly, when he pulled in the driveway, David was packing up a U-Haul.

"David, where are you headed?"

"I just received word Aunt Benita passed away. Since it came out in the trial that Bea had killed Grandpa, I'm her only living relative who is *not* in prison. She changed her will and left everything to me. I spoke with her a couple of days before she died, and she made me promise to move to Phoenix and live in her house. I'm moving to Phoenix and I plan on using a large portion of her money to start a Foundation to help kidnapped victims. I want to call it Never Give Up. You know, Bea kidnapped those kids years ago, and eventually everyone stopped looking for them. If they would have never given up, they might have found them sooner and stopped the vicious cycle which consumed my mother. She lived her life as if she were above the law."

Officer Butler put his hand on David's shoulder. "I'm really proud of you, Son. I knew you were going to be the one to break the cycle and make a difference."

"Thank you, Sir . . . that means a lot."

"What about school? Have you given up on that?"

"No. I've enrolled in the University of Phoenix. I'd like to major in criminal law."

"Glad to hear it. Oh, before I forget, I have something for you." Officer Butler reached in his car and grabbed the journal. "She wrote this for you. Maybe someday you'll want to read it when you're ready to forgive her."

David took the journal and smiled. Officer Butler knew it would take some time, but he also knew, that eventually, David would forgive her. She was, after all . . . his mother.

The End

Coming soon . . .

Not My Mother's Son

R. K. Avery

After Beatrice Miller is sentenced to thirty years in prison for the kidnappings, David makes a decision to start the Never Give Up foundation, an organization dedicated to finding and returning exploited and missing children safely to their families. With all the bad things his mother has done, David feels it is his unspoken duty to do something worthwhile.

Hesitant at first but determined to mend their broken relationship, each time David visits Bea in prison, she ends their encounter with the chilling statement, "Remember, David, things aren't always what they seem."

As word about the agency spreads, the services of Never Give Up are requested time and time again to help where others have failed. That is, until the police come knocking on David's door and arrest him for the murder of a baby boy. The entire world turns their back on David—and his mother's testimony is the only thing that can save him. As everyone in the courtroom holds their breath, you will too . . . remember, things are not always what they seem.

ᐸᔡ About the Author ᔡᐳ

R. K. Avery, a recent graduate of the Institute of Children's Literature, discovered one thing during her coursework—she loves writing adult fiction. Having been kidnapped from a beach as a small child, she has pondered time and time again what her life may have been like if her story didn't have a happy ending. R. K. Avery lives in Macedonia, Ohio, with her husband, two kids, three dogs, and her wonderful mother-in-law. This is her first novel.

CPSIA information can be obtained at www.ICGtesting.com
Printed in the USA
BVOW032040220911

271839BV00005B/1/P